Marilyn Pavlovsky

THE REVEREND'S DAUGHTER

The Reverends Daughter

Is published by – Marilyn Pavlovsky
Other Titles Currently Available
By this Author:

BURNING SUNSHINE

(2008)

HONORABLE LIFE

(2009)

TAINTED MAGNOLIA

(2011)

Two children's books:
Going Downtown (2010) & Cody (2011)

Publisher: Marilyn Pavlovsky
Language: English
Country: United States
Edited by: WRGA Edit – S. Short, Editor
Edition: First Edition
Version: 2
Storefront: ID: 8171913 LuLu Publishing, Inc.
Websites   www.book-burningsunshine.com
                www.marilynpavlovsky.com

Library of Congress Catalog Number 2011901281

ISBN 978-0-615-43999-0

Dedication

Dedication of this book was to be to those of my generation while we remembered the days of our sheltered lives and the happy days of our music.
But
While writing these books about a family whom I gave the fictional name of Dahl, I was not aware there would be still more pain and tragedy come to these wonderful people. Even before the trilogy of fictional books about their lives was complete, another tragedy struck. On August the third of 2009 - a beautiful little ten year old boy was killed. He was killed while playing on a golf cart upon that magical old farm. The family has been through so many tragedies. While hearts are bleeding:
I now want to dedicate this final book about this family to Levi.
Rest in Peace our sweet beautiful child.
You will live in our hearts forever & ever!

*"Turn off American Bandstand,
(PLEASE!!) How many times do I have
to tell you to not dance with that
Frigidaire door?
You know you **are** going to break it
right off!"*

Chapter 1

She was beautiful, extremely intelligent, naive, all grown up, childlike, talented and stupid as HELL! I guess that would be the best way to describe Hannah Jane Dahl. Hannah was a minister's daughter. She grew up in a small town. When speaking of small towns, in this case the town was a village of about twenty families. Hannah's ancestors had arrived in this area as pioneers and the town was created. The town was named after her family.

Hannah was held by the strictest of religious rules. Her father had become a minister when he was about thirty-five years of age and he was very impressible. During the late fifties a new minister arrived at the father's home church. This minister had a background of what one could call scare tactics. Or, maybe what one may call holly rollers because he was something to behold. His sermons were all very full of HELL, FIRE & BRIMESTONE! Hannah's father was so very influenced by this minister. The small country church soon began being ruled and controlled by the good Reverend Wyatt P. Jenkins. The impact that this one man would have upon Hannah's life would be immeasurable!

In the beginning, Hannah was delivered to an eighteen year old mother in a small bedroom of a farm house. The house was her paternal grandmothers and it was located only a few miles from her current home. The Midwestern state in which she lived was mostly farm country. The county she lived in was most likely one of the least populated in her state. One could drive for miles without seeing a house.

Hannah and her grandmother slept in the very bedroom that she was born in. She could remember the white sheer curtains blowing in from the windows of this room. Hannah loved the wallpaper. It was of a white background and placed ever so far apart were little yellow flowers. A door to this room was like a castle door. The wood was planked up and down and the door was arched at the top. Big black cast iron hinges attached this door to the wall. The door latched by a large bar that was also made of black cast iron. Hannah always felt there was something magical about this room. All fairy tales read to the little girl seemed to come alive in this very room.

Hannah's grandmother, being born in the late 1800's, had never changed any of her ways. She still used all of her old home remedies. She still cooked on a wood cook stove and she still hated electricity. Upon a shelf behind the massive bedroom door were items that would seem very strange by today's standards. There was a large tin can that was about two inches high and about seven inches in diameter. This can held a stinking red salve. The ointment in this can was used for everything that ailed a person. Alongside of this salve sat a bottle of whiskey. This was most strange for a Quaker type lady like Hannah's grandmother. This grandmother did not believe in drinking, yet she used her whiskey as a medicine. She would take one teaspoon of whiskey along with a teaspoon full of sugar when she felt she needed it for her lung problems. Other items upon this shelf included a fine toothed comb for the grandmother to comb her hair. The comb was used while combing those one-hundred strokes she felt that she needed each night. The grandmother's hair was so long that she could have sat upon it. Hannah never understood the combing of the hair upside down over a newspaper. She guessed this was to be sure there were no ticks or debris left in the old lady's hair after a hard day of work upon the farm.

The Dahl bunch worried about their mother and wished she would slow down once in awhile. She had almost died on them on one terrible occasion. The entire family was called in that night, but Rebecca Dahl pulled through. The family knew at this time that their mother's days were numbered.

Hannah's father James sold gas ranges and tried his best to place one such stove into his mother's home. She would have none of that. She was sure that the contraption would blow up and kill the whole family.

Most all of Hannah's aunts and uncles now lived away from home. She had one aunt who had married a man from the large neighboring farm. This aunt and her family still lived in the countryside woods. With purchases, the Dahl farm acreage had increased over the years. With the aunt's marriage this gave the family even more property for everyone to work and play upon.

Hannah, her siblings and her cousins roamed these large beautiful old farms while they played and enjoyed every minute of each day. They would turn somersaults the whole way to the barn gate. They would do cartwheel turns on every tree branch upon the farm. They would sit in the old white buggy that had been left in an old shed. Or, they would swing in the big swing upon the front porch. They would crawl through the tunnels of their uncle's stacked hay bales that were in the upstairs of one of his large barns. The children would jump into hay stacks while the family was still thrashing. They would make stages upon wagons where they would use cans and broom sticks for a sermon or a hit parade show. They would play in the old abandoned train depot behind the aunt's house by day and they would catch lighting bugs in jars at night.

Although much fun was had by all, it was not just fun and games for these descendants of the Dahl family. There were also many chores for these children to complete each day. They did much of the planting and hoeing, then the harvesting of the gardens. They would pick fruit off of the trees or from the ground and then they would gather and clean eggs. Feeding the animals and milking cows were also often some of their duties. These youngsters rarely saw the inside of a house other than for eating and sleeping purposes during the summer months. Winters, they would go through old trunks and play house in the upstairs of their grandmother's home. On the days they were permitted to go outside, they would sleigh ride down the snowy hills or they would go to the large old plantation house of the cousin's grandparents and skate. They would be dressed in their winter rubber boots. They would skate upon a frozen shallow pond.

Summer months the children would build playhouses in the gardens and bury each other in the wheat bins. Life was wonderful, healthy and fun for the descendants of the Dahl family. Then when Hannah was seven, her parents built their own home in the small village of Evertton. They moved the grandmother into their new home with them. This caused the aging woman to become very sad. She hated to leave her wonderful old home place, but sadly she had become unhealthy and unable to care for herself.

Okay, growing up in the late forties, the fifties and the sixties may have been wonderful carefree days, but who remembers how naive we all were? Many grew up inside of a glass globe while being protected from all of the wrongs of the world. At least that is the way Hannah Jane Dahl was raised. She knew nothing about the outside world on the day that she left her childhood home.

Hannah was born to this nice country couple who had lived their entire lives working hard, loving hard and going to church each time the doors were open. The family was now living in the most modern of a 1950's home. Hannah's father was a farmer first, then a businessman and then a minister/businessman. Her mother was a stay at home mother who did everything the Beaver Cleaver way. She bought only the good brand named items. She made her children brush their teeth with Pepsodent so they would wonder where the yellow went! She cleaned her cabinets inside and out with Murphy's Oil soap once every week. She scrubbed around floor corners, sinks and toilets with an old toothbrush. She would make a perfect list for her order from the milk man who delivered milk, cheeses and dairy products at the house once a week. She sewed her own little house dresses and wore one neatly starched and pressed every day. In a drawer she would have a stack of neatly sewn, starched and pressed darling little aprons that she would wear over the neat little dresses. To top this attire off, she would wear a fashionable shoe. Most usually the shoes would have a wedged heel. Every hair upon her head had to be in the perfect place. She would often place a ribbon or a pretty comb in her hair. If it was a summer month you may find a pretty flower adorning this young mother's hair.

Mrs. Dahl's children had to be just as neat as she. She would drive them crazy with the washing of their faces and their hands. Hannah's younger sister was not as patient as she. She would give her picky mother fits most every Sunday morning. The mother had sewn, starched and ironed the most perfect of little frilly dresses for the youngster to wear; only to have the child throw a fit about wearing such things. The mother would reason, scream, cry or even spank the little girl after trying one dress on after another. Stubborn was the word one may have used for the not wanting to wear these beautiful dresses. However one must live in this child's world just a short while to realize the pressure of being clean, neat and perfect at all times. In the end, the mother and this child would almost always walk the two block distance to the church after sending the father and the others on their way.

Both of the Dahl parents were very pretty people. The father was big and he was strong. He had black wavy hair and the bluest eyes anyone had ever seen. The mother was a raving beauty. She had been a platinum blonde in her younger years but later she was having a case of her hair turning forever darker. This lady was petite and shaped really well. She could brag of a twenty-four inch waist. Of course these parents were fairly young to have Hannah. Most of Hannah's friends had much older parents than she.

Being raised by these two God fearing and fun loving people was possibly the most wonderful and wholesome way for one to grow up. However, it had major problems for a teenage girl. Being raised in the strictest of ways caused little Miss Hannah Jane Dahl to believe that her teenage years could have been more teenage friendly. This young lady was protected and loved. However, she stayed completely depressed for the whole of her time at being a teenager. Due to the influence of the minister of the family church and Hannah's father with his belief system; Hannah was not allowed to do anything that other children were allowed to do in school. She had no outside activities. She was only allowed to go to church.

The young lady felt very, very cheated. She wanted to be in the band and she had been for a short time before the new minister arrived. She wanted to be a cheerleader or a majorette. She wanted what every teenager wanted. Things like going to school functions, hang out with friends and maybe even go to the drive-in. She just wanted to be *normal*! Yet things must have lightened up by the end of her schooling because she *was* permitted to take the lead part in the school's senior play where she played the part of Mrs. Tilly in a play named, 'Mrs. Tilly Goes to Town'! To her surprise, she was also allowed to go with her classmates on a *Senior Trip* to Washington, D.C.

Hannah had not been permitted to dress as other children. She had not been permitted to wear makeup of any kind, even including lipstick as a teen. Pants or slacks of any kind were completely forbidden. The inventive young lady finally learned how to get around a little of the strictness in her senior year. The community was so unpopulated to where bus trips were long for all of the county's children. Hannah would get on the school bus and find a seat in the very back. Skirts were now of a mini style and all of Hannah's skirts were longer. Thankfully, her mother had taught her to sew while she was very young.

Hannah would take a needle, thread and scissors to school with her each day. She would sit in the back of the bus and hem her skirt to the desired length. The young lady had also purchase an eyebrow pencil on a Saturday trip to Gallipolis. She somehow got away from her parents long enough to do this. The money had been saved from the money she was given for school or church. Hannah would line her eyes and paint her eyebrows while bouncing along the rough country roads. She probably looked strange because she had no training in this department. Then as evening approached, she would get back on her bus and find a seat in the back, preferably alone. She would then complete the task of removing her make-up and the removal of the hem in her skirt. She had also found some sort of capsules that colored one's hair. It would wash out with each wash but Hannah had gradually darkened her hair as well. One might say that she had become a very sneaky young lady!

Only as an adult did Hannah appreciate her healthy and wholesome childhood. However; she somehow knew that her protective childhood had not prepared her in any way for the real world. In many ways she was extremely lucky, but in many other ways she was so very deprived. She felt there could have been a middle ground somewhere. For the remainder of Hannah's life, she seemed to have many mixed emotions about her childhood.

Hannah's paternal grandmother had been a constant in her life. The move to the new home had been a small one and the grandmother had moved along with the family. James and his family had only moved two miles from the farm. Both sides of Hannah's family now lived in large cities. This was somewhat sad, yet okay because on the weekends the families would come to visit. The children were all so very close. The cousins were more like brothers and sisters than they were cousins.

The Dahl's new house had the most modern of conveniences. The new house was wonderful. This home had the kind of conveniences that was almost unheard of in this particular neck of the woods. Most country homes were that of a farm house and many did not have inside bathrooms or other necessities. Very few had any sort of plumbing in their homes. But the Dahl's had water running through copper pipes throughout their new house.

Hannah's father, James George Dahl, had completed most of the work on his new home by himself. He had created a very neat modern home for his family. The home came with a full basement. This basement had a coal bin on one side to supply the stoker furnace that stood directly in the middle. There was a window of sorts in the wall with a cast iron door that did not look that unlike the actual furnace door. Delivery trucks would back up to the wall and open this window type door. They would then place a shoot through the opening and dump a ton or two of coal. The basement had many other uses as well. All laundry was completed in the basement. A dark cool room was used for a cellar.

The middle floor, or as one may call the ground floor since this house was built into a hill, consisted of a front living room with what was known as a picture window. There was a large kitchen, a nice hall, two bedrooms and a bath. Between the living room and the kitchen was a large arched Spanish looking door that was built so Mr. and Mrs. Dahl could see each other and visit while cooking. In the living room there was still a smaller arched door leading into the hall of the house. Still another door of a normal rectangle style led into the kitchen from the hall. This created a circle that the children could run around.

In the very middle of the large arched door was a very big register. In other words, a closable grate through which warm or cool air was forced through a household heating system. In this case, the register was for very hot air. During the summer months a large rug would be placed so as to cover this register. During the winter months this large grate heated the entire house. Directly above this very hot machine was still another, much smaller register in the ceiling. This was so the upstairs of the home could be heated. This was quite a simple idea by later standards of building.

Looking backward, Hannah questioned as to how the house was never burned down because of the coals. Her father would use large tongs to remove a cluster of coal ash developed by this furnace. The large clump of ashes would be taken up the steps, out of the back door and then dropped onto a stack of the same coal debris in the backyard. These coals would glow red or orange sometimes for hours, maybe even days.

On weekends when the extended family members were at the home, the children would be awaken by the smell of bacon or sausage frying below. The smells floated ever so freely through that upstairs open register. These smells made for the most wonderful memories for the entire group of children.

At the top of the steep stairs there was a twin bed. This bed belonged to Hannah's little sister. In the middle section Mrs. Dahl had put a couch and a chair for a recreational section of the home. A roll-a-way bed was covered and folded neatly in the corner for those week-end guests. During these visits, children were often lined up cross ways of the bed to make room for four, five or even six to sleep. Due to the very steep roof of this house, there were deep low walls on each side of the upstairs. James had built two small closets that went back very deep into the small part of the walls. Between these closets there was placed a rod and a full curtain. Beyond that curtain was Hannah's room. This little room was at the very front of the house. Hannah could look out of her small window and see the highway on one side of the steep porch roof.

Before Hannah became a teenager, her mother had fixed up her daughter's room by decorating it in a cute style. Upon the floor she had laid a light grey shag carpet. The mother had decorated a dressing table with lavender taffeta and organdy. A nail keg was covered with a ruffle and matching pillow. It was used as a stool. The mother had sewn pretty tieback organdy curtains of the same color. An antique secretarial was against one wall. The chest was an old wash stand that still had the bar across the top for a towel. The bed slid back underneath the lower part of the ceiling, thus making a little cave like atmosphere.

Hannah loved her new room, but often seemed to have a fear of it because her parent's room seemed to be so very far away from hers. There was a huge dark attic on the other side of the stairs that only had a curtain hanging over the door. This could have been, and most probably was, the reasons for the young girl's fears. When the little girl was first moved into this large upstairs, she was the only child to sleep up there. She could not have been more than seven or eight years of age. For a short time after the move, and before Hannah became of any age, she and her brother had twin beds that they had shared in the second bedroom downstairs. This room was just on the opposite end of the hall from her parents.

The older Hannah became, the more she appreciated her room. This room gave her the privacy she wanted while listening to music and doing what she called her thing. One year she had received a record player for Christmas and was happy when she could buy a few forty-fives to play on it. She loved the Everly Brothers and about any rock and roll song she could get. By the time she was in the seventh grade, Hannah was deeply in love with music.

Hannah's junior high years had been wonderful. They were filled with music. Times were changing. Younger and newer teachers were coming to her country school. In junior high, Hannah had been in the band. She had also been in a singing group of eight girls that was called the 'Ivy Leaguers'. The group had purchased matching white shirts and black wrap around skirts. Hannah absolutely loved the skirt. It had a silk black and white striped lining. The outfit was topped off with a black and white striped beanie type hat. Suddenly the group was singing at all kinds of functions. They sang on the radio. They sang in restaurants. The group was becoming, what Hannah believed to be, famous in their small local circuit. In reality at this time, little Miss Hannah did not seem to have a care in the world. *THEN*, her whole life changed drastically. The new minister *came* to her church! He frowned upon just about everything anyone did, what they said and what they wore. He frowned upon everything that Hannah held dear. One thing that was so hard on the whole Dahl family was that this man did not believe in having a TV set. He called it the Devil's box.

Thankfully music was not completely cut out of Hannah's life. Her taste in music was not so appreciated by her parents, but her father loved music and he appreciated the fact that his eldest daughter loved it too.

Hannah's cousin Carolyn also loved music. She was three years older. Hannah absolutely worshiped her. Carolyn's family owned a T.V. From the time the young lady was about ten, she loved to go and visit. She and her cousin would dance to songs such as, 'You Ain't Nothing But a Hound Dog' and sing together. This cousin was her salvation. Hannah was fortunate enough to have Carolyn's wisdom and knowledge shared with her. She often felt if she had not had this wonderful cousin, she would have been even more lost in the real world than she was.

Teenage years, in Hannah's way of thinking, did not seem to be very kind to her. She would always hold sort of a grudge at her father for being so very, very strict. She would hold a grudge about the fact that she was not permitted to do the things that most other teenagers were permitted to do. She felt like a freak for the whole four years of her High School. In some ways she was possibly more blessed than many of the other teenagers. She could not see that! From a child's view point, all she could see was that the other children seemed so very happy and carefree.

Hannah *was* permitted to drive vehicles at a very young age. Not that this did her any good, because she could absolutely go nowhere without her parent's permission. They rarely gave her permission to do anything. She felt that her teenage life had been completely ruined. She felt that she was held entirely too strict. She blamed it totally upon the new minister's religious belief system. She could remember praying that he would be gone before her Junior Senior Prom because he did not believe in dancing. But he stayed at her church until long after she had grown up.

Hannah knew that her hurt could not be held against her parents forever. The years were the 1950's and the 1960's. Everyone's life was held back by one old fashioned standard or another. Music was just coming into its own and the music is what saved this generation. Hannah often wondered, without the music where would we be now?

Hannah lost herself into the music. She could play a piano some, but only by ear. Her mother's baby brother could make a piano talk. There were not enough keys on one piano for him to use, so he would take the back off of the piano and play the strings as well. Summers he and his young family would often come to visit and spend a week or two. During these years no one had air conditioners and doors were left swinging wide open with only the use of a screen door. While Hannah's uncle visited he played the piano every day.

Hannah also had a cousin on the other side of the family who was about two years younger than she. This cousin was taking piano lessons and preparing to be a concert pianist. She too came to visit often. She would also play the Dahl's piano beautifully. Once Hannah would return to school in the fall, a neighbor child would tell the teachers that Hannah was an expert at playing the piano. Odd, but she never corrected that assumption! This was one thing she could feel good about even if it was a lie. She was proud of her relatives for their talent and for some reason she would just let that little lie hang.

Hannah was a pretty, but shy child. She had a few neighbor children she befriended and she had a couple of friends at school. A neighbor boy was about her age and he picked on her constantly. The styles during her younger youth were that of a wide sash being tied in the back of a little girl's dress. This neighbor boy would often rip these belts from Hannah's dress. Medal lunch boxes were used and this boy would often hit Hannah over the head with his or her lunch box. It seemed that every time she was hurt, she would have to tell her parents that this little neighbor boy had done it. So, one embarrassing day Hannah's daddy cornered the young neighbor. He asked for him to please pick on someone his own size. Mr. Dahl never forgot the answer that he received from the little boy on that day. He answered by saying,

"Mr. Dahl, she is my own size!"

Mr. Dahl told of how he looked down and saw the two little heads standing at about the same height. Hannah remembers her father laughing uncontrollably about this day and she believes nothing else was ever said to the young boy. Needless to say, Hannah had to learn to defend herself. Also needless to say, all through her childhood this lad was one of her only friends.

During Hannah's early teen life, a family moved into the neighborhood that had two boys and two girls. These children were not that far from the ages of the four Dahl children. The family was very kind people. The father was a big jolly man and the mother was as sweet as she could be. She welcomed all of the neighboring children into her home with open arms. One of the wonderful things to Hannah was that this family owned a large TV set. Hannah loved to go to their house each and every evening to watch American Bandstand. Hannah's parents would eventually get a TV of their own, but at this time in history they did not own one. The music of the times was the highlight of Hannah's life. As a younger child, Hannah's cousin had taught her the jitter bug. In junior high she had learned to dance the stroll. By high school she was well trained in such dances as the twist, mashed potatoes and the bunny hop. Music seemed to keep this young lady sane.

At church, Hannah was a main vocalist. She often played the piano and sang a solo for the entire world to hear. At home she sang with the radio and she danced with the refrigerator door. This usually kept her in hot water with her parents. They would complain that she may break the door off. But if she moved to the other room, they feared that she was going to wear out the beautiful mohair carpet in the living room. Things of this sort were quite common in Hannah's life. Her father would tell her that he was going to send her to a country where there were tribes that had dances around the fires. He told her that this would be a saner place for her to be because the American people had carpets, doors and furniture that needed protected.

Even with all of the strictness, many things were funny in Hannah's youth. Her maternal grandmother was a wonderfully funny, sweet and beautiful woman. She was always so cheerful and so very happy. The only problem was that the grandparents lived so far away and visits were very few. Evangelist ministers who came to their church for revivals would always stay at the Dahl's home. This was whether it was one week or two. Some of these ministers were funny. One young man used to walk on his hands. The Dahl children always got great fun out of that.

The uncle who played the piano so beautifully had a young son. Actually he had three children in total, but this one young son gave everyone great laughter during one of their visits. Hannah's father had built an outside toilet while building his new home. He had never taken it away and used it often when he was outdoors. One fine day the children and the parents were all frolicking in the backyard while having fun with a game called croquet. The young son had to go to the bathroom. It was closer to go to the outside toilet rather than running all of the way up to the house. The small child reluctantly went inside of the small building and latched the door. After a while the young lad came out of the building. His father said,

"Johnny, did you flush the toilet?"

A much confused look came over the little boy's face. He stood still for a minute and then went back into the small wooden building. He stayed for what seemed to be the longest time. Finally the beaten little boy came out with his head hanging low. He said,

"Daddy, there is no flusher on it!"

Needless to say, the women were aggravated that Hannah's uncle got such humor out of such a thing, but everyone did have a good laugh.

There were many other things one may find funny about Hannah's childhood. She often tells of how she was nine years old before she realized that a piece of chewing gum actually came in a whole stick. Her mother and her aunts would always offer their children only one-half of a stick of gum. The offer of the gum was most usually when one was at church. It was not meant to be a treat. It was only meant to make sure everyone had the freshest of breath. The only other choice would have been to take one of the Dahl father's Sen-Sens and they were very strong in taste. Later generations would have no idea what a Sen-Sen was. It looked like a small piece of coal. It was formed into a very small black triangle. It was packaged to give a person good breath. Created in the 1890's, Sen-Sen *'Throat Ease & Breath Perfume'* was the first commercial breath freshener in the United States. Sen-Sen's blend of licorice and rare herbs effectively masked odors and freshened one's mouth. Each pack contained around a hundred mini mints. The pack looked like a small envelope with a top that folded down. A pack of Sen-Sens was always in the father's suit pocket. Hannah's father used these mints religiously.

Goodies were not something that was handed out to these children on other occasions. After becoming an adult, this was not the only thing that Hannah loved to tease her parents about. She would tease her father often about how she was twelve years old before she realized that her name was not Edith Bella Hannah. Her father would often say the two names of his younger sisters before he could ever get Hannah's name out of his mouth. The joke was often made into a question as to whether she should have worn a name tag.

Chapter 2

As a whole, Hannah Jane Dahl's family life was very wholesome. She lived in a bit of a bubble, but in reality life was nice. The family knew everyone for about fifty miles around. So, the bubble was a large bubble. All neighbors and friends were good wholesome people who sheltered their children from the knowledge that any other part of the world could be different from theirs. Neighbors, family and friends were just as concerned about the proper upbringing of all of the children the same as they were their own. Everyone watched out for each other's children.

At a young age, Hannah discovered death. The death of her paternal grandmother was extremely painful. This was not the only death she would have to face as a youngster. When she was in the fourth grade she had lost a classmate to cancer, but as a teenager that death somehow seemed to be so far in the past. Then, right after her senior year she lost still another classmate. This may not seem to be a lot of deaths to many people coming out of one school, but it was quite a few in this case judging from the size of Hannah's school. She started to school with twenty in her class and graduated with about sixty.

On graduation night her friend, whom she had accompanied to many classes for four years, ask Hannah to meet her in the ladies restroom. Hannah did just that, per the request, and to her surprise her friend stuck her finger out to show a wedding ring. She announced that she had married on that very day. She was celebrating two events on this same day. She was celebrating her wedding and her graduation. Although completely in shock, Hannah hugged her friend and congratulated her. A few months into that very summer after the graduation this friend had died of a gunshot wound. This was caused by her and her new husband while they were playing around and scuffling over a gun. Hannah went from a graduation with her good friend to carrying flowers in honor of this friend at her funeral.

With these sad happenings behind her, years became better for Hannah shortly after high school. There had been much talk by her parents about sending her to the Circleville Bible College. All of Hannah's cousins had or would be attending this college. Hannah had overheard her father say,

"If Hannah never does anything else with her life but marry and have children, at least by sending her to the Bible College she will have met the proper kind of man to marry."

Somewhere along the line these ideas were either changed, or Hannah begged enough for her parents to change their minds. Either way, this was changed. Hannah was permitted to attend a more local, run of the mill college. This college was enough miles away from home to where she could stay in a dorm close to campus during the week, thus giving Miss Hannah the freedom she so much desired.

During the years of college life, Hannah met her first love. She had never been permitted to date while in high school, so her new found freedom paid off when she met the man of her dreams. Every day she would walk down a hall and see this handsome young man and his friend at a water fountain. Hannah had met a girl with whom she had become friends and they were always together. As fate would have it, Hannah's friend had somewhere along the line started dating Ted who was the nice looking young man's friend. This caused the girls to often stop and chat with the lads.

Hannah knew of nothing to say or to do in the dating department, but she was very adventurous. She wanted so much out of life. She felt the straps of bondage had just been loosened and she was *free*! She wanted to see the world. She wanted to do everything that could be done in life. She loved bright lights, big cities and fun. However, this young lady had nothing to prepare her for the life she so desired. She knew that this young man seemed to be much older than she. He was so worldly. This may have been one of the reasons she was so attracted to him. He was tall, dark and handsome. His looks were all she could think about when she looked at this young man. That alone should have explained to her that she was still very immature. Mostly, the only time she would allow herself to look up at this nice looking man was when his back was turned. So one could imagine the shock on the day that this young man swung around and said,

"Hey ladies, how would you two like to go bowling with us tomorrow night?"

Hannah had never looked this handsome man in the face before. She knew he wore his clothes like no other. He seemed to be the neatest person she had ever seen. His body structure was to die for. He had very broad shoulders and he had large upper arms. His body came down into a very neat smaller waistline. He had a walk with a sway to where he seemed to have a hint of a right kick with his right leg. This caused a most sexy walk. Hannah knew that he had the most beautiful hair she had ever seen on a man. It was almost black and very, very thick. It had a hint of a wave going up and down the combed backward style. Beautiful, was the only word Hannah could think of when she looked at this man's hair. But not until this day did she have any clue about his eyes. Oh she knew his face was gorgeous. She could she that each time she would steal a glance at him as he would walk by. However, she did not realize until this very day that this man had the most beautiful, mesmerizing eyes that anyone could ever behold.

The beautiful eyes were of a powder or a sky color blue. They could make anyone melt just at the site. At this very minute, Hannah knew these eyes were making her knees buckle. She could not look any longer. She was sure that she would surely faint dead away. Somehow she was able to speak enough to thank the kind young man for his invitation, while her friend accepted. She remembered murmuring something about the fact that she had never been bowling before. She remembered the kind young man had said he would teach her how to play. Little did Hannah know this chance meeting would cause her to learn everything there was to know about life?

The following day Hannah could not concentrate upon her classes. She had learned that the man of her dreams had a nickname of Hugh. She did not know what his real name was but she knew everyone called him Hugh. Music being her life, she caught herself humming all of the day long to the tune of,

"I'm In Love With You, You, You, Only you will do, do, do!"

She was changing the (you) to (Hugh) as she would sing,

"I'm in love with Hugh, Hugh, Hugh. Only Hugh will do, do, do!"

She would stop herself at times and then feel that all of these things were proving her lack of maturity. She wanted so for the world to believe that she was completely grown up. Although Hannah believed she was now an adult, if truth be known, she was about as green and wet behind the ears as anyone could ever be.

That night and the next day were filled with worry, anticipation and fear. The evening finally arrived. The girls had worried much over what the proper attire was for a bowling alley. Oddly enough, both girls had a minister for a father. Although the girls had never met, Hannah knew this was one of the reasons that they had become friends. They had so much in common. Finally both settled upon plaid wool pleated skirts and ruffled dress blouses.

The bowling alley seemed so very large to Hannah. She had never been anywhere as large as this before other than some churches, church camp, a skating rink and a few department stores. The lighting was wonderful. The whole place gave her a big city adult feeling.

The gentlemen met the girls at the counter where they were to rent shoes and the games began. Hannah learned that the handsome stranger bowled on a league. Of course that had to be explained to her as well. The night was going to be a very nerve racking night for Hannah. She was going to do everything in her power to try to fit in. She was going to try to pretend that she was not from the total backwoods. She was going to try to show that she was actually an adult. Her handsome stranger was a city boy. He was born and raised in Cincinnati, Ohio.

As the lessons began, Hugh put his big arms around Hannah to show her how she should hold the bowling ball. Hannah did not believe she would learn a thing in this way. All she was aware of was the warmth and the heavenly feel of Hugh's wonderful arms around her. The rest of the evening went along pretty much the same. The lessons on bowling were very thorough and the fun was plenty. After about a half of an hour, Hannah could feel her tensions lessen.

The date, of sorts, started something. In the following weeks Ted and Hugh would offer to take the girls to one place or another. One might say that both couples were dating at this time. Hugh and Hannah had never been alone. Hannah was uneasy about that day ever coming. She had learned enough about her new friend to know that he was very experienced in everything. She had also learned enough to know that her father would never approve of him. Oh my, she knew there was going to be a major problem! That would be true even without her father's strict religious beliefs. Thankfully this young man had a religious background. She learned Hugh had been raised as a very strict Catholic. He was Irish. His real name was Ambros Cooney Hughes. No wonder everyone called him Hugh. By this time, Hannah had looked up his full name in a book that she had found at the library. She found the meaning of each of his names from an Irish Catholic baby name book. Ambros meant (Divine). Cooney meant (Handsome). Well he certainly was all of the above.

Hannah's father was a very strict Protestant, who was also a Scottish/Englishman. However, this would most probably be the least of her problems. The remembrance of her father's sayings about the boys from her high school made her shudder. He would often say things such as,

"That boy is no good!"

Or something like,

"His father drinks!"

Another saying was,

"He is nothing but a heathen!"

Then there were the many, many other excuses her father had for her not being able to date this or that young man. The biggest fear of all was the realization of this young man's age. She was very sure her father would not be happy with the big age difference. This young man had already served a term in the Navy. He had delayed his college education until after these duties. Hannah was shocked to learn that Hugh was about to turn twenty-seven years of age. She should have realized that his worldliness compared to the immaturity and dependence of her life could only make the two completely incompatible. Hannah had graduated high school at the age of seventeen and was not even eighteen at the time of her meeting the marvelous Hugh. These things, although quite true, did not hinder the romance that had started.

In the following weeks, Hannah and Hugh were inseparable. They walked everywhere within the college community. On one occasion it rained during their walk between classes. They ran upon someone's large historical porch while they waited for the rain to stop. They giggled and held each other close. After much uninvited time upon this porch and the realization that the rain was not going to stop, they did not have to say a thing to each other. They looked each other in the eyes, giggled, locked hands and started a steady walk along their way. The rain was hitting them in the face but they still just walked. Occasionally they would look at each other behind the funnel of water flowing down over their eyelids and laugh out loud. These things were the making of a wonderful romance. The year's difference in this couples age just seemed to disappear after the first few weeks. Hugh liked to smoke a pipe. Hannah loved the smell of his pipe. He would mix some sort of an Indian blend with a cherry mix. Other than the pipe smoking this handsome young stranger seemed to have no other vices.

Hugh's voice was very, very, very deep and with sound rasps. Hannah would laugh about how he could make her chest rattle when he spoke loudly. She felt this voice to be quite sexy. Hugh also had tattoos. This was most uncommon around the area of Hannah's birth. The only tattoo Hannah had ever seen was on her uncle's ankle and he was also in the Navy. His was well hidden and no one knew it was there unless he showed it to them. Besides, it was a nice picture of his wife with her long flowing black hair. Only people in the Navy would have received such things. These tattoos proved Hugh was in the Navy. Therefore Hannah knew her parents would realize the age difference from the get go.

Although Hugh tried to hide his tattoos, it was quite obvious that he had them. He had a lady with a large boat steering wheel and an American flag covering her nakedness below his elbow. This lady's feet went down to his wrist on his left arm. Then he had a completely nude girl covering the same part of his right forearm. With his large muscles, he could make the covered girl and the nude girl dance. This was always a big hit at a party. Each wrist was wrapped with two large braided bracelets of chains and butterflies. Hugh told of how someone had used what was obviously a dirty needle on him and he had spent thirty days in the Hawaiian Islands while recovering from blood poisoning. Hannah wondered if the tattoos had been worth it all to him. Hugh most always wore long sleeved shirts. He either felt uncomfortable with the tattoos, or he worried that others may be uncomfortable about them. Even buttoned long sleeved shirts could not cover these drawings. Nothing would keep these tattoos from the watchful eyes of Hannah's father.

The couple was becoming closer and closer with each passing day. Hannah knew she was cruising for some sort of a disaster with her parents. But she also knew she wanted to be with Hugh at all cost. She believed she was falling in love. She was hoping Hugh felt the same. She knew that they enjoyed each other's company completely! Believe it or not, Hannah already felt like an old maid. Most of her school mates had already married. These young marriages were most common in the farm area.

Three months had passed now and Hannah was invited to Hugh's dorm, of sorts. Several young men shared a large old house on the outskirts of town. Hannah and her friend Majel were to join Ted and Hugh for dinner at their place on a Thursday night. The girls were guaranteed that the only two gentlemen in their house that night would be the two of them. All others were out on the town or completely out of town on this holiday week night. School had ended on Wednesday. Hannah had not told her parents of the school outage because of her date with Hugh. She was going to let them believe Friday afternoon was the last class for the week. Her father would pick her up at his regular time. Sneaky as this seemed to be, young girls with the strictness that Hannah endured often caused them to tell a white lie or two along the way.

Upon arrival at the boy's home, the girls laughed amongst themselves when one whispered to the other that they were sure they would be having pizza this night. Ted had picked the young ladies up and Hannah had questioned the absence of Hugh. She was told that he had to get dinner ready. Someone chuckled and the conversation was changed. Finally they arrived at a big old fashioned home. This was now a fraternity house for these young men. Hannah was very surprised at the homey look. It was so nice to where she had to remember that this was a place for college students.

As the ladies walked into a large meeting or living room; a most wonderful aroma was coming from another room. Ted took Majel by her hand and led the way down the three steps into a dining area. The girl's eyes popped as they saw the feast that had been placed before them. There was the most beautiful of tables covered in a fashionable lace tablecloth. Upon this table was beautiful china. Tall long stemmed glasses stood high with mauve colored neatly fan folded napkins inside of them. Standing in the very middle of this table was a beautiful bouquet of mixed colorful flowers. There was a lit candle on each side of this arrangement. Close to the center of this beautiful table was a pretty cake that was standing high upon a tall cake stand. As they moved closer to the table they realized this cake was a German Chocolate Cake. A silver holder of ice was close by and it held a chilled bottle of wine.

Majel made a joke when she asked,

"When did one of your mothers arrive?"

Hugh swung around while his white baker's apron showed. He said in a whining type voice while pretending that his feelings were hurt,

"Hey, did anyone ever think that maybe a man can cook too?"

Hannah and Majel were most pleasantly pleased to take a seat before this wonderful meal. Hugh had fixed steaks that would absolutely melt in one's mouth. He had stuffed baked twice potatoes, a delicious salad and many other side dishes. This meal was comparable to one a person would find in a five star restaurant. To everyone's shock and surprise, Hugh was a gourmet cook. The food did not only taste delicious, it also looked wonderful. He had not missed one thing.

This night when Ted left with Majel, Hugh told Hannah that he would take her home later, so she stayed. The evening was spent with the couple doing dishes, and then retiring once again to the dining room table. Here they drew pictures, practiced printing and had a good time in general. Hugh was taking drafting classes so he showed Hannah the proper way to write. This was a much needed lesson for Hannah because she had the handwriting of many doctors. She believed this was caused by three reasons. No one had taught her how to hold a pen or pencil correctly and she had developed a knot on a finger due to this

36

problem. Secondly, her father wrote so poorly that it was mostly illegible. Maybe she had inherited some of that. Then thirdly, many of her teachers, especially a history teacher who spoke very fast, expected their students to write down each word they said. This made Hannah's practice of writing to be extremely fast. Her handwriting was what one would call *pitiful*. Of course she would not heed to the much given instructions. Once Hugh realized this, the tone of the evening changed. He started writing the word Hannah upon the large sheets of paper. Under about the tenth writing of the name, he wrote in what was beautiful block letters,

"I'm in love with Hannah Jane Dahl."
Hannah was surprised. She knew they were getting closer and closer. They never ended an evening without a long drawn out kiss anymore, but she did not expect this at this time. She knew he was so much more seasoned and aware of the world around him than she. He had lived a much different kind of life than Hannah Jane Dahl. She knew she was in love with him, but did not want to tell him first. What would he have thought? Would he have laughed at her? Would he think she was so wet behind the ears that she would not know what love was? All sorts of thoughts had crossed her mind. But, now there it was. It was out in the open and she had not been the one who had said it first!

Hannah picked up a pen and wrote directly under Hugh's writing,

"Hugh, Hugh, Hugh, I'm in love with Hugh, Hugh, Hugh. Only Hugh will do, do, do. I'm in love with Hugh, Hugh, Hugh!"

Hugh rocked back on his chair and laughed loudly. He then reached out and took Hannah into the warmth of his big arms. She realized their age difference did not make any differences when it came to nerves. Hugh dropped his arms and told her that he had been so worried that she may not feel the same way about him. He told her of how he was afraid to tell her how he really felt. He picked up the pen again and this time he really did make Hannah nervous. He wrote her first name, left out Dahl and then he put his last name at the end. She worried he may be teasing her until she looked into his beautiful eyes. They were clouded over with affection. Hannah believed at this minute she was loved very dearly by this beautiful man.

It was getting late. Johnny Carson had come on TV. By now, Hugh and Hannah had retired to the large living room. Hugh had lain down upon a large leather couch and he had taken Hannah into his arms. The couple stayed side by side throughout the whole show. They had watched a big part of Johnny Carson, but both had fallen asleep. One of the roommates walked into the house awakening the couple. The TV shows were completely off and it was making that horrible sound that it made after twelve o'clock at night. This noise had not awakened the couple. So, they were thankful that the roommate had made noise upon his arrival. Hannah whispered to Hugh that she must go home. As they drove along, both were very quiet. All of a sudden Hugh said,

"Hannah, I would like to meet your parents."

Hannah had not expected this and felt the panic come from the very pits of her soul. Her throat swelled and she could not speak. Oh dear God! Her parents! What would they say? She had separated her two worlds. She had felt safe in both as long as they were far apart. Was she now allowed to date or was she only dating because her parents knew nothing about it? At this time in history one had to be twenty-one to do anything without their parent's permission. That was the age that was considered the adult age limit. This was not just ethics. It was the law!

Chapter 3

School was going very well for Hannah. She loved math and her accounting classes moved along as expected. She was taking Accounting 101 this freshman year and she loved it. She had a typing class and for someone who could only type about forty-five words per minute in high school, she was shocked when she was tested once at over one-hundred words per minute. Of course that only happened the one time, but she was averaging speeds of eighty to ninety-five words per minute on a regular basis. The only school things she hated were the very same things that she hated in high school. Those classes were algebra, calculus, and the new math. No one ever knew that she was stubbornly not learning these things properly. This was because she could always arrive at the answer. She just couldn't arrive there in the same formula that was desired. She was starting to realize this was a pattern in her life. She could always get to the end results of something but only by taking the forbidden path. This reminded her of her piano lessons when she played by ear while listening to her classmates learn the actual notes. She started questioning as to what was wrong with her.

Hannah's boyfriend Hugh was quite an item at the school. Hannah could not help but notice all of the girls wanted to be around him. His ego had to be very large. One afternoon, several of the girls in Hannah's dorm decided to adorn bathing suits and lay out on their hot roof for a suntan. This roof was floor level to the second floor of the building and the flat part of the roof could be entered by climbing through one of their bedroom windows. Hugh was not allowed to join the girls in their dormitories, but he was allowed to climb the bank that reached one side of the roof. Hannah, who did not own a bathing suit or even a pair of slacks, had to sit upon the roof in a skirt and a blouse. This day was not a happy one for Hannah. She watched as her handsome young man floated from one towel to another while putting suntan lotion upon each and every girl's back. Jealously was sitting in after one girl said,

"Hannah! Where have you been hiding this one?"

Hannah realized that Hugh was enjoying this. She also noticed he was much practiced in this kind of behavior. He spent very little time with Hannah on that afternoon. To make things even worse, other than a glass of wine they had for that special dinner, Hannah had never seen Hugh take a drink. Today he had a couple of six packs and he was offering everyone a beer. When she refused his offer he called her a wimp, even though there was only one of the other girls who took a beer. This behavior was very odd for Hannah to understand because she had never been around anyone who drank *ANYTHING!* As a matter of a fact, her family believed any kind of drinking to be a horrible sin. If one should drink an alcoholic beverage, then one would surely go straight to Hell.

That evening when everyone went their separate ways, Hannah and Hugh went over to his place. When they arrived many couples were scattered about on the floor in the large meeting room. Someone had in their possession a set of bongo drums. They were passing these around a circle of people and different people were playing the drums. The person playing would pick out a song and then everyone else would sing along. By the time the bongos got to Hugh, he took them and started playing and singing, 'It's Cherry Pink and Apple Blossom White.' The young man did have a nice singing voice. He looked over the drums at Hannah with those mesmerizing blue eyes and said,

"I love you!"

Those eyes were dancing in the dim light. Hannah knew she was hooked. She knew she could not stay mad at this very, very handsome man for very long. She had never seen anyone on TV, on the street, or anywhere else that she had ever been that could be compared with this man's looks. He had to be the best looking man alive. She felt so very fortunate to have his attention.

On the following Friday evening when the good Reverend Dahl arrived to pick up his daughter from school, he had the pleasure of meeting Hugh! Hannah was scared to death! She had not told her parents she was seeing anyone. Hugh was the one who was so very determined to meet her parents. She had a fear this would be the end. The end of everything! Hannah feared she may be removed from school all together. No one could ever understand the fear that Hannah had of her father and mother. She had been trained to have complete respect. She had been trained to never question anything. She also knew any word from her father; whether it went her way or not, that would be the law, the rules, and she could never question it. Then she thought of how Hugh would realize the size, the strictness and the strength of her father. But then again, her father would realize that this was not a harmless boy, but a determined man. As all of these thoughts were rushing through her mind she knew she was screwed about anyway you could cut it.

To Hannah's surprise, Hugh walked over by the car and stuck out his hand for a shake just as her father was picking up the luggage that she had placed at the curb. Then he said,

"Reverend Dahl, it is such a pleasure to meet you. My name is Hugh, and I am in love with your beautiful daughter!"

Hannah felt the ground leave from beneath her feet. You know the way the sands move from under your feet when you are wading in the ocean. This is the very way Hannah felt right now. She believed she would fall down at any minute. Oh Dear God, now she has had it. If Hugh had only introduced himself, she could have possibly explained him away as just a friend. But,

"I'm in love with your beautiful daughter?" How could she explain that away? What was going to happen next?

Hugh continued to smile, Reverend Dahl continued to be corrigible and Hannah continued to fall apart. Hannah turned her head as Hugh tried to place a kiss upon her mouth. He ended up kissing her on the cheek. She slid into the car seat as if she were a snake. She slithered into a small little ball while hoping not to be seen. She knew the thirty-five miles home was going to be the longest ride of her life.

As Hannah and her father waved goodbye to Hugh, the car pulled out of the driveway with great speed. Hannah's father always drove fast so she was not sure as to whether she should put much importance on that or not. She was feeling so much steep emotion at this time to where she could feel the wetness in the palms of her hands. She wished her father would just speak. She knew that she was going to be in for the sermon of her life. Finally the Reverend did speak,

"Hannah, are you seeing that fellow?"
Okay, what was there to say now but,

"Yes Daddy, I am."
The next statement from her father's mouth was,

"Has that boy ever seen the inside of a church?"
Hannah knew her father was very upset. She knew that she had better tread lightly. She hesitated and then she answered,

"I am told he went to a Christian school, Father!"
She never mentioned the fact that it was a Catholic school, or the fact that he had been ask to leave because he smarted off to a nun. He had later graduated from one of the largest public high schools in the nation, Hughes High School in Cincinnati, Ohio. Hannah knew she was hiding much of the truth. She also knew that with the beliefs of her father, a child learns to evade the truths with much terseness.

There was a long silence and then all of a sudden Reverend Dahl cleared his throat as he said,

"I don't know what to think of a boy who upon the first time he is to meet his girl's father, he has a beer can in his hand."
Oh My God! Hannah had been so concerned about everything else going okay to the point of where she did not realize Hugh had a beer in his hands. The difference in their beliefs was so strong to where Hannah knew that Hugh and his

family found absolutely nothing wrong with having a beer. She did, however, know that her father felt this was one of the largest sins.

The rest of the way home was quiet. Hannah knew her father was very upset. Upon arrival at her home she noticed that her father did not trouble to get any of her luggage out of the car. This task was left entirely for her to do. She knew her father had gone straight to her mother to explain the situation. Now the jitters were coming back because she now must face her mother too. To her literal shock, her mother was quite pleasant when she met her at the door. Her mother spoke and she said,

"Your father tells me you have a boyfriend. He said he is a very nice looking young man. He also said he was quite pleasant to talk with."
Hannah knew that her mother was only telling the good things that her father had said. She knew there was a whole other paragraph that her mother had kept to herself. This was a family rule. If you could not say anything good about someone, well then you must not say anything at all.

While Hannah was placing her bags in her room, her mother followed her. She said,

"Hannah, why don't you invite your young man home with you some weekend? We would love to get to know him."

With that her mother left her room while leaving Hannah in complete bewilderment! Nothing else was said to Hannah's face about Hugh over the entire weekend. However, she could feel the tension in every room of the house for the rest of the time she was home. She knew her father was most dissatisfied. She knew that she had been groomed to be a missionary or a minister's wife. She was not to go out and fall in love with a worldly man. Especially one with a beer can in his hands!

As Hannah's father and she were loading the car for her trip back to school on Monday morning, her father ran back into the house for something. Hannah's mother stood by the door as her daughter got into the car. She reached in and hugged her daughter as she said,

"You're in love, aren't you honey?"
This was no surprise to Hannah. Her mother could always read her like a dime store novel. Her mother had a sense about her. Many would call it ESP. Hannah did not answer her mother immediately, she only smiled. She was comforted by the fact that her mother understood. Her father returned and the trip went off without anyone killing the other. However, not much was said on the trip back to the school that day.

A few weeks passed and Hannah got up the nerve to invite Hugh to go home with her on a weekend. This was mainly because of the pressure she was getting from Hugh. She had now explained her family's religion to him and she now wished she had done that earlier. She was somewhat embarrassed about the strictness of her religion. Hugh promised to be on his very best behavior. His eyes would dance as he would make these promises. Hannah knew he was almost in disbelief that anyone had that kind of a belief system. This was completely foreign to him. She somehow felt he was getting humor out of her demise.

On the following weekend, Hugh was to go home with Hannah. She had made arrangements to ride the distance with him. Upon arrival at her family home, she could not help but notice the atmosphere had changed completely. She was much aware that her mother had given a talk to her father. She was later to learn that her mother had believed if they interfered in this relationship they would lose their daughter. The mother was much aware of the deep love her daughter now felt for this young man. She had bluntly asked her husband if he wished to lose his loving daughter. She had informed him that she knew if Hannah had to make a choice at this point in her life between her parents and this young man, she knew in her heart that Hannah would choose the young man. With the fear of losing their daughter forever, the Dahl's were determined to make Hugh feel most welcomed at their home.

The weekend went beautifully. Hugh had a very charming personality. By the end of the weekend, he had helped change the local preacher's tire. He had whipped up meringue for pies for Mrs. Dahl, and he had attended church with the family. He had dressed in a nice pair of black dress pants and wore a white shirt with a narrow black tie. His shoes looked like they had been spit shinned. To Hannah's surprise, he was fitting in quite nicely. Hannah knew he used much restraint to make the very best of impression. She was so very proud of him. She even heard her father tell her mother,

"Did you notice the attention Hugh gave the sermon this morning? I wish my own children would show half that much interest!"

Now she was proud of her father until she heard more, when he said,

"That boy soaked up that sermon like he was a heathen. It was as if he had never heard a preacher preach before."

Hannah figured her small, loud, country church was most probably a shock to Hugh's practices of a more quiet and professional service. She resented her father calling him a heathen. However, she could not help but wonder what Hugh thought about this distant and completely different world from what he was accustomed. But, she realized that her worries were more based towards her parent's wishes more so than Hugh's. She knew with his humor, he was most likely getting a charge out of the differences.

Chapter 4

Hannah continued to date Hugh throughout college. By the second summer the couple was extremely close. Habit was that Hugh would accompany Hannah to her village just about each and every weekend. It was now expected that the young couple would more than likely marry.

Hannah's father was not the happiest person on earth about this decision even though no one had said a word about marriage to date. Hannah was still very afraid. She knew if she asked her father, he would say no. She knew if she ran off and he found out about it, he would have the wedding annulled. He had said as much.

For all of these reasons Hannah and Hugh **_DID_** run off and get married on June the second during that very summer. They went to visit Hannah's family as usual for the weekend. They were only going to stay Friday night and Saturday morning. Hugh and Hannah had told Hannah's folks that they wanted to go to Hugh's parents so that Hannah could meet them. Hannah had purchased a beautiful yellow dress. Yellow was definitely her color. She had darkened her hair so much by now to where it was almost black. Her pale skin looked pretty in the soft yellow color, while it showed off her dark hair. Other times the dark hair seemed to make her complexion sort of washed out looking as many people would say. Others believed her to have the most beautiful peaches and cream complexion.

The yellow dress was of a very modern style for the year. Many called this dress a sack dress. This one had a taffeta shell. It was then covered with a yellow lace that had the designs of roses. Roses were Hannah's favorite and had been ever since she and her cousin had found a beautiful old skirt in one of their grandma's trunks that was covered in roses. Hannah loved this pretty yellow dress. Hugh had purchased a very handsome black suit. The two could not have looked better. They were a very handsome couple.

Knowing the couple was going to run off together to get married the following week; the two had decided not to include anyone. This was to be a very large secret. Hugh had been sideways with his family for about eighteen months. Hannah did not know the cause of this and she did not ask. He wanted his parents and his family to meet Hannah; however he made it very clear that he did not want any of them to know about the wedding. He also made it very clear that he did not want any of them at the wedding. Hannah knew her reasoning for the same things, but did not quite understand Hugh's.

Saturday morning the couple got up and dressed in their wedding attire. They would take the clothes off shortly, but they hoped to get some pictures. Hannah asked her mother if she would take some pictures of the two. She told one of those now famous white lies to her mother when she said,

"Mother, I am meeting Hugh's parents for the very first time and Hugh said they will want a picture of us. We can't go to a photographer soon enough for this visit, but we can go to one of those one hour places and have pictures developed."
Hannah will never know why her mother bought that story, because it did not even sound too sensible to her. In any regards, Hannah's mother was happy to take the pictures of the pretty couple. Hannah's mother was none the more aware. These

pictures would be their only wedding pictures. Hannah knew this to be true because they were getting married on Tuesday.

The plan was to go to Cincinnati, visit Hugh's parents, then head back home on Tuesday. They were instead going across the state line to a Justice of Peace Tuesday morning. There was a town in that state that performed blood tests, licenses and weddings all within a couple of hours. There was no waiting period. Hannah, like all other girls of her time, had always dreamed of that beautiful church wedding while wearing the pretty white gown with all of the family and the flowers. She had saved herself for this wedding. Or, she had been forced to save herself, she was never quite sure of the answer to that question. However, she knew she wanted to marry Hugh and this seemed to be the only way to do so.

Hannah was a nervous wreck the whole weekend long. When they left her parent's home she could not help but feel the dread of what would happen should her parents find out her plans. She knew if she and Hugh were able to pull this off, her father would have her wedding annulled the minute he found out about it. Being a good typist, Hannah was able to falsify her birth certificate. This was scaring her to death. She had visions of going to jail for doing such a thing. She had ask Hugh over and over again,

"Isn't this illegal?"

Hugh would just give her a nervous laugh.

The trip to Cincinnati was a quiet one. Hugh knew that Hannah was very nervous. He would look over and smile ever so often as he would say,

"I Love You!"

Or

"You surely look beautiful today!"

Finally, Hannah felt the car come to a stop. She had almost dozed off into a sleeping land. The trip had been a long one and it was now dark. She heard Hugh say,

"We're here honey. I am almost as nervous as you are! As I told you my family has been a little sideways with me for quite a while."

Once again he did not explain why. He just left that hanging in the air.

As the couple walked up some concrete steps at the street's sidewalk, Hannah noticed the personal sidewalk continued to the front door of a very large dark house. It also led around the corner of the house to a backyard. Hannah could hear voices there. Hugh hollered,

"Hello everyone! What's up?"

As they arrived into what seemed to be the backyard, Hugh said,

"I brought someone I would love for you all to meet."

Hannah could not see one thing. These people did not have on any lights. You could smell charcoal. You could smell good smelling food, but there were no lights at all. Hugh did his introductions and Hannah said hello to the invisible people. Someone lit a cigarette at which time she could see a face or two. The family was having dinner in the backyard. They were in the process of having a cookout when it got dark. They were enjoying it so much to where no one troubled themselves to turn on any lights. They were talking, laughing and enjoying themselves. Hugh joined in on the fun and lit his lighter in front of Hannah's face, while saying,

"Isn't she pretty?"
The whole family said,

"She sure is. Where did you find her and does she know anything about you?"
Everyone laughed and it looked as if any trouble Hugh may have had with his family was all forgiven. Mrs. Hughes fixed Hannah a plate and said,

"Here dear, enjoy!"
Hannah had never tasted better food. She knew that this was a steak. She also knew that she did not ordinarily like steak, but this was delicious. There was a baked potato with sour cream and chives. There were grilled vegetables, and someone put a drink in her hand. She remembers being asked what she wanted while many alcoholic beverages were offered. She heard vodka and orange juice so she asked for just the orange juice. She thoroughly enjoyed her meal and the comradely while eating in this pitch black darkness.

The evening went on very smoothly. The family sat in that backyard another two hours while laughing, joking and drinking beer. Hannah was thankful by now that the lights were off. She could imagine what the night air was doing to her hair. She had just enough natural curl to be aggravating. Her hair did not have enough curl to look good if she left it natural, but it had enough curl to make it fuzzy in damp climates.

As the evening came to close, everyone started going into the house before going their separate ways. Everyone had carried their plates to the kitchen so they could be washed. There was now a large gathering in the kitchen. Hannah was happy to see everyone's faces and realized this whole family was very attractive. Hugh had very handsome brothers. His father was a very good looking elderly man with snow white hair. Hugh's mother was a short little woman who looked every part of the loving grandmother type. He had one sister and she was a hoot. She had a boyfriend with her. Hannah could not get over her attire. She had on a mini skirt and boots that came up over her knees. She too was a very attractive lady. She was much older than Hugh. Actually she had a daughter with her that night. This daughter was about the age of Hugh. All of Hugh's siblings were much older, except for one brother. Hugh had explained that his Catholic religion did not approve of birth control of any kind. He told Hannah that, yes in fact the older brothers and sister were old enough to be his parents. His parents in their older years at about the time of his mother's change had two surprises. Those two surprises were Hugh and his brother John. His brother John was about eighteen months older than he.

Hannah tried to be as corrigible as she possibly could be, but one thing was driving her crazy. She looked down at the plate she had carried into the kitchen and she realized that her steak had been close to raw. How could anything have tasted so wonderful and not been fully cooked. She did not realize how very much she was out of her element. Everyone seemed wonderful and welcomed her into their lives with open arms, but she knew she was from a totally different world. Everyone smoked. All of the men said words she had never heard before and they drank so many alcoholic beverages.

Hannah noticed that the father of the group did not drink. She was later to learn that he had a bad heart condition and had been forbidden to drink. She knew she was not to judge anyone. She also knew she was very naïve and that her belief system was not the only belief system in the world. Her church did not believe in drinking. The Catholic Church found it not to be a problem as long as it was done in moderation. However, Hannah could not see much moderation in this jolly Irish family tonight. She did feel much more comfortable visiting with her soon to become father-in-law.

That night sleeping arrangements was also most uncommon to Hannah. Mrs. Hughes had prepared a bed for Hannah and one for Hugh. She must have been clairvoyant like Hannah's own mother or Hugh may have told his mother what their plans were. She could see he and his mother were extremely close. Of course they would be, since he was her baby son. Mrs. Hughes had put the two in the very same bedroom that night. They were to sleep in twin beds, but they were sleeping in the same room. Hannah made Hugh promise that he would stay on his side of the room. Mrs. Hughes had made a remark very similar while letting out a slight chuckle. She had said,

"Now you stay on your side of the room Ambros!"

Hannah was already nervous enough about her wedding night. Never being with a man and being taught that she had to save herself for her marriage made this young lady extremely nervous about what was going to happen on Tuesday night. There was something else that was making Hannah very uncomfortable. The whole family called Hugh, Ambros. Of course they would because that was his name, but in the other world everyone called him Hugh.

The rest of the weekend and the following days went along just fine. Hannah realized she enjoyed the Hughes family very much. She had probably judged the family a little harshly on that first night, but she found they practiced their religion just as seriously as they did their fun. Sunday morning Hannah was told that the family was going to Mass. The whole family got up and dressed to the nines. Hannah had always worn church clothes, so she was very well prepared. What Hannah did not own was casual or sports clothing.

As the large group started out of the door to get into various cars Mrs. Hughes handed Hannah a beautiful lace scarf. She asked her to please put it upon her head, while handing her some pins so she could place it in her hair. Hannah did not want to mess up her hair because it had been teased and sprayed heavily. Regardless, she did as the older woman asked mainly because she wanted to make a good impression on her mother-in-law to be.

After arriving at the very large cathedral, Hannah understood the scarf. A bigger church Hannah had never seen. Every woman in the place had a scarf or a hat upon their head. Hugh had whispered an answer to Hannah's confusion, while telling her that it was proper for a lady to cover her head in the House of God.

All of a sudden Hannah felt so back woodsy. This elegant place with these elegant people made Hannah feel less confident than she had ever felt. She had no idea what to do. Each family member knelt at the entrance of the church and then they washed their hands in a bowl full of water that stood on a pedestal. So many things she could not understand. She did not know how to say the prayers or how to make the hand movements. Then the priest spoke in Latin for a big part of his sermon. Hannah felt like a fish out of water. She did however; feel that everything was quite beautiful. She also realized these people took their religion just as seriously as her family took their religion. She consoled herself by repeating under her breath,

"Thankfully there is only one God."
Then repeating that phrase to herself again and again,

"There is only one God. There is only one God!"
She knew people may have many different ways of showing their faith, but she knew they were all worshiping the same God and that they were all trying to go to the very same place when they die.

Chapter 5

Hugh and Hannah were married on that Tuesday. They went back to the school, work and their lives without anyone knowing what they had done. They told their closest friends who had helped them celebrate but they did not tell either of their families.

Hannah's schooling was over at this point. She had received her degree and had been offered a position in Columbus, Ohio. Hugh had still another semester before he would be graduating. The separation was hard on the newlywed couple. Several week nights Hannah would run down to Hugh's school. She would leave during the next early morning hours to guarantee that she would be at her job on time. On one occasion of doing this, it got her caught up in a mess with her parents. She had overslept and was going rather fast through the town of Chillicothe. Right above the city on Route 23 a Highway Patrol Officer stopped her. This may not have been so devastating had the silly girl had in her possession some money. Or, it may not have been so bad had she worn something besides a pair of shorts. It would have also helped if she had not been barefooted. To add to her demise she had rollers in her hair. Hannah at this time with having her own money had now purchased more worldly clothing. On this day her life would have been better if she was still adorning her old fashioned attire.

Hannah was caught for her speeding and was asked to follow the police officer back to the precinct. Unlike later years where an officer could just give a ticket and let a person mail in the fine, at this time in history a speeder had to have the money available upon their arrest. The police officers in this precinct had told Hannah that they would have to lock her up if she could not come up with the money immediately to pay her fine. She was scared to death. There was nothing left to do but to call her mother. Hugh would be in school by now. She had to call her mother. When she did call, she got all of the questions as to why she was where she was to get a ticket and so on and so on! She tried to avoid telling her mother the truth. She cut her mother off short and warned her that the officers were going to put her in jail if she did not hurry.

Hannah's mother did not drive and the closest town was something like twenty miles away. Cell phones were non-existent at that time, just as any other form of communication. Telegrams and money grams were about the only thing that could be sent anywhere. Hannah's mother told her that she would have to wait until her father came home from one place or another.

Hannah called her work and told them that she would be very late today. She had called her mother collect. She then had to charge the call to her work on her parent's home phone number. She knew this was distressing her mother since the telephone company would have called her mother to ask permission to charge this call to her phone. Now, Hannah prayed her mother could find her father soon. Lunch time came around and an officer at the front desk said,

"If you wish to eat, I will have to put you in a holding cell."

The fear of jail in anyway caused Hannah to not have an appetite. So, she just sat there worrying about when and how her mother would get the money delivered to this office.

The front desk officer had, of course, seen her driver's license. She still had her maiden name upon them. Now the officer was asking questions,

"Are you related to so and so, *or* so and so?"

He named just about everyone in her family. She knew her family was very well known, but she had no idea someone was going to know her over sixty miles from her house. But this officer did know her family and he was trying very hard to embarrass her. She just wished he would let her worry in silence. The bench was hard, she looked awful, and people were walking in and out of the precinct all day long. She had finally taken the rollers out of her hair and placed them in her purse. She asked on two or three different occasions if she could please go to her car and get some other clothing and a pair of shoes. She was refused with each request. The officer made another remark without warning when he ask,

"Do your parents know that you smoke?"

Hannah now smoked cigarettes and her nerves were shot by now so she had asked the officer if it was okay if she had a cigarette. He had responded with a,

"I don't think so young lady!"

Then to make the matter even worse, the now irritating officer was saying things like,

"Does your family have any idea you drive at those speeds?"

Or he would ask her just what she was doing that caused her to go through his town at that time of a morning. Then he said the one thing that had always gone right to the core and disturbed this young lady completely. He said,

"Your family is such a respectable and well loved family. Remember your name little lady and count its value. A good name is not something that a child should try to destroy!"

How many times had Hannah heard about her good name? How many times had she been told to not destroy her precious name! As of right now she only wished she could go far, far away where no one had ever heard of her last name!

Finally the nightmare was over. Hannah's parents had wired the money for her ticket and she was free to go. She hurried to her place of employment and worked the last hour of the day. She was worried about her appearance because she had put on the clothing that she had worn the day before. There was not enough time to go to her apartment for a change before closing time. She had the fear that being as new as she was on her job that they may fire her if she did not show up at all. Hannah was now living a secret. She was living a forbidden life. She was telling lie after lie because of her fear of her parents. The happiness she believed she was going to have was starting to crumble down around her.

The summer finally ended and Hugh had graduated. He was taking a position just a few buildings from Hannah's job in the city of Columbus, Ohio. They were both working for the State of Ohio. This was wonderful because they could live together, ride to work together and meet for lunch. Finally, all seemed to be coming together in this adult world. Hannah could not admit to herself that she was not quite an adult as of yet. Oh, she believed that she was. She acted the part. She believed the part. Her only problem was that she had been raised in a small community and knew absolutely nothing of the *REAL* world! Not to worry, she was about to get real dozes of that real world.

By October of that same year, Hannah worried she may have become pregnant. She wanted to be excited, but she was scared. She had hoped that Hugh would be ecstatic. *That* did not go as planned! There was the fact that something like this could not be hidden from one's parents. She knew she may never be able to see her loved ones again. How could she ever explain to them that this was the life she had chosen without their permission?

Hannah's first project was to find out for certain if she and her husband were indeed expecting. Then the second project would be to tell her husband. The third thing to do was to tell her parents. This was a whole lot more scary. She had thoughts of how she could just never go home again. This would break her heart because she really loved her family. She loved her parents. She had siblings that she missed. One little brother was but five years old and she idolized him. There were times that she had pangs of worry about whether she really wanted a child at this time because of her love for her little brother. She did not want him to be jealous of her baby and she worried as to whether she could even love another baby as much as she loved her little brother. Her mother had been sickly during his baby years and much of the care for this brother had fallen upon Hannah. Now her heart would break when she thought of the outcome she could possibly be facing. Then as if getting a second wind, she would have little talks with herself like,

"I am an adult after all. An adult does not have to have permission from her parents to have a child."

She did not have to have their permission! As far as that goes, she did not have to have their blessings! This was her life! Of course she knew this was only the rebellious side of her way of thinking.

Every time that Hannah thought about telling her parents the old fears would all come back. She had not reached twenty-one to date. She was still considered a minor. She was scared to death of her parents and the fear of God that they had put into her. She had been taught to have an uncontestable respect for them. She wanted to talk with Hugh about all of this, but she knew he could never understand. Anyone not being raised as Hannah was could never possibly understand. Being the oldest child and being a girl only complicated the situation more. She was raised by the Bible completely. She honestly believed that no one could have been raised as strictly as her. She loved her parents dearly, but was completely horrified of *EVER* being caught doing anything against their wishes.

Hannah was sure that she would surely die if she ever crossed either of her parents. Worse, they would annul her marriage and send her away somewhere. Her daddy had always said if his daughter did not do as he said, he would send her up the river. Hannah knew this to mean he would send her to Marysville where there was a women's prison. This may sound silly and impossible in many circles, but it really could have happened in Hannah's world. Her father knew every judge or lawyer in his county and he considered each and every one of them as dear friends. All she could think about were these things over and over again while she would say to herself,

"Unless one was raised in such a home as mine, one could never understand my fear."

Now with the possibility of being pregnant, Hannah's parents would void her marriage and then possibly send her to a home for unwed mothers. Being the Christians that they were they would raise the child as their own, but they would disown their daughter forever. She would be their shame. If they had not approved the marriage, it was not Christian in their eyes and it would not be considered a marriage. They would believe that they had not been strict enough on their daughter. She would now be the horrible sinner that they knew her to be. If she ever mentioned any of these ideas to Hugh, he would only laugh at her fears. He would surly laugh at her now. He could have no idea of how very serious these things would be should her parents decide to act upon any of them.

Hugh and Hannah had started riding a city bus to save on gas and the cost of parking downtown. Hannah had by now sneaked to a doctor and yes, she was expecting. She had not gotten up the nerve by this date to tell her husband. One evening the couple had jumped on the city bus only to find there were no seats where they could sit together. This often happened so neither was distressed. Hannah had been creative this day with the way she planned on sharing her news with her much loved husband. She had taken a napkin, a small safety pin and some mustard and folded up this mess to make it look like a tiny, dirty diaper.

While getting bored at all of the stops and the length of the bus trip home this evening, Hannah asked her neighboring seated person to please pass this gift back to her husband. Each person who passed it on had a laugh. Finally the package arrived to Hugh. The shocked look upon his face bewildered Hannah. The whole bus crowd cheered and laughed. They all seemed very happy for the nice looking couple. One old lady seated near Hannah asked,

"Is this your first?"

Hannah answered with a big smile while saying,

"Yes!"

Hugh just sat there completely bewildered! Hannah could not read his expression! Actually, she did not know what to think. She believed and she had hoped that her husband would be very happy. She knew it was way too soon after their marriage and in reality they had not been able to spend very much time together at this point. They had been separated so much of the time since their marriage due to the distance to work and the need for Hugh to finish school. They had been married less than four months at the date of conception. Possibly this was much too soon for Hugh.

"Oh well!"

Thought Hannah.

"It's too late now!"

Hannah had taken birth control pills and could not understand why or how she could have gotten pregnant. But she did. Now she hoped all was well with her husband and that everybody would be happy.

That evening Hugh said very little. Hannah made some grilled cheese sandwiches and opened a can of soup for dinner. Usually Hugh did all of the cooking because of two reasons. One, he was a marvelous cook. The other reason was that Hannah only knew how to make spaghetti, mashed potatoes and cakes. You could really get sick of that combination. Tonight however, Hugh drowned himself in the TV and hardly looked towards the kitchen.

At about 7:00pm Hugh brought his bowl and plate into the kitchen where Hannah was spending her evening. He reached over and took her hands into his and said,

"Come On!"

She said,

"Why? Where are we going?"

He really did not answer that question and Hannah was worried. They got into the car and drove to a neighborhood bar. Hannah had been in the bowling alley's bar a time or two while in school. She had also gone looking for Hugh one night at another fairly rough looking place. But, as a whole she had never spent any time inside of a bar. Actually these places made her a nervous wreck. Everyone was loud. Most were drunk and obnoxious. Many tried to hit on Hannah the minute she walked in. All of these reasons always made Hannah very willing to stay at home when Hugh really wanted to go out. Tonight she really did not have a choice. Hugh was acting very strangely and he *requested* her presence.

After a few beers and talking with some people at the bar, Hugh came back to the table where he had left Hannah waiting. He ask,

"Would you like a coke or something?"

These were the very first kind words the man had said directly to her since the funny way of telling him about the baby on the bus this afternoon. Hannah answered by saying,

"No Thank You!"

It came out in a hurt sort of a way! Then Hugh brought his beer to the table and slid into the booth beside of her. He did not go to the other side of the table as one would expect. Instead he slid in on her side beside of her.

Hannah could tell that her husband was getting high. He drank at least three beers while standing at the bar. He had also ordered two shots of whiskey that she could see from where she was sitting. It could have been more. She was worried as to who was going to pay for all of this when she heard him say,

"Put that on my tab!"

Now she realized he had been at this bar before. On many nights lately Hugh would just disappear. He would be gone sometimes for hours. When questioned upon his arrival at home, he would always mummer something about being with friends or of how he had to meet a guy or something. Hannah was too naïve to ask any more questions.

Finally on this unusual night after many drinks Hugh took out his billfold. Hannah was relieved. She believed they may be going home shortly. To her surprise that was far from the reason his billfold came out. By now Hugh was being belligerent. He was actually being rather nasty with Hannah. At one time he looked at Hannah and said,

"Gee, your nose is long! I've never noticed that before!"

Hannah knew this was the swelling she had been getting lately from the pregnancy. She was already self-conscious enough about it. The cause was most probably because her husband had taken up most of the refrigerator with his beer and she only had celery to snack on. She seemed to be craving salt.

Hannah had never seen this side of her husband before and she was getting her feelings hurt really badly. Then for the longest time Hugh left his billfold open upon the table. He would take a drink and mess with his billfold. After several more drinks he finally unfolded a large chain of pictures. There were pictures galore of children. There were also many pictures of a dark headed woman with these children. Bewildered, Hannah asked,

"Who are all of these children?"

In the same tone of voice that was bordering nasty, Hugh answered through gritted teeth,

"Mine!"

Hannah felt it was twenty minutes before she could even breathe. She wanted to scream,

"You *#//*#//# ! You have got to be kidding me!"

But she could tell by the look on her husband's face that this was no joking matter. Finally she said,

"Why have you never mentioned your children to me before?"

All of a sudden she realized that her husband could be the ultimate smart ass. The impertinent man said,

"You never ask!"

For a young lady who had been raised in a totally different world these words came down upon her with a terrible blow. Now she knew she was one gullible little girl. Now she knew that she was that green little hillbilly girl that her husband had talked of so often. Yes, she was stupid. She knew absolutely nothing about this world. She knew nothing about judging someone's character. She was a lost little girl in an all grown up world. Right now it felt like a horrible world that she did not understand nor want to be in.

As the conversation continued, Hugh informed Hannah that he did not want any more children. Then in a belligerent kind of way he screamed out over top of all of the noise in the bar, **"I HAVE ENOUGH!"**

This is when Hannah realized probably why Hugh was sideways with his parents and family. Being Catholic and not believing in divorces she was sure they were a little bit more than upset with him over his divorce. However, as he continued to *finally* tell Hannah about his life, he told of how he had married a girl who already had two children. He had married her while he was still in the Navy. A bigger shock was that he was not married in the Catholic Church. Hannah was finding out quickly that her new husband had fallen far away from his Catholic belief system. Even so, the divorce from his wife and leaving his children must have been the reasons for his family's discontent. Shockingly, no one in his family had mentioned these things either. Of course Hannah had only met them that one time.

Hannah also found out that her husband had difficulty separating his faith from his chosen world. He had forced the lack of birth control on his ex-wife and now he had four children of his own by the young age of twenty-seven. Now

Hannah was wondering if he had done something to cause her pregnancy. Maybe he was some kind of a saddest or something. Judging from his actions tonight over the pregnancy, surely he had nothing to do with disturbing her pills. She just could not understand how she could have gotten pregnant while she was on the pill. At this point Hannah was completely confused and she was hurt. She was so very hurt! Her thoughts were jumping back and forth rapidly. She had heard a jokingly, but very disturbing remark from her good time acting husband a few nights before when he had said to someone,

"The way to keep a woman is barefooted and pregnant!"

What was she to believe? Would he have messed with her birth control? Surely not! He was too mad right now for that to have happened.

The night finally ended with Hannah completely bewildered, hurt and very confused. If she thought this was shocking, she was in for more big surprises after this night. Hugh started going out every night. He only came home after the bars had closed. Every morning he was completely hung over and could not get up. Within days he had quit going to work. Hannah was devastated. She knew he had probably lost his job within a few days of not showing up for work. Their tiny apartment was barely large enough for the two of them. How could they ever afford a larger one for the baby if Hugh did not work? Most days anymore he would not even trouble himself to get up until in the afternoons. Hannah started to get into a deep, dark depression. She wondered if the pregnancy had brought grief and pain to Ambros.

Then one Saturday morning while Hannah was doing dishes in her tiny little kitchen, she was not aware as to where her husband may be. She noticed that he had gotten up in the middle of the night and left. This was starting to become common practice anymore. Or, he would leave of an evening and just not come home until the next day.

Hugh was so arrogant and Hannah was so depressed of late to where the two had not spoken much about anything. Then on this Saturday morning, one of the strangest things happened to Hannah. A young woman opened her apartment door and calmly walked in. She walked past Hannah's backside, through the very small kitchen and she opened the refrigerator door. She acted as though she lived there. She was also very much aware of her surroundings. Hannah felt that this woman had been in her apartment before. The young lady got something out of the refrigerator. As she turned around and started back out of the door, she said flippantly,

"Hugh wanted a beer!"

She had a smirk upon her face. Hannah just stood there in complete shock!

All of a sudden Hannah realized that she had met this girl before. Now she went into a nervous shock. Her hands began to shake. Tears flowed down her face and a heat wave engulfed her whole body. She watched out of the window to see where the girl was going. She realized now that the young lady had an apartment in the very next building. Hugh had posted a note or possibly had someone else post a note upon their door this very morning that had said he was going to the pool for awhile before coming home. This had been about three hours ago now. Earlier Hannah had thought about checking the pool area, but was worried about doing so.

By this time Hannah had her married name upon her driver's license. Since her husband was now doing nothing but playing, a few weeks ago when it was a little warmer Hugh had taken advantage of this fact while he was drinking and in a party mood. Hannah had walked up on him at the pool while he was lying upon a towel with a half-naked woman. Hannah knew that she had to be freezing at this time of year, but this woman was brown as could be and she had on a bikini. Beer bottles were all around them. This woman had to be drinking enough to where she could not feel the cold. Hugh, thinking he was being funny, started making fun of Hannah for being so white skinned. Then his attempt at having fun became nasty. He asked Hannah to show the young woman her driver's license. She did as he asked, then she realized why he wanted her to do this. As she walked away angrily from the pair she heard Hugh say,

"See, I told you she was my sister!"

So today instead of heading for the pool Hannah tore off her apron, dried her hands and decided to follow the girl who was just in her apartment. When she got to the girl's apartment door she could hear Hugh's voice. He was laughing and talking in a drunken state. Hannah started to knock on the door, but decided differently. Instead she ran back to her apartment and threw all of her clothes and her belongings together. She ran out to her car. A car, that was by the way, in her name. She jumped into her car and tried to leave. To her complete shock, Hugh had been at the car first while he had anticipated his wife's next move. She opened the hood only to find that he had removed her distributor cap. Beaten and hurt, all she could do was to take her things and go back into her apartment and rest.

As Hannah let her tired body fall into the couch, she started to realize that she *did* know this girl. She had seen her before! Now she realized where and when. On one night while she was working in the city and driving down to see Hugh at school, she had to hunt him. Hannah had traveled down to the school city about every two nights of a week. On this night someone had told her that Hugh was at a local bar. She found the bar and she went inside. It was dark, smelly, and noisy inside of that bar. She was only hoping to find her husband and to get out of there.

Suddenly, Hannah remembered seeing this very same girl in that far away town. On that night of her search the girl was in that bar. She was leaning over some of the chairs in a drunken state herself. She was holding onto Hugh's necktie. She was looking straight into his eyes while calling him Hughie, Hughie. Hugh was melted into the attention he was receiving from this wild woman. Hannah had gotten upset at this sight and to Hugh's shock and embarrassment she had informed this young lady, in no spared words, that her husband's name was not Hughie. Hannah had excused this episode as being in a bar with a drunken woman who could not have meant anything to her husband. She knew people did stupid stuff when they were drinking. Now she remembered that evening completely! This was the same girl. Thoughts rushed through Hannah's mind. Hugh must have brought this girl up to the city so she could live close by. Had they always had a relationship parallel to hers? Had Hannah been that big of a fool? Or, was this girl just taking advantage of the disagreement Ambros and Hannah were having over children?

Oh Dear God! Hannah was putting pieces together and she did not like what she saw. How could she be so foolish and with blind eyes? How could she be so completely naïve about her marriage to this now seemingly wild man? Had Hugh kept this woman as a girlfriend? Was all of this going on while Hannah was working towards their future in the city? Hannah had worked hard for that future over sixty miles away from her husband's obvious playground. Thankfully this night Hugh did not come home. As a matter of fact, he did not come home for the whole weekend. Hannah did not know how she would have handled that. She was a complete wreck. All she could do was cry.

Monday morning came and Hannah had a problem in getting to work. She needed her car. She was not able to drive to the bus stop now because not only had her husband taken the distributor cap, but now the whole car was missing. As the fact at hand soaked in, another realization came to the naïve Hannah. She suddenly realized that her husband had not tried to stop her from leaving. He was only trying to keep her from having the car. He knew he would want to use it later.

After Hannah had walked to the corner to use the pay phone to call her job and to tell them a lie about being sick, Hugh walked into the house and headed straight to the bedroom. It was plain to see he was having one big hangover. Hannah looked out of the window and it was also plain to see that the car was still missing. She was now very mad. She woke her husband up and asked him where her car was. He kept saying he did not know. Hannah told him she was going to report it stolen if he did not tell her where it was. She got no answer.

Hannah later wondered as to how she got through that day. She was so upset to where she could feel the baby in a knot for much of that day. She knew she had to calm down for the precious little life that was trying to survive inside of her. She finally forced herself to relax and went to sleep upon the couch. This is where she spent the night. Then the following morning she walked the three blocks to the bus stop and went on to work. Being at work was a relief. It helped keep her mind on other things. This continued for the rest of the week. Hannah would get up early, lose her insides from pregnancy, get dressed then walk to the bus stop and go to work. She knew better than to start a fight with her drunken husband. He was staying that way this whole week. He must be drinking all day and every day, because when she arrived home at about 6:30pm he was always either gone or he was in the bed while passed out.

Then one evening when Hannah arrived home she found a nice meal cooked and a sober Hugh sitting at the table. He had candles lit and was in a strange mood. Hannah hated him right now! She wanted absolutely nothing to do with him. He put a plate in front of her and asked her to please eat. She did not want to touch a drop of this food. For all she knew he could be trying to poison her. Or still a bigger fear was he may have found some way for her to lose her baby. She wanted him to just go away. Instead, he wanted to give her an explanation. Now that he seemed to be sober, Hannah lost some of her fear of him and started blowing her top. Hugh, being the older and stronger individual took complete charge of the situation. He said,

"I am sorry! I was so shocked when you told me you were pregnant to where I got drunk and made some terrible mistakes!"

He left that hang in the air as he dug into his meal. Hannah being mad enough to chew nails by now, said,

"*T-h-a-t i-s i-t*? *You are sorry*! You were shocked I was pregnant and that excused you to go out on me, sleep with another woman and stay drunk for days!"

Then she knew she was even madder than she had ever been because she started to cry. Not one of those misery cries, but a mad cry when she screamed,

"You sorry -^*!!^**#!-! Where is my CAR?"

Now she had made him mad. He stood up and threw his food all over the kitchen. He went over to the stove, picked up the pans and threw that food into the air. Hannah watched as it dripped down from the ceiling to the floor. He ran out of the door and knocked it off the hinges. Hannah was left with no answers, no marriage and a big mess to clean up.

Chapter 6

Hannah and Hugh separated. Then they got back together time and time again. This rocky relationship was not going to work. The two were from two totally different worlds. Hannah did not understand the ways of an older adult man who had never grown up or had what he called grown up years ago. She was still but a child. She still believed in a man riding up on a white horse and the pretty little white fences around a happy couple's yard. Hugh said he could not deal with having a child for a wife. Many times he would tell her that he would run off just to be with someone whom he felt was an adult woman. After the first big shock to Hannah's very strict moral attitude, she never ceased to amaze those around her when she forgave and took her husband back time and time again. Hugh had now somehow convinced Hannah that much of his shenanigans were caused by her not being a grown up woman.

Hannah's car was found. The young woman who had walked into their home and helped herself to the refrigerator had used it in fright to get away from Hugh and his much upset wife. Hugh was unable to tell Hannah whether he had loaned the lady the car or whether she had just taken it in a stupor of drunkenness. Since the car was located in Southern Ohio, Hannah's father and brother had retrieved it and it was now parked at her parent's house.

Hannah only knew they could not pay the rent without Hugh working and that her check would not carry the heavy partying that her husband partook of lately. Therefore, when Hugh insisted that they move to Cincinnati, Ohio, what else could she do but what he suggested. Hannah turned in a notice at work and began working it out. The couple gathered their few things, took a bus to Hannah's parents and picked up their car.

As if bad luck was following poor Hannah around, within a few days after arriving at Hugh's parent's home the car was broken into. All of Hannah's hand designed clothes were stolen. She was devastated! Knowing now that she would need maternity clothing shortly, she purchased only a few loose type items. Hannah's first project must be to find a job. Living from paycheck to paycheck and her husband's lack of concern over money, she knew she had to have a job very fast. Since she had always worked civil service, she knew her best bet was to apply for a civil service position. She got one within two days of applying. This position was in the basement of a mental hospital. There were long tunnels going everywhere and Hannah was told to watch every step that she took. There were some criminally insane individuals housed within these walls.

Hannah's position was to type from a Dictaphone. This was a hard position because she was not trained in medical terminology. She had to use a medical dictionary with almost every other word that she typed. Thankfully Hannah was a fast typist.

Hugh did not find a job and Hannah wondered how hard he tried. On many occasions Mr. Hughes would have to take, or come and get Hannah from work because Hugh would want the car for that day. He always claimed he was looking for a job but often would come home very late and with the smell of alcohol upon his breath.

The couple seemed to be getting along much better in this Cincinnati land. Many nights Hugh would tell Hannah that he was having pregnancy cravings. Hannah thought this to be odd but went along with his ideas. He often told her that he could be very sure that this baby was his because he was having all of the same sicknesses as Hannah. She had never heard of such a thing, but went along with his impositions.

Hannah would even go as far as to get out of her bed and drive to a Skyway Chili Restaurant as late as three o'clock in the morning because Hugh was having a craving. Hannah knew she was stupid at this point because no pregnant woman in her right mind would cater to the husband in these times. Everyone knew things should be in the reverse! She excused all of this simply because she loved Skyway Chili too. This Chili could only be found in Cincinnati, Ohio. It was a form of a wonderful chili that gave the customer a choice of one way, two ways, three ways or four. Hugh and Hannah both loved the four way chili. This was chili over some noodles that caused a saucy type bowl. Then one would add shredded cheddar cheese and onions. This was then served with oyster crackers. This made for the most wonderful combination and the cravings could be considered quite normal by men and women alike.

For a month or two Hugh and Hannah stayed at Hugh's parents. Finally they acquired an apartment in College Hill. This was by Hugh's doing and was an apartment that had to be shared with another couple. Hannah did not complain because the apartment was beautiful. It was in a large beautiful home that had chandlers and hardwood floors.

The couple did not live in this apartment for many weeks. Hannah could not remember Hugh being at home during this period. He was in his own stomping grounds and he knew far too many people to stay at home with his wife. One evening he did take Hannah to a VFW. This VFW was clear across town and up Reading Road. The two stayed really late this evening. It was fun because Hugh's parents were there and several of his family members. This was also a night that the Shriners came through. They were playing a game to where they were collecting earrings and trinkets for their hats. Hannah had to keep telling the men that she loved her earrings and they were not welcomed to take them. Everyone had great fun.

Hugh was dressed in a light beige suit this night and he looked so very handsome. His beautiful eyes danced tonight and Hannah knew once again that she was so very much in love with her husband. The extremely handsome Irish man, with his thick dark beautiful hair and his pretty blue eyes of a pale blue powder had lost some of that attraction to his wife while she was holding a grudge against him for fooling around on her. She knew that tonight she had forgiven all of his transgressions as she danced in his strong arms across the floor. She basked in the warmth of the love that they shared this night. TV shows of the times were that of Dr. Kildare, Dr. Casey, Bonanza and Peyton Place. About every show was filled with rough and tough handsome men. Hannah knew that none could hold a candle to the looks of her handsome husband.

Hugh's big broad shoulders and his thirty-two inch waistline, along with the way he was dressed was making Hannah melt tonight. She had never seen her husband look more handsome. Tonight those dancing Irish eyes seemed to be dancing only for her. At one time she looked over while they were dancing and noticed a wall lined with ladies who were watching her handsome husband dance. Hannah felt so proud tonight to know that he was *her* husband. He did not belong to anyone else, just her!

Hannah knew that her handsome husband, who stood about six feet tall with the sexiest of walks and his good looks, was so tempting for all of the women around. She knew that he dressed so very nice. She knew that every woman who saw him melted in her tracks, but she also knew that she had ironed his shirt and that when all else was said and done, this man belonged to her and he was going home with her. She thought for a minute and then silently said to herself,

"That is all that matters!"

Hannah laughed out loud when she remembered the young ladies who would stand along the walls of the college halls to watch her handsome husband walk by. Tonight was no different. Women were watching the couple dance from the side lines. Tonight Hannah felt very lucky to have won this man's affections. With a twinkle in his eye, Hugh said,

"What?"

He looked at her with those questionable blue eyes while they were floating across the dance floor. He said,

"What are you thinking about?"

Hannah told him she was thinking of how she must have fallen in love with him the day that he walked up to the water fountain directly beside of her. She told him that she had realized at that very minute that she could not find any flaws in him. She told him of how she had believed even his hands had been pretty. Then she told him how she believed him to be so very masculine. Hannah told her husband that she had fallen head over heels in love with him long before he ever knew it. He was in an exceptionally good mood this night. He said as he pulled her closer to him,

"I fell in love with you on the first day we met too baby!"

Tonight all was well with the Mr. and Mrs. Hughes.

Wedded bliss continued for a while. Christmas came and Hannah had never missed a Christmas with her family. The Hughes family had a large gathering this joyful season and everyone was having great fun. Hannah had believed the plan was to visit with the Hughes family first, then go on to Gallia County to visit with her family. As Christmas Eve approached, Hugh was showing signs that he did not want to go anywhere. This devastated Hannah. In later years she would come to know that Hugh's wanting to be with his family was not that unheard of and possibly he would have enjoyed his family as much as she would have enjoyed hers. However at this young age, all Hannah could see was that Hugh made a promise and now he did not want to keep it. Therefore, Christmas Eve was spent at the Hughes.

Christmas morning Hannah knew that her family had expected her. She tried once more to get Hugh to go with her to visit her family. He was solid in his desires and he would not budge. He kept saying that they would go to her family on New Year's. During the early morning Hannah told Hugh that she was going to go by herself. She knew nothing about Cincinnati and she had made her husband mad by this time with all of her ranting and raving. Hannah begged for Hugh to please draw a map. He did! He put down every alley and side street he could think of to get her out of Cincinnati. He was so mad to where he was hoping she would get completely lost.

The tires were bad on the car and the car should not have been driven anywhere, much less one hundred and fifty miles. They were what her father referred to as, 'May Pops'!

It took Hannah hours just to get out of Cincinnati. When she finally made it home her nerves were shot. Her parents had waited and made the children wait for their big sister to arrive before opening gifts. Hannah felt so guilty over this. There is no way that the children should have had to wait to open their gifts because her husband was so stubborn. She felt so ashamed.

The rest of Christmas day went wonderful. Hannah was sick a big part of it. Her nerves probably had played a big part in that. She realized the pressure and stress of coming from Cincinnati alone without knowing where she was going had taken its toll on this pregnant lady.

Hannah had been able to disguise her pregnancy from her parents up to this date. Being only three months along, she really was not showing much at all. All she had to do was unbutton a button here and there, put on a big loss top and no one was the wiser. For this visit she had worn a very large and long knitted sweater over matching stretch pants that had straps around her feet. This was a new modern style and Hannah loved it. The pants were so very comfortable and the sweaters were so soft and fluffy. There was no way anyone could have ever guessed that she was expecting. But then there was her mother!

Hannah spent that night with her family, but the following morning she knew she had to get back to Cincinnati. She would have to go to work the day after that. As she was saying her goodbyes to her loving family, her mother walked with her to her car. Just the same as the time her mother had ask if she was in love, this time her mother asked,

"Have you been to the doctor yet?"
Hannah said in a shocked way,
"What!"
Her mother repeated her question and this time with more determination.

"Have you been to the doctor yet?"
Hannah almost fainted. Not only was her mother not supposed to know that she was expecting, her mother was not even supposed to know that she was married. The couple had been able to keep this a total secret from Hannah's parents. Hannah had told so many lies to her parents to where she was sure she was crossing herself up. When one tells too many lies, it is so hard to keep them straight. She had told her parents that she had wanted to be close to Hugh, therefore she had taken a job in Cincinnati and his parents had been kind enough to give her a room. It seemed as though her parents had accepted that fact and they had accepted the fact that Hugh and Hannah were a couple.

While the couple was in Columbus, Ohio, Hannah had told her parents that she was the one who had the apartment. She was able to get away with this because she did share her apartment for a short time with a high school classmate. This was while Hugh was still in school. She had told her parents that Hugh supposedly had his own apartment in the very same complex. She neglected to tell her parents that her friend had moved out of her apartment when Hugh came to Columbus. Hannah felt these lies were to protect her from the threats of her family's religious beliefs and the strictness of her father. Now she finally believed maybe she had told so many lies to only destroy herself. She had gotten in so deep by now, what was she to do? Surely her father would not try to void a marriage when his daughter was pregnant. Could he even do that? She was not sure! How was she going to answer her mother?

Hannah thought about jumping into her car and speeding away while leaving her mother standing there in disbelief. She knew she could not do that. So she thought out her words very carefully as she said,

"No, mother I have not been to the doctor! What are you talking about anyway?"

Her mother said,

"Don't lie to me little girl. I know you are expecting!"

Hannah felt like a ten year old child again. She had just turned twenty. Yet her mother was treating her as a child. Finally, after glaring sternly into her mother's eyes she knew she was trapped. So she said,

"Yes mother I am expecting, but it is not what you think!"

She wanted to say,

"When you run to tell Daddy this let him know that I am very afraid of him. I am three months pregnant and I am happy about that. You guys can go off and be upset with me or whatever. I cannot take this anymore! I just don't care anymore!"

Hannah, of course, could not and would not ever say anything like that to her parents. She knew she couldn't. She never would and never had spoken to her parents in that way. Besides, she did not know but what she would have the rage of God come down upon her should she ever disagree with her parents in any way! Hannah's hands were now shaking. She was starting to get sick again. Finally in a weak voice, she ask her mother,

"How did you know?"

Her mother seemed to show sympathy and hugged her daughter as she said,

"Mother's always know!"

Hannah wondered why she always had such a guilt feeling about anything and everything with her parents. She was feeling big pings of guilt for being pregnant because she believed her parents were not approving. What kind of fear was this? Away from her parents, she was extremely happy to be expecting. Even though her marriage had ups and downs, she was extremely happy to be married to Hugh. She felt like an adult and she was happy. Or so she thought! With her parents she became a ten to fourteen year old child again who was scared to death of any consequences she may receive from displeasing them or their belief system.

Finally, Hannah asked her mother to please get into the car with her. The mother did as she ask and Hannah started to explain. She hung her head down low and would not look up at her mother when she said,

"Mother, I am so sorry. I have been dishonest to you and Daddy for way too long. You are going to explode. If you don't, I'm sure Daddy will! All I am asking is that you do not destroy my happiness. Please do not destroy my life, mother. I love Hugh!"

Then in that same half voice, half cry, she said,

"Mother, Hugh and I got married June the 2nd."

There, it was out! Now what would her parents do with this information? Would she be in so much trouble to where the family would demand an annulment? Would they try to annul her marriage to Hugh? She worried about everything clear down to her car. Would she lose her car? Her daddy had co-signed! Would she ever see her parents and siblings again? Fear overtook the young lady while she gripped the steering wheel so tightly to where she could feel her long fingernails cutting into her flesh. She prayed for her mother to speak, or for her mother to get out of her car so that she could just run away. It seemed like it took forever before her mother did say anything. When she did speak, she looked saddened as she said,

"I wish you had not run off to get married. Daddy would have come around. You could have had a proper wedding."

Then she laughed a nervous laugh as she said,

"I am however, very thankful that you are married!"

She let out that nervous cover up laugh as she reached over and put her hand on Hannah's stomach while saying,

"We would have had a problem with Junior here if you had not been married!"

To Hannah's surprise, her mother seemed somewhat happy. Maybe her mother was also scared and she was only putting on a good front. Either way, the mother slid over in the seat and hugged her daughter as she said,

"Congratulations to you, well I guess to us! Now get out of here before you are dark getting home! And *Go to the Doctor*!"

With that her mother got out of the car. She waved goodbye to her daughter. While smiling, she said,

"I love you!"

Hannah felt a relief flow through her veins. Her parents did love her. She knew that, but how would her father react to all of this?

Chapter 7

Cincinnati was not offering a job to Ambros Cooney Hughes. Most of January passed and Hugh could not find a job. Hannah was panicking. They were once more living with her husband's parents. This was not a very good arrangement in Hannah's book. She believed they should have an apartment of their own by the time the baby came along.

A few weeks into January, Hannah did not quite know what had happened. She arrived home one night by way of Mr. Hughes once more. Hugh had now told his parents about their marriage. Mr. Hughes was such a good old gentleman who did not seem to mind running all over the city to pick up his daughter-in-law. Actually, Hannah knew that the elderly gentleman thought a lot of her. She had to laugh at him because he must be like her mother. One evening, the Hughes had company. Hannah sat down into a small child's rocking chair. She was tall and thin and this was usually an easy accomplishment. Tonight, when she finally positioned herself into this seat, the father-in-law said,

"It would be easier wouldn't it little girl if you weren't carrying my grandson!"
Hannah looked at him in shock. He only laughed. She should have known he already knew she was pregnant. She knew there was something wrong with him a few days ago when she tried to eat a cream horn pastry. The elderly gentleman had taken this cream horn from her and thrown it into the trashcan. It turned out that years before refrigeration, the father had a friend who had died

from eating an obviously spoiled cream horn. He was being so over protective of Hannah. He had guessed about the pregnancy all by himself, because Mrs. Hughes had said nothing. Hannah realized that her husband had no intentions of telling them, obviously, until the day the baby was born! She chuckled to herself about that thought and wondered how he was expecting her belly not to show somewhere down the line.

This night Hugh was in a very strange mood. He did not act happy. When all of the company left the home, Hugh and Hannah retired to the bedroom. Hannah could not find her gown and rob. She asked Hugh if he knew anything about it. He said,

"Yes, it is all packed!"
Hannah twirled her head around to face Hugh and said,

"Why?"
He said,

"Because we are leaving."
Hannah was beside of herself. What did he mean? While the visitors were there he had taken all of their luggage to the car. Now he asked her to stay dressed because they were leaving tonight. She could not understand why, so she said,

"To where?"
Hugh told her that they were going to her parents for awhile. He was using the excuse that he could not get a job in Cincinnati. He stated that maybe he could find one there. Hannah questioned this because she came from such a small area. If her husband could not find work in Cincinnati, Ohio then how on earth could he find work in Gallia County? Finally, she talked him into waiting until she could give a notice on her

job. It took hours to convince him, but she finally did. He went to the car and returned all of their belongings back to their bedroom. Needless to say, Hannah was very tired the next day. She was never to understand what had happened that day because the parents acted the same and everything seemed to be quite normal at their household.

There was nothing to do for Hannah but to quit her job and move to her parent's home of about one hundred and fifty miles from the city of Cincinnati. Hannah knew that she must get a position at this residence very quickly. She could still get away without anyone knowing she was expecting. Who would hire someone who was with child? She did feel blessed in some ways. At least with the baby coming she would now have the much needed comfort of her parent's presence.

Hannah had never had any problem getting a position. She was smart and had a degree under her belt. She always knew she wanted more education, but knew she would have to work hard to get it. The first thing that she did after they had settled in with her parents was to go to a neighboring college city and get a position at the school. Being tall and very thin, Hannah was able to disguise the fact that she was expecting even during this month of February. She was now five months pregnant. She had to have a job. She could not tell the truth about the upcoming birth of a child.

Luckily, Hannah got a very nice position at the correspondence course department at the Ohio University College. Once again, she was thankful for knowing the importance of giving a notice when she was leaving a position. That, plus the fact that she was still working civil service gave her a boot in securing a nice position. Since her degree was from a satellite school of that college, this made everything seem okay to Hannah. She hoped to continue her education while working at this school. At this point she was not sure that she cared what her husband did. She was becoming very frustrated that he could not, or possibly would not, find a job. She was soon settled in with her parents. They had accepted all of her facts and she had her old room back. She had three square meals a day, so what else mattered. Daddy had furnished her with transportation and her life was getting back to normal. Hugh was becoming a liability.

Hugh would respect Hannah's parents to the point that he did not drink alcohol in their home. Hannah had learned that he really was trying to break his nasty habit. He told her that the very first time he had been drunk he was but nine years of age. Hannah had never heard of such a thing and thought to herself some of the thoughts she had heard from her father like,

"He must be a heathen!"
He told of how he got so drunk at that very young age to where he had fallen overboard of the family yacht. One of his brothers had to pull him out of the Ohio River. He also told of how his father used to drink too, but had since quit due to his poor health. Hannah never once realized that she was being judgmental. She was being all of the things she had hated so badly about her religion. She was now judging her husband and his family. She felt badly afterwards, because his family had been nothing but very kind to her. Her husband was the playboy. Her husband was the one who

cheated on her. Her husband was who she was mad at during this period.

Hugh told Hannah of how he never considered drinking alcohol to be a sin until she had pointed it out. He would laugh and ask her why Jesus would have turned the water into wine if it was a sin to drink alcohol. He would make light of Hannah's thoughts and tell her she was such a wet behind the ears prude. In reality she probably was. She came from such a strict way of believing and he came from a, what he called, more normal world. He said that the drinking socially was just what his family had always done. He said,

"We just believe in having fun! Did you ever think that maybe people drink for entertainment and to loosen up and to have some fun? Your family is so uptight, how on earth do they stand themselves?"

Hannah knew it was hopeless to explain anything to this man. She now only hoped he would get a job.

Hannah's parents had a building that had been a store and they were no longer using it. Hugh started to put up partitions of fine wood and started to build an apartment for him and his wife. Hannah was getting excited. She loved the idea of being able to have a home of their own. Hugh had nailed up slanted tongue and groove boards upon what was to become the most beautiful living room wall. He had then put white paint upon that wall, only to wipe it off quickly. Then he let it dry in the knot holes and the grooves. Later he had varnished the wall to a high shine. The store already had hard wood floors. The home was going to be very pretty. Hannah was pleased with this idea.

On many days Hugh would get dressed and go to work with Hannah. He would go to the movies or look for a job. There were many times the couple would just fight. But there were also many times they had fun. One evening of the much fun was while traveling the thirty some miles home from Hannah's work. Hugh told Hannah of the movie he had watched that day. The movie was called,

"Hush, Hush, Sweet Charlotte!"
Hugh would talk like the actors and repeat some of the things said in the movie. They laughed and joked most of the way home that evening. It was true. This couple still could have fun together.

Shortly after the move to Hannah's parents, Hugh did get a job. He was working construction on a high rise that was going to be a coed dormitory for the college students. This worked out marvelously for a while. Hannah, believing that they had a new lease on life, bought another car. After her father had found her old car parked in the country at the other woman's house, it never seemed to work quite right after that. This woman too had moved to her family's home around Colton, Ohio. The car had been found due to Hannah's father knowing so many people in law enforcement. This is how he had located the car. Hannah chose not to press charges and the car had been returned, but it was not in such good shape after that. It needed replaced.

Sad was the fact that Hannah's parents were now seeing the situation that their daughter was in. They started to try to help. Hannah's father made arrangements to trade the car in for a better one.

94

Her father had a cousin who owned the largest Ford car lot east of the Mississippi. The day of the trade, Hannah picked out a pretty black Pontiac convertible but the father's cousin refused to sell it to her while stating that it had some problems. So, they picked out something that Hugh fell in love with. It was an older 1959 Ford that had a retractable top. This Ford was hot pink and white. It was covered in chrome. Even the motor was covered in chrome. It had chrome skirts with Cadillac tail lights sticking out from the rear. The old car was traded in and everyone seemed happy.

Trips to and from work seemed to be happy times for Hugh and Hannah. She was starting to show her bun in the oven by now. Luckily everyone at work was happy about the announcement she had to make. Hannah knew this could have been a touch and go situation. She was lucky in the fact that she was a very good employee and a hard worker. She was also lucky enough to be able to take a few classes while her husband worked a later shift. These few months were much like the months of romance the couple had enjoyed while attending school the years before. Hannah seemed to once more be happy.

Then the partying started again. While working on this construction job with a large crew from New York City, Hugh started partying once more. The crew was away from their families and had nothing to do of an evening but to stay in a bar. Lucky for them, in less than a block from their positions stood a large restaurant/bar where they could spend their entire evenings. They could eat dinner; then party the night away.

One day it had started to rain a cold icy rain. The job was shut down for the whole day.

Hugh spent the rest of his day in the bar with his working buddies. By the time Hannah got off from work he was inebriated, smashed, intoxicated or any other word that could have fit his situation. Thankfully he did not fight Hannah when she insisted that she drive. In the past he had joked if he was high about how he may not be able to walk, but he could still drive. Thankfully tonight he did not say such things. However, she had not managed to get him to leave the bar until closing time. Therefore, she was very tired for the long drive home.

Living in the rolling hills of Ohio, there are many curves. Hannah and Hugh took a road less traveled because it was of a shorter distance to Athens, Ohio. On this night when Hannah took the largest curve of them all, Hugh opened the door. Hannah almost wrecked because she had to stop quickly. Her husband was dragging his feet upon the pavement. When she finally got stopped and placed his feet back into the car she ask,

"What on earth were you doing?"

He said,

"I was cramped up in here!"

Needless to say, Hannah slowed down for the rest of the trip. Then once more he about wrecked them before they arrived at her parent's house. This time he was throwing his arms around. He got his arm caught in the steering wheel at one time. Hannah with being pregnant was having a horrible time driving and getting sick all at the same time from Hugh's shenanigans. She knew saying anything this night would be futile. However, she intended a long talk to come tomorrow about endangering the lives of both of them and the baby.

96

On other occasions, the couple had lots of fun. They would walk hand in hand across the campus. Hannah was now wearing maturity clothing, so they looked the complete happy family. Often the couple rode home from the college with the top down on their collectors 1959 Ford. The top was a retractable top, meaning it was a hard top car with the exception that a button could be pushed and the top would retract into the trunk just like a convertible. Though getting old by this date, the car was beautiful. Hannah loved the color of 'Hot Pink and White'. She had broken out one of the tail lights while in Cincinnati because of all of the hills. The car was a straight shift and Hannah had a deadly fear of rolling backwards on the steep hills in the City of Cincinnati. She did just that on one day. The clear Cadillac tail light busted when she rolled into another car, but no damage was done to the other person's car. They were yet to replace this light, but the car was still very pretty.

On one evening, as the couple was riding home with the top down, it started to rain! The button was pushed and the top started to come up. They knew that they should stop before trying to close the top, but for some odd reason Hugh did not stop. He just tried to close the top while going down the highway. Suddenly, the top got to a certain point of standing straight up in the air and would not come down any further. Nor would it retract again. Hannah knew they were surely a site to be seen while traveling along these country roads in a hot pink car with the top standing half way up in the air and the female holding an umbrella over her head. Instead of stopping to try to rectify the situation, all Hugh and Hannah could do was laugh. They laughed all of the way home. When they walked into the door at Hannah's parents they were soaking wet. But, they were laughing uncontrollably. Hannah's mom laughed with them when she heard the story, but told them they deserved each other because they were both nuts! The condition with the car was something minor and Hugh had no problems in fixing it once the rain stopped.

After a while Ambros, or Hugh as Hannah called him, started to never show signs of drinking even when Hannah knew he drank most of the time. Hannah never understood that. There was someone that she knew who came to a summer function the family attended who was most usually drunk, or well on his way to being drunk each time they saw him. Hannah believed that is how someone should act if they drank, but Ambros rarely showed a sign. He started handling his liquor very well. His moods changed and Hannah could always tell when he had been drinking. She did not believe others could tell. He had a wonderful personality when he wasn't drinking, or when he was sober. He was just a little more nasty with Hannah when he was drinking. Everyone seemed to love this friendly, handsome man. No one was ever the wiser that he drank something constantly. Beer was like his only beverage. The only times he would really get completely nasty with anyone was when he drank hard liquor.

This way of living was not that unusual for anyone but Hannah. Her upbringing had not prepared her for any of this. Many women would have joined their husband and had fun. Hannah could only see that everything her husband did was horrible. She tried, but she just could not get the training she had out of her system. Hugh was just as bad, he could not get his training and life style out of his system. He did not have that desire. This couple was doomed for failure from day one.

Chapter 8

During Hannah's seventh month she realized that Hugh had stopped working on the apartment. Actually the only thing he had completed was the wall of the living room. He seemed to have lost all interest. Hannah did not understand. Then one weekend he told Hannah he wanted her to meet his other children. So they left for a small town outside of Cincinnati to see them. They arrived at a large old farm house where the children and their mother resided. The children were beautiful and the mother was corrigible. They visited for a while and then Hugh asked the mother if he could take the children home with him on some future weekend. The mother agreed. A few weeks later Ambros started to get the children on a regular basis. Hannah assumed that the mother must have wanted to know her better before sending her children off somewhere strange. She knew that she would have felt the very same way. She could not help but believe that this lady was a good and wholesome mother. Hannah's watchful eyes also could not help but to see that this woman was still in love with Hugh.

One weekend during the seventh month of the pregnancy Hugh went to pick up the children alone. He never returned. Hugh and the car were both missing. When Hannah finally found him, he was in trouble in the county where his other family lived. He had missed a few child support checks and was now a guest of the county jail. During that period, Hannah visited only to find that the ex-wife was visiting with Hugh regularly. Obviously, she and Hugh had worked something out regarding the back child support. When Hugh was released a couple of days later, he went home with his ex-wife. There he stayed!

Hannah did not see nor hear from Hugh until his new son was three months old. Though now a mother, she was still so naïve. She was still but a child. Yes, she was still green and wet behind the ears! After it all, she still believed herself to be in love with this man even though she had to go through the delivery of her first child all alone. Her heart would break when she would see another father being so proud of his new born child and of his wife. She could not help but be jealous of the other mothers.

Hannah was so naïve, but so-o-o-o-o in love with her husband to where she stayed in a state of depression the whole time Hugh was gone. Oh, she was completely proud of her beautiful little son. He was bringing her so very much happiness on that side of the coin. He was so very beautiful. On the day he was born, he looked just like his daddy. She knew that no one would ever question if he were a boy. It was so very obvious that he was a boy! He was so very handsome!

Hannah had worked for one half of a day on the Saturday of a day right before her new son was born. That Sunday she had attended a family reunion. That Sunday night she had to have her teenage cousin drive her to the hospital several miles away. The seventeen year old cousin was so worried and so scared. However, there was no need to worry. The young mother had a hard delivery and was in labor for fourteen hours. The baby was born the following Monday.

Hannah did not hear from her husband. She knew that he knew exactly when the baby was to be born, but he never called. He never came to the hospital and he never called. The young lady was so very hurt. Before his great exit, Hugh and she had many talks about what to name the baby. Hannah liked the name Jeffery, but Hugh was completely determined that if it was a boy he would be named after him. This son would be a junior. Even without the presence of her husband, Hannah **DID** name her son after his father with the Jr. at the end of his name.

Then as fast as Hugh had disappeared, he returned. The baby was then three months old. One day Hugh just showed up with the intentions of moving right back in and acted as though nothing had ever happened. Strange, but he and Hannah never discussed the reasons for his leaving. Nor did he explain anything at all. After being back at Hannah's mother and fathers for about two months, Hugh had not found another job. Hannah had gone back to work and was working every day. Now to keep her husband from having problems with his ex-wife, Hannah was making sure the child support payments were being made. Hugh was staying home during the days with her mother while getting acquainted with his beautiful son.

Hannah awakened one morning to Hugh telling her that he wanted the family to move to Texas. One of his brothers was in Corpus Christy, Texas and he was in the Navy. Hugh thought maybe he could reenlist. Hannah was scared. She had never been away from her family. Never had she been further than a little over one-hundred and fifty miles to Cincinnati. Traveling all the way to Texas was very scary. **But**, Hannah loved her husband and she wanted her marriage to work. So before she knew it, the little family was off and on their way to the big State of Texas!

Hannah was the first to get a job in Texas. Hugh finally landed one in a half working condition and a half reserves type position at the base where his brother was a high officer. They were bringing in good pay checks now, so they started to look for a home of their own. To this date they were staying at his brother's home. They were sleeping in the living room on a daybed while their son was in a baby's car bed beside of them.

They were now miles away from Hannah's home and her way of life. Here, the brothers partied heavily. The sister-in-law had a baby too and the women just stayed home and watched after their children. Before long Hugh and Hannah were fighting constantly. After one big blow out, Hannah moved into a small apartment by herself. She called her parents to have them wire her the money to come home. BUT, Hugh went home with her. He explained as to how he just wanted to party. He did not want to lose his wife. Hannah had no choice in the matter.

Shortly after the arrival back to Ohio, Hannah discovered that she was pregnant again. This time, she did not tell Hugh. She had gotten to the point where she was afraid to tell him anything about anything. He drank so heavily and he had become very nasty more than once at this time. Hannah knew he was no longer only drinking beer. He was now using strong alcohol. He would sometimes drink a fifth of something a day. If anyone offered a stay awake kind of pill he would take one of them as well. These combinations caused Hugh to often become a complete stranger.

Hugh would more than likely leave Hannah should he find out that she was expecting again. Once again, she was on the birth control pill. Once again, she could not understand how she could have gotten pregnant while on that pill. Once again she questioned whether Hugh had replaced her pills with something else. She knew that he was deadly against any form of birth control even though he swore he wanted no more children. Hannah was justified with her thoughts. She was not being paranoid. Lately, she had to replace her pills on more than one occasion because Hugh had flushed her packet of pills, one by one down the toilet.

The need to tell Hugh about the pregnancy was short lived anyway. Once the couple arrived back to Ohio, Hugh left Hannah once more. The couple had gone back to Columbus, Ohio. Here, they had once more rented an apartment. Then during a heated argument Hugh headed right back to Cincinnati and he did not come back. This time he did not go to his ex-wife. He just went to his hometown without Hannah. This time, Hannah knew the drill. She was comforted by having her mother and father to protect her and to help her along. Once again she went back to work. Thankfully her father was always able to provide her with transportation. He always had an extra car around. Hugh had once again taken off with the car. By now the old car was pretty much shot anyway, so Hannah started working towards buying another.

All through the pregnancy, Hannah worked. She had a babysitter who let her son get hurt by a bookcase one day. She immediately found another babysitter who kept a terrible looking house.

Hannah hated watching her son cry after her while standing at that screen door. Then, she found that this lady did not use the stack of diapers given her each day. Hannah came to believe that this babysitter was possibly giving her baby something to make him sleep all day long. Within a week, she did not take him back to this babysitter either. Luckily, she had many relatives in this city. However, most of them worked during the day. She had an aunt who was a school teacher and she helped when she could with the baby. Then summer came and Hannah's younger sister came to babysit for her. Thankfully, a while before the delivery of the second child, her mother was able to come and stay with her.

Hannah worked up until the very day that the doctor had told her that she should deliver. The company where she worked had a policy. It stated that after the delivery of a baby, a woman could not return to work until the baby was six weeks old. Hannah was devastated! How could she and her children survive if she could not work?

To add to Hannah's demise; she nor the doctor could be quite sure as to when she had become pregnant. They had either miscalculated, or the baby was really late. Hannah was home weeks with no pay before the baby was born.

Hannah's mother did not drive. Therefore, at the time of the baby's birth Hannah drove herself to the hospital. She would pull over, have a pain and then drive on. Even with all of her mother's worries, they arrived safely.

The hospital had many interns and students. Big groups of students would come up to Hannah's bed side. They would be carrying their little clipboards while asking very intruding questions. They were kind enough to wait while she would have a severe pain. Every so often, one of these students would think that they were saying something nice to her with a,

"Oh no, don't you worry about us now. You just go right ahead and let your emotions show with your pains. We will wait for you to answer!"

They were asking dumb questions like,

"Does it hurt for you to have sex?"

This was all happening while she wanted to scream and while she was driving her long fingernails straight into the flesh of her hands. This normally calm and sweet girl hated these people right now.

Delivery was long, but well worth it. It brought Hannah the most precious daughter. When she opened her eyes she saw the most beautiful little girl she had ever seen. She knew all was well with the world once more. Once more she found herself in the hospital all alone for days while she watched the other fathers interacting with their new babies. Her heart was breaking for herself and for her new baby. She was somewhat embarrassed that she did not have a husband around. With the many Victorian beliefs that most everyone still seemed to have in her circle, she only prayed no one believed that she was a single mother. She had been raised to believe that would be the largest of shames. Hannah caught herself flashing her wedding ring at everyone who passed.

Maybe it was bitterness. Maybe it was hurt, but in a selfish kind of a way Hannah was happy to have her beautiful little daughter all to herself. She knew this baby was the most beautiful little girl that had ever come into this world. Her little head was so very perfectly shaped. She was just beautiful in every way. Hannah counted her little toes and fingers. She kept taking off the little hood the nurses had placed upon her head. She wanted to see that beautiful shaped little head and look at her high eyebrows. This mother could not take her eyes off the prettiest little face that she had ever seen. She believed that this was the most beautiful little girl in the whole wide world. This was Ambros Hughes's loss and the baby was *all* Hannah's now.

Upon the release date from the hospital, Hannah felt she had a new lease on life. She knew that she had the two beautiful children and that had to be all that mattered in the world. She had missed her son so very much on the days while she was in the hospital. Now, she knew she was going to do everything in her power to keep her wonderful little boy and sweet baby girl forever safe from all harm. She intended to pour all of her love over these beautiful children for the rest of her days. She would go back to work immediately to provide. She believed herself to be completely done with their father forever.

As Hannah was wheeled down to the hospital office, her mother took the precious little baby from her arms and went to the car. Hannah's son, who was only fourteen months old, awaited his mother in her parent's car. Granted, she had been eight months pregnant when she finally went to the doctor. This was due to her husband's abandonment and limited funds. She could not afford to go any earlier. Hannah felt so stupid sometimes. She was still so naïve about everything! She had believed that she had everything arranged for the birth of her child. She had made arrangements with her doctor to pay a monthly payment of $200.00. He had agreed. She believed this to be the whole fee. Unbeknownst to her, she was not going to be permitted to leave the hospital without full payment of the hospital bill. All the poor girl could do was stay in her wheelchair and cry.

When the young lady was not delivered to the family as promised, Hannah's father came back into the hospital office to see what may be the problem. He was informed that Hannah was not free to leave the hospital without full payment of the hospital bill. Hannah hung her head in shame while her father wrote a check for the full amount due. It had to be done. They would not release his daughter.

Hannah had already been through so much of the pressures of the time period. No one alive believed that a woman without a husband could do anything alone. Her doctor was a nice man but since many of her relatives used the same doctor, someone had told him of all her problems and of how she was all alone. Most likely the conversations were that of pity and worry. The person must have gone into deep detail with Hannah's doctor about her husband Ambros. Instead of anyone thinking that maybe this young lady had the ability to make a living and a determination to protect her children, even the doctor she respected was now questioning her. Hannah knew she was smart. She knew that she was going to make a better world for her children even if she had to sell her soul.

On one of Hannah's visits to her doctor, a conversation brought up by him nearly destroyed her. She was asked by her doctor if she wished to put her daughter up for adoption. Hannah's eyes got large and fire came up into her throat. She knew her face was ablaze. How on earth could *ANYONE* ask such a horrible question? Hannah blew up at her doctor! She cussed, she screamed. She **hated** that doctor at this minute. Ready for her examine, she had nothing on. She was most usually the most modest person alive, but on this day she got up from the table. She threw down the sheet and she started throwing her clothes on right there in front of the doctor and his nurse.

Hannah did not know who could have made her out to be someone who would ever have the slightest thought of giving up one of her children. Maybe the doctor came up with that on his own. She did not know! Never had that thought crossed her mind. What a *HORRIBLE, HORRIBLE,* thought! Why would she give up either of her children? The doctor might as well have taken out a knife and cut out her heart! She was so extremely aggravated, hurt and very mad! She did not remember ever being that mad before! Needless to say, the doctor begged her to calm down. He begged her to remain his patient. He acted embarrassed that he had asked such a question. Hannah finally calmed down and she accepted her doctor's apologize. From that day on the doctor never mentioned it again. The good doctor had realized, although he was more than likely trying to help from his misguided information, that the statement had hurt Hannah very badly.

Hannah had loved her son more than life itself. She had already loved the baby that had been moving around inside of her. Even before the delivery, she had felt so close to her new baby to where she knew it was a girl. Hannah had only picked out a girl's name. How could anyone ever believe she would want rid of this child. Her children were all she had. Her children were her heart, her life and her everything. She was so very hurt and mad that someone would have questioned her ability to raise her children.

After the birth, attempts were made to contact the father once more. Hannah's parents could not understand their son-in-law. Everyone tried, unsuccessfully to get hold of Hugh. Hannah was sure by now with the attempts of notification that the whole Hughes family was very much aware of a new addition to their family. But, she did not hear from any of them.

Hannah went home with her beautiful little girl to her beautiful little son and tried to make a go of it. She could not wait until the end of her six week period to return to work. She had an apartment and she had expenses. She had to pay her bills. If not, she and her family would be out in the street. The poor girl was not yet twenty-two years of age. She was so thankful that her mother had decided to stay on with her for a while longer. She had no idea of how she could afford babysitting with both of the children. Many people would not take a child that had not been potty trained. Hannah now had two babies. Her children were only fourteen months apart and she had not trained Ambros, Jr. as of yet.

The young lady found a solution to her money problem. She went to a temporary service and applied for a job. She tested high and was sent immediately to a manufacturing company. She thought she would take the temporary job and try to stay on that job until she could go back to her regular position. She made the decision not to tell anyone connected with any positions that she had just had a baby. She was back to work within a week after the delivery. Hannah had a hard time for a while. She would go into the bathroom, lay her head upon the sink while throwing cold water into her face to keep from passing out. Thankfully no one was ever the wiser. She told no one that she had just delivered a baby. This company liked her very well. They made her a better offer than she would have received once she returned back to her regular position. So she took the job with this company as their payroll and accounts payable clerk.

During the baby's first months, Hannah was so happy to have family members stopping in all of the time. Everyone believed her children to be absolutely beautiful and they wanted to visit as often as they could. During this time Hannah had a stalker. She would have been scared to death had she been all alone. Many mornings when she would go out to get into her car, she would find twelve long stem wine colored roses in the handle of the door. This was very eerie, especially since the color of these roses was her very favorite wine color rose. After a while the roses stopped. Hannah was never to find out who was behind this jester.

It seemed that many unusual things happened to this new mother. Both of Hannah's children had to wear real cloth diapers. They were allergic to the paper kind. Hannah had to go the Laundromat almost every night. She now owned five dozen diapers. She worked every day and cared for her children every night. Her parents knew that she needed help badly. So they sold their much loved home and moved to the city where they could care for their grandchildren. Hannah felt blessed.

Hannah's mother would become her constant babysitter. The lady was fascinated with her first grandchildren. This was such a relief. When Hannah needed a car to carry her to and from work, or the children needed clothing, medical attention or other needs; the security of having her parents was immeasurable. This also made it easier for Hannah to take a second job when needed. She had to have extra money often because there would be no child support. It was as if her husband had completely fallen off of the map.

One sun shining day, when Hannah's daughter was eighteen months of age, Hugh showed up once more. The grandparents had purchased a home in the city. Hannah had made enough money and had now become secure enough to have moved with her small children into a very nice apartment. She was getting her life on tract. Her apartment was one that was based on her income, but it was a nice new apartment and she was very happy. She had purchased a newer car and life was getting better for the troubled Hannah Hughes. Her wages were better and her parents were staying in Columbus, Ohio to babysit. These children being the Dahl's first grandchildren caused the grandparents to love this duty. They never once charged for any of their services, which helped Hannah and the children to survive nicely.

One evening after Hannah had picked up the children, she had stopped to buy some groceries on her way home. Upon arrival at her

112

apartment complex, she got the shock of her life. Hannah and her children lived on the third floor of the apartment complex. She started walking up the enclosed wide steps with a bag of groceries in one arm, her daughter in the other while holding the hand of her small son. The little boy had to walk slowly up the steps because of his short little legs. Finally Hannah and the children were at the top of the stairs and they had walked down the hall to their apartment. She sat down the bag of groceries to get her door key from her purse. She had been aware someone was behind her upon the steps. She had not turned around to look at the person. Many people lived in this apartment building, so she assumed it was most likely another tenant. Just as she got the door opened a large foot came up and opened the door wider. To her total shock and disbelief, it was her husband Hugh.

Hannah had told no one who knew her husband where she lived. She thought she was safe. She was through with him forever! She was making a life for herself and her children. That life was working for her. She needed nothing to do with this man. Ambros had found her by watching outside of her parent's home. Somehow, he had found out where they lived. He had parked down the street and waited to follow Hannah home. Although Hannah's family Christian belief was that when one marries they must stay married forever; Hannah had decided that she was completely finished with her husband. He had left her one too many times. Even with the strong belief system she was just waiting to get enough money together to get a divorce. She blamed that belief system and believed that had been the force behind her staying married to this man as long as she had. Now the man was back. What was she to do?

Ambros just never left. The new marriage bliss that he had decided upon only started after weeks of sleeping on the couch and Hannah refusing to let him back into her heart. Finally, like any good wife she weakened and he was back into her good graces, hook line and sinker. She felt like such a fool, but she knew that she still loved this man.

Hannah had been doing fairly well without her husband, but she had missed him no matter how hard she tried to deny that. She could not shake the love she felt for this man. She knew this love was very hazardous to her health. Once her parents found out that the husband was back in the picture, they were not happy. Her father had told her that she would have permission from God to get a divorce. He had told her that one could divorce if the reason was because of fornication. See, her church had given her an out.

No one in Hannah's family had ever gotten a divorce and she was scared. Plus the fact that Ambros could be the real charmer. He was not ready to let her give up on him just yet. Even with this, God only knows what number of a chance this was. It also was not very long before the husband was back to his merriment ways. He had now met a big group of people that he considered to be his very best friends. Parties started to happen in her own apartment. One night Hannah realized this situation was *ALL WRONG* when her two year old son got a beer can out of the trash and drank what was left in it. She knew the differences in the way she and her husband were raised would always be a conflict over how to raise their children.

Then one evening Hugh came home with a friend and said,

"I'm going to Florida. Don't know when I'll be back."

Hannah got really mad. She followed him to the parking lot with many of his clothes in tow and asked him what she was to do with the rest of them. She screamed,

"You will not be coming back. Not now, not ever!"

He screamed back,

"That's fine with me! Why don't you just burn the clothes?"

Once more, Hugh was gone for several months. It did not seem to matter what Hannah said. Hugh always seemed to know he could come back. Once more, and then again, each time he would return. Each time Hannah would take him back. The struggles continued between this couple. They went back and forth while getting back together time and time again. *Finally*, after six years of marriage they got a divorce. Hannah filed for divorce the first part of the year and on March 19th their divorce became final.

Hannah was now riding a city bus every day to work because of the financial problems that the marriage had caused her once more. She had lost her latest car. The pain of her divorce was heavy upon her mind. No matter what had happened, Hugh was like an addiction to the pretty Miss Hannah. She believed she could never love again. She was grieving! She saw the morning paper lying on the seat beside of her one morning while on her way to work. She turned straight to the marriage and divorce section. She knew Hugh was living with another woman by this time. But she was not prepared for what she was about to see. There it was, right in front of her! There was a marriage license announcement for Ambros Hughes. Hugh was to remarry on April the 4th. This was less than one month after his divorce became final.

Hannah was devastated! She was hurting beyond belief. That little naïve girl had now become a woman. She really was a woman now! She was hurting indeed, but she had become a woman! Now, she just needed to be strong. She needed to be very strong. She had two beautiful children to raise. She knew that she must get a hold of her feelings. The times being as they were, many believed not having a husband would put her out there as a failure. Hugh had finally made her feel completely useless. Her pretty face was now dragging the pavement!

Chapter 9

Life became most difficult for Hannah as she tried to raise her children. Thankfully, she had her parents to lean upon. Had she not had them, she would have surely been lost. Even with this large support system, Hannah tried to run from her pain. This woman now became a runner. She ran from pain, hurt and devastation. She ran as fast as she could run. She was moving from place to place while meeting more and more new people. She was leaving her tortured world behind. She tried every path that she could find upon her journey, while hoping that she could stay just one step ahead of her grief. She was a very attractive young woman, but she could not see that. Many men kept interest in her, but she dated very few. Each time she tried to have a relationship with anyone, she would find out quickly that he was not what he seemed to be. She suddenly believed she must be a magnet for the worst kind of a man.

One would believe Ambros had moved on after the divorce, but Hannah had many problems with him for a long time. He claimed he had never wanted the divorce. He claimed that Hannah had listened to the other woman instead of taking the time to discuss it with him. Hannah reminded him if that were so, what was the reason for the sudden marriage? Obviously, Ambros had ideas about having his cake and eating it too. In reality once Hannah thought about it, she realized that Ambros never did say he actually wanted the divorce. He had only hung his head while his girlfriend told her that Mr. Ambros Hughes wanted a divorce so that he could marry her. Maybe he really did not want one. However, if this be true, she never knew him to listen to anyone. She never knew him to be submissive in any way, so she had a real hard time believing anything he was telling her. After all of that, he kept trying to come back to Hannah.

While Hannah's world was falling apart, she realized that Ambros must not really know what he wanted out of life. She found comfort in the fact that he was more than likely miserable. Maybe the grass was not so much greener on the other side. Of course, she realized he had problems letting go of his first wife as well. Later she learned that the other lady had been expecting when she divorced Ambros. He was most surely caught in a problem.

Hannah finally took enough hurt, enough Ambros, and she left town. Within two years after her divorce, she had moved herself and her children to another state. In the very beginning she was happy after the move. Even though she loved her parents and she loved the care they had given her children, she knew that due to her need to work so many hours that her children seemed to belong more to her parents than to her.

Hannah's parents went into a protective mode with the children. Their religious beliefs hit face on with their disrespect for Ambros. They also had lost respect for a daughter who had returned time and time again to a husband such as Ambros. This made them overpower Hannah in about every way. Hannah knew all of this was because she had to depend on them so very much. She had lived with her parents for an extended amount of time after her divorce. She had moved in and out of their home so many times to where she could definitely understand their dismay.

The deep emotional differences and the disrespect of Hannah's choices in life caused her parents to teach the children in their beliefs. The mother and father were the children's controlling factors. Hannah was just thrown into the stack somewhere along the line as an unruly child. She was treated as one of the little children. Whether she had a right to feel this way or not, she did feel hurt. She felt moving away would bring her children back to her. Through no fault of her wonderful parents at this time, Hannah felt like a victim. Ambros Hughes had given her that feeling of always being the victim. This was hard to overcome.

With Hannah's low self-esteem and with the failure of a marriage that she had wanted so badly, combined with her parent's religion output of their never approving of anything she did made her feel like she was the person who was always in the wrong. She could only be ashamed for the sins she had committed. She would often question what she had done so terribly wrong that brought her world crumbling down around her. She felt all that she had done was to fall in love with Ambros. Obviously he was the wrong man, but everyone could not be as fortunate as her parents had been in finding each other. The strong beliefs kept Hannah considered being a sinner, even in her own mind. She always felt she just had to get away. This would turn out to be another one of her, now obvious, mistakes in life. She was naïve and she was doomed by her own despair.

Once Hannah got her own apartment and a new job in a new state, she landed herself upon her couch one night and said,

"I'm free! This is now my world. My kids are my kids. This is my life. This is our NEW life!"

Happiness was short lived. Shortly after arriving in the Northern part of a state that did not have the good economy that Ohio could brag of at that time, the bottom fell out of everything. The position that Hannah got just days after arriving into town was cut back to only two days of a week. Now the little family was struggling. They were struggling badly. It felt like they were a million miles away from anyone who cared about them or anyone who could help.

Hannah had to break down and ask her parents for help once more. They again came to her rescue by sending her money when needed. Hannah would not ask until there was absolutely no food for their table. Now, with the stress and the loneliness of being so far away from home, this young woman became depressed. She was not even thirty years of age yet, but she felt like she had lived a dozen lives. She became very, very depressed. One may have called her depression, 'Clinically Depressed'!

Hannah smoked heavily at this time and she let her health go down the tubes. On her thirtieth birthday she almost died of pneumonia. When she finally came to her senses, she did not remember anything that had happened for several days. Her little children had covered their mother up with coats and anything they could find. She must have told them that she was cold. The poor little ones had pushed chairs up to the cabinets and they had been eating only things such as peanut butter and bread. Feeling guilty when she realized that her children had been sick as well, she felt terrible knowing that she had not been coherent enough to care for them. Not until Hannah saw the clothes that were stacked in a large heap in the bathroom floor, did she realize that she must have been out for days. At this point, she had no funds, no insurance and *no hope*. Had it not been for her two day employment, no one would have ever known that she was so sick. A lady from her job finally brought over some medicine that had been given her children. It was packed with antibiotics. Plus the lady had brought along a lot of fresh squeezed orange juice. Finally Hannah, with her small frame of one-hundred and fifteen pounds, was back on her feet. She would forever admire her little children for their brains and their bravery. She thanked them for knowing to stay around home while their mother was incoherent.

At this point Hannah should have been wise enough to pack her belongings, her beautiful children and head back to Ohio. She would not do this, thus giving her family more reasons to believe that she did not have good judgment.

After many months of struggling to keep her head above water and while working part time as a home party hostess, someone bought the company for which she worked days. Thankfully, shortly thereafter she was back to work on a full time basis and receiving a full week's check. It was still very rough for this young lady, but she soon learned how to manage with the funds that she received. She did the best that she could.

Due to the failed marriage and anyone whom Hugh and Hannah had known turned out to be only Hugh's friends, Hannah realized she had never really had any friends. Now she would not let herself get close to anyone. The apartment complex in which she lived had a few single women. Obviously, none had lived the life that Hannah had lived. Their ex-husbands were still much involved in their children's lives and they were always available when one of them was needed.

These apartment women would gather together and decide to go out. This was what they called a 'Girl's Night Out'. They were to do this once each week. All had children. So it was decided to rotate the women. One would stay home each week to care for all of the children. Hannah went one evening under the pressure she was receiving from the others. Due to the places she had been with her ex-husband and a few dates in between, this caused her to look around. She looked up at the band. She looked around at all of the people who seemed to already be high. She looked at the darkness of the room, then a man came up to her and asked her dance. She refused. Suddenly, she asked herself just what she was doing there. Thoughts ran through her mind like,

"Been here, done this! Don't want to do this anymore!"
She had fought too many years to make a life for her and her children. Now, this very night her children were at a stranger's home. She made her excuses and she never went out with these ladies again.

Hannah's life became work, worry and stress. She missed her family terribly and she knew her children missed their grandparents. She tried to travel back for visits as much as possible.

Many times this was done in an old car that could barely make it the five-hundred miles she had to drive. Many nights she would leave straight after work on a Friday night. This endangered the whole lot of them due to the fact that she would sometimes become very sleepy along the way. This was a very nervous young lady anyway. She was afraid of the mountains. Especially the ones you could look down over and see forever. Her hands would always start sweating when she crossed what she called the Jellico Mountains. There was only one little road up on these mountains at that time. It went to nowhere. It was called 'Stinking Creek Road'. A major problem was that the weather could be totally different on the top of these mountains. Many times the fog could be cut with a knife. Other times the valleys would be dry, only to find flooding rain on the top of these mountains.

Over the years of traveling this route, there were many problems along the way. One trip, thankfully without her children, Hannah had a terrible fright! All traffic was stopped on top of her fearful mountains. This was due to an ice storm that had formed on the very tops. The lower lying areas did not have any ice. No one knew when they climbed the mountains that they would be in such a contrariety. One had to keep their cars running to keep themselves from freezing to death. Hannah's car became very low on gas. That was not the worst part. After not being able to move for several hours, her car started to slide. This was while it was still in park. Thankfully by this time the National Guards were moving everyone down the mountains ever so slowly and with much care. Once she reached the bottom, she found that they had closed I-75 completely. Though relieved to be safe, people slept in churches, private homes and on every chair or empty floor space left within the few motels at the exit just below.

Another trip was during the time of the tornados that were tearing Xenia, Ohio into pieces. Hannah had no idea this was going on. She came through the worst storms imaginable while driving through the State of Kentucky. She could barely see if she was on the road. She was amazed at a site she had never seen before. Large frogs were hopping to safety over the roadways. This time she was headed north and her children were asleep in the back seat. She left them asleep so as not to worry them. Her hands were sweating and she was very fearful.

Another such trip was while the gas crunch was on. There were lines at every service station. Hannah got into the State of Kentucky once more and turned onto I-64. This was the last leg of her journey. She traveled along at an even pace, only to find that she was nearly out of gasoline. She started watching exits and found that all of the stations on I-64 were closed. There was nothing left to do but pray! Her children were asleep and she prayed. She really prayed to the God of her youth. It is funny how she could lean upon her family's belief system when she felt she needed it. She continued to pray! Somehow the big ole' heavy car made it all of the way to her parent's home. What was so ironic with this was that the following morning the car would not even start due to the lack of gas. This renewed Hannah's faith in the God of her father. During winter months these visits were very short. The little

124

family would arrive in the middle of the night on early Saturday morning. They would leave on Sunday. However, these visits were very much needed for both Hannah and her children.

Hannah did not realize that she was still running. She had such a beautiful extended family. She was depriving herself and her children of that great love. During her running she missed birthday parties, school plays, weddings, funerals and just everyday occurrences. Running is what Hannah did best. She had started running when she was very young and now she could not stop. She did not know how to stop. *Lonely* and *Sad* were words she truly understood. *Happiness* was not so common of a word in her vocabulary. Hannah realized that she had started grieving over her marriage shortly after she had married. She also realized she had probably been grieving over her life since the day she had turned fourteen.

After a few years and still more mistakes, Hannah began to be more comfortable in her adult world. The people who had purchased her company seemed to be very stable. They were very kind to her. On the day of the purchase, she had been asked to bring coffee to one of the new owners. She was wearing the styles of the times. She had on a white gored mini skirt that had a big colorful scarf tied around the waist. She had on a black puffy long sleeved taffeta blouse and she was wearing tall white boots. Her hair was long by now and she had colored it a very light blonde. These were the styles of the day. Somewhere along the way, Hannah had picked her face up off the pavement and by now she was quite comfortable in her own skin. She had been told very often that she was very pretty. Thankfully, her losses and her upbringing kept her from believing many of these compliments.

For some reason, on this day, Hannah did believe a compliment that was given to her. She felt her face turn a bright shade of pink. Just as she delivered the tray of coffee into the office, the man whom she had seen pull up in front of the building driving a beautiful Corvette was watching her every move. This was a small company with only two women who managed the office. They both did all secretarial, all bookkeeping, and all reception work together. Hannah acted as the receptionist upon this gentleman's arrival. She had noticed he was extremely attractive. She also noticed he was dressed to the elevens instead of the nines. This man was all together in every way. Just as she put the large tray upon her boss's desk, the gentleman said,

"She looks like that and she can cook too!" The men both laughed. Hannah was so embarrassed. As she walked back into her office she told her coworker what had happened, only to be told that this is the man who was purchasing the company. He and another man would be merging the small company in with their larger company.

The compliment turned to fear when the other lady told Hannah that the purchase was to be completed this day and that she was not sure of how many of the employees the new company would be taking with them. Why had no one been told? Hannah could not lose her job. She had two children, an apartment, utilities and a car that was going to break down on any given day. She had gone to court to get child support on several different occasions while still in Ohio, only to have given up. Each time she was either not given the money. Or, she was told she must give her ex-husband visiting rights from 8:00p.m. Friday to 8:00p.m. on Sunday. With Hugh's behavior, she would do without child support rather than put her children in his care. This is the way it was left and she received no funds to help with the rearing of her children.

Finally when all of the moving was complete and decisions were made, Hannah still had a job. She was hired as the office manager and the financial officer of the newly merged company. The company had all of these people in place, but they liked the looks of Hannah's resume and her work ethics. So much to her surprise, they put her in charge of the office and its employees. This was wonderful to Hannah because it also meant a larger weekly check. The downside was that her small family would have to move. The company would be moving to a neighboring small city. Hannah hated the fact that her children would have to change schools once more.

Chapter 10

Hannah knew her road to success was a very long and hurtful path. She had already reached a time in her life when most people believe their life is set in concrete and it can never be changed. Now, she had a wonderful job that she could pour herself into. She became close friends with everyone she worked with and she was happy in everything but love. She was adjusting and her children seemed to be happy.

For several years Hannah worked each day alongside of her new boss. He was handsome, smart, settled, a father and a <u>devoted husband</u>. This man and Hannah became very close friends, but their relationship stayed above board and only as boss and employee.

Then it happened. The boss's wife left him and filed for a divorce. It was common knowledge that this relationship had always been very rocky. Hannah tried to be sympathetic to both. By this time everyone at this company was the best of friends. They all hung out together. They did cook-outs together. They went on picnics with each other's families. Everyone's children played together nonstop. The boss's little boy spent more time at Hannah's house than he did at his own. A divorce would make this little family community change.

After several months and the divorce coming ever so much closer, when work weeks started everyone had to forget about their problems and their personal lives. One normal working day, Hannah and her boss were headed to a CPA's office with all of their tax information in tow. The boss had volunteered to take Hannah. She could have handled this meeting by herself. The only problem was that she had not learned her way around some of these small town areas. She did not know how to get to the CPA's office. So early on this Monday morning Mr. Wright parked in front of the office to await Hannah. He was somewhat impatient as he said,

"Come on, I am going to carry you!"

Hannah, feeling mischievous this morning, just stood in the same spot without saying a word. Everyone at her job teased her constantly about her Northern accent and the things she would say. She was in the South now and the Southern people spook totally different from her. She must have been one heck of a site by not moving while carrying those large and heavy accounting books. Her boss stared boldly at her and asked,

"Is something wrong?"

She said,

"No! But I thought you were going to carry me, so I am just waiting on you to come and get me!"

He looked at her with a hard and hateful look as he said,

"J-u-s-t *get* in the truck!"

The long trip to the CPA's office was traveled in a company pick-up truck. It had a long bench seat where Hannah had placed the large books between she and her boss. The two had never ridden anywhere together before. She had never been alone with this man. She felt much more comfortable with the large books between them. This man drove like a maniac! She was to learn later that he had once owned a race car and had driven it himself. He was using all of those techniques this very morning. Hannah had much fear. She noted that it was a good thing that the company had a good mechanic whom she hoped had checked the brakes on a regular basis. If he had not they would surely be killed, because this man did not even attempt to put pressure upon his brakes until he was within a foot of a red light.

Hannah's boss was very friendly this morning. They talked about their children. They talked about the company and some of the customers. They talked about fellow employees. They joked about the word 'carried' when Hannah said,

"I don't understand the usage of the word *FIXING* either! I've heard of preparing to do something, getting ready to do something, but never have I heard of *FIXING* to do something!"
They laughed and talked for the whole twenty miles. The boss did most of the talking. Hannah would pick up all of the ledgers from the floor after each curve or braking. Her boss seemed unaware that he was dumping this important information into the floor with each of his actions.

The meeting was over and Mr. Wright invited Hannah to go to lunch with him in the neighboring city. Even though they were alone for the first time, she was starting to feel comfortable in this man's presence. She respected him so very much. He was such a hardworking man and his hard work had paid off. He was a very, very successful man for his age. He had a beautiful home. He had a cabin in the mountains. He had condos in Florida and he owned the biggest share of the company that Hannah worked for. She was extremely impressed by his achievements. This day she was just enjoying the conversation and being alone with him. The two seemed to have at least their love of music in common. The radio had blasted during the trip. All of the same songs that Hannah loved so much were what her boss was playing.

Several weeks passed. Workloads became more heavy. Everyone was just cordial with each other at work. Mr. Wright had called Hannah into his office one week day and she thought she had done something wrong. Another girl in the office was very afraid of this man. She did not like his short fuse at times. For some reason, Hannah felt completely comfortable with her boss. He was only a year older than she and the couple seemed to have a good working relationship. Their sons were within days of each other's age. She loved the interaction this man had with her children. If they weren't at home, they wanted to be at the boss's house and he seemed to thoroughly enjoy having these children at his home. Hannah's children really cared for this man. He started to become the father figure that they did not have.

The meeting requested in the boss's office confused Hannah. She believed she was a good worker and she knew that all of her bosses were impressed by her knowledge and her work ethics. When she knocked and was ask into this very nice office, she could not help but notice the expense that had been put into decorating. The rich mahogany desk was large and engraved with scenery. It had a matching credenza behind it with tall rich mahogany shelves full of books floating atop. Diplomas lined the walls. The desk chair was large and of a black leather. The other seating in this office was that of burgundy leather with brass tacks holding the covers in place. The walls were of a rich wood. A large medieval type chandelier hung in the middle of the room. The site of this handsome boss sitting behind that massive desk in his expensive business suit could be most intimidating. Hannah had never lingered in her boss's office before. She had rarely sat down. She worked so hard and fast to where her duties were always completed on a run. Today, Mr. Wright asked her to please have a seat.

This unnerved the now thirty some year old Hannah. Oh, the whole office was casual and friendly in an off hour atmosphere, but never during working hours had the boss requested her presence without asking for something work related. This world was a very professional world and everything worked better in that way. The boss would often ring her desk to see a certain balance sheet, a ledger, bank statement or maybe just discuss the behavior of one of their employees; but NEVER had he ask her to just come in and sit down.

Today Hannah's boss was being very mysterious. He was so powerful and he held her world in his hands. He could either make or break her. Finally after she had sat down, he began to talk in a friendly manner. He noticed that she was looking at some sculptures that were of Spanish men playing some sort of guitars. These sculptures were of distressed silver and were quite charming. As Mr. Wright watched her look about, he said,

"Those came from Mexico. The chandelier above your head also came from Mexico and the Sun Calendar on that wall came from Mexico."
Hannah had noticed the large round jade piece and believed it to be very pretty. She did not want to

admit that she had no idea that it was a Sun Calendar. Turns out that Mr. and Mrs. Wright had gone to Acapulco for their honeymoon, years ago.

Hannah knew a courier had stopped by her desk and ask for Mr. Wright earlier on that day. The courier would not give his package to Hannah or any of the ladies in the office. He said he must deliver this package directly into the hands of Mr. Wright. Hannah could now see the opened large brown envelope lying in the middle of her boss's desk. She had guessed as to what she believed it to be. She had also witnessed a firing this morning. Needless to say, she was getting nervous. She had gone back into the plant when she could not reach her boss by phone. He had an important phone call and she felt she should find him. As she stepped out onto the dock she looked down to see an employee under one of the large trucks. He was on a wheeled wooden carrier made for that sort of thing. She had watched Mr. Wright being very mad as he pulled the wheeled carrier out from under that truck with the employee on it. He had screamed,

"Get your stuff and get the Hell out of here. You're FIRED!"

She had questioned others and only one person thought he knew what had happened. He said that the employee had cussed at the boss and called him something nasty in a mad spell. The mood of this day was all the more reason why Hannah was not real sure as to where this meeting was headed.

Hannah had always wondered how anyone could just stare at another, or be in a room with people and not talk. She had come from a talkative, social background to where if it got quiet in a room, she talked. She could never just sit there saying nothing. She often caught herself filling in words to about anything to keep the conversation going. Today, Mr. Wright was just staring at her and not saying one word. He fumbled with some paper clips upon his desk. The man had actually connected each and every one of them like a necklace. It looked to be a whole package of paper clips in this one chain. In the sunlight that was coming through one of the windows, she could see that his eyes were changing colors. She had noticed that he had blue eyes, but today it looked as if they were changing colors.

Finally, after much silence, Mr. Wright said,

"Hannah, I have a nice cabin up in the mountains. It is only about seventy miles from here. How would you like to take your children up there for some weekend? I am sure you and your family would enjoy that. Hannah choked back the fear that she had been having and answered by saying,

"That would be very nice Mr. Wright! Thank you!"

With that he said,

"You just let me know when you want to go and I will give you a map and the keys!"

Now the room got really quiet again. For what seemed like the longest time and after Hannah had wondered what to do, she had stood up and was about to leave the room when Mr. Wright said,

"Hannah, I consider you to be one of my only friends. I need someone to talk with."

He then picked up the large envelope and said,

"I got my walking papers today!"

Taken aback, Hannah said,

"I am so sorry!"

He started to talk now as if no one could make him still. He asked for Hannah to please sit back down. She did and her boss poured his heart out to his employee. He told of how he loved his son more than life. He told of how his son had always been with him. Hannah was very much aware that this little boy was definitely a Daddy's boy. He went with his father everywhere.

Mr. Wright said,

"Hannah, can you please quit calling me Mr. Wright. That seems so inappropriate for you and me. My name is Samuel and you can call me Sam! Please?"

Hannah nervously said,

"Okay, Sam!"

Sam went on to tell Hannah of how he felt at times that he did have a good marriage. He said that he knew the two were entirely too young when they got married. He also stated that he knew he was gone away from home so very much, especially in the first years of his marriage. He stated that he was only trying to make a better life for his family. He said that he and his wife had lost about all of their caring for each other in the last few years. He said all that they did lately was fight. What did they have to fight over, but their son? He told of how he would buy something nice for his child only for his wife to go out and buy something bigger and better. He told of how that is the way their life had been now for several years. This, of course, kept their little boy right in the middle of their discontent. He told of how he did not believe there was anyone else in his wife's life. He just knew she wanted out. Then he hung his head and said,

"I'm probably not the best person on earth to live with either!"

Hannah was surprised that her boss was opening up to her about his personal life. Actually it made her nervous, but her heart went out to him. Then he murmured something about how he had given his wife everything she had ever wanted and of how she had a good life. Hannah remembered a day during one of their big fights of how mad his wife had gotten over the fact that Hannah refused to write her a company check in a large amount. She had felt since Hannah worked for her husband; she needed to do as she asked. Hannah refused to write a check out of the company check book without the permission of her boss. Mrs. Wright then blew up at Hannah, to whom she had been so kind to on all of the occasions before. This taught Hannah that the lady had a horrible temper. She also remembered being very shocked at the remark Mrs. Wright had made during that mad spell, when she said,

"He *WILL* keep me in the way I am accustomed!"

Hannah looked down to see diamonds dripping off of every finger this woman had. She also knew she had never seen this lady in the same outfit more than once. She always looked like a million dollars and Hannah felt sad when she watched the lady stomp out of the office and jump into her personal Corvette. Hannah had always liked this lady, now everyone was involved in their divorce. Mrs. Wright had always been good to her. She had given her all kinds of stuff. She had helped her get home parties when she needed extra cash. She had taken her little girl with her on many shopping trips and she would always come home with something nice that the lady had purchased for her. So, Hannah did not like being in the middle of this very nasty divorce. But now she caught herself taking sides and the woman did not win. Hannah's sympathy went completely to Samuel.

After one of those silent minutes that Samuel Wright seemed to be a pro at, Hannah snapped back into reality when he said,

"Hannah, would you have dinner with me tonight?"

She looked at him strangely. Then he quickly added,

"Oh, we'll take the children! I just don't want to be alone tonight. I need you to pick up my son at school when you get your children. He is still living with me at this date. I don't know if my wife is going to fight for custody later, or on down the line. Right now, my son refused to go with his mother."

Hannah could see the sadness in her boss's eyes. She realized the conversation was over and she also knew it was about time to pick up the children. At least this had not changed. She had always picked up her boss's son when she picked up her own children. She had always taken him to school. She had always had to endure the fight the three would have over who was riding in the front seat. She would make them take turns, at which time she would have two boys in the front seat and one girl in the back, or she would have one girl in the front seat and two boys in the back. Her son and her boss's son seemed to be constant companions. The question was not, would she pick up his son, but where did the boys want to stay tonight. That was usually the problem. It had gotten to the place to where most of the son's clothing had ended up at Hannah's. Even on the days that the lad stayed with his mother, she would drive over to Hannah's in the early mornings to get him some clean clothes for school.

Hannah finally agreed to go to dinner with Samuel. She had asked him what restaurant he wished to go to. He had told her. She said that she and her children would just meet him there. He seemed pleased. As usual she was concerned. Her boss had been the one to ask her to go to eat with him, but was it only because he wanted company? Would he be footing the bill? He had chosen a fairly nice restaurant and it would be a wonderful treat for her children since they were not in a habit of going to such places. She just could not afford it. Even though this restaurant was probably considered to be a middle of the line restaurant, Hannah still worried about spending the money. She knew from experience that the wealthier people did not understand her dismay. They would not have thought as to whether she may be able to afford something like that. Hannah and her children were accustomed to entertainment at a cheap fast food restaurant on Friday night and then a $1.00 movie. This was their family night out.

On the way to the restaurant, Hannah told her children to be sure and let her see what they wanted to order for dinner before telling the waitress what they were ordering. She was going to keep the cost down, but hoped for the children to have a nice evening. Hannah had taken her time to get dressed. She chose a nice pull over top that was form fitting. Then she covered it up with a black thin jacket. She was of a fairly large chest,

138

so she buttoned the jacket neatly. She then placed on a pair of matching slacks and hoped she did not look too professional for a casual dinner. She honestly did not own casual clothes. Her whole life was working in an office and she could not afford more clothing than she may use. Therefore, if she ever purchased anything it would have to be professional work clothes. So tonight she did not put on any classy necklace or pin and she left the top button of her jacket open after a little thought of how that may look more casual. Then just as she walked into the restaurant, she thought maybe that jester made her look too sexy! Too late, Samuel Wright was by the door and staring straight at her by now.

The well behaved children watched their mother's eyes as they picked out what they wanted to eat. Samuel noticed what she and the children were doing. He obviously <u>did</u> understand her finances. She guessed maybe he should, as he is the one who decided how much to pay her. He did pay her a decent women's salary for the times, but with two children, school clothing, food, rent and keeping up a car, there never seemed to be enough to go around.

Hannah had cried one Christmas, during the downfall of the economy, when she had no idea up until Christmas Eve day of how she was to get anything for her children to put under the tree. As the mail ran that day, there was a $200.00 check from her uncle. Never did she feel that God had answered prayers any better. She ran quickly and purchased what she could for her precious little children. These are the kind of times the poor girl had. Suddenly, Samuel laid the menus back in front of the children, at which time he said,

"Tonight is my treat. You order anything and everything you want off that menu!"

The children looked at their mother with big bright eyes as if in question. Hannah smiled and said Thank You to Samuel and said,

"Okay children, this is your night, just do not buy so much food you get sick later."

The couple and the three children ate and sat at that table until it was almost closing time. Samuel seemed as if he did not want to go home.

The following weeks went along very busily. Hannah's boss had taken her son to his parents so the boys could go to the cabin with them for the weekend. This was starting to be a habit. Hannah's son enjoyed this very much. A few times, Samuel's ex-wife would come and get Hannah's daughter and take her shopping. All seemed to be well with everyone at this time.

Chapter 11

Hannah liked to sew and it seemed instead of fun, this hobby had become a duty as of late. She had made her son one pair of pants after another. Every night he would come home with the knees out of his pants. Hannah's favorite sewing was not that of making clothing. She had to do enough of that when she was growing up. Every time she would want something new as a teenager her parents would go purchase her some material and then say,

"Here, you make it."

Or since her aunt was the postmaster of the town and she wore very nice clothing, Hannah was such a skinny child to where when her aunt would give away her used clothing, Hannah would take it all apart and make something pretty for herself. The materials were always of the best of quality. Her desires now were to make drapes, cover furniture, make pillows or redecorate a whole room. She got so more satisfaction out of things like that.

Once her son got into soccer, his roughness slowed on the playground fields and at recess. Hannah realized by the site of her poor child's purple legs from his knees down that he was getting all of the roughness he could handle from his new found sport. So, the making of pants slowed down.

Hannah's beautiful daughter took classes as a majorette. She was a tiny little thing and Hannah had somehow saved enough extra cash to buy the sparkly little uniform and the things that she needed for this activity. She had been able to do the same thing for her son's soccer shoes and so on. Her children deserved so much better than she could give them. They were wonderful little ones. They were very smart. People would stop Hannah on the streets to tell her of how beautiful or of how well behaved her children were. The children, being so close in age, caused them to have little disagreements amongst themselves. They could drive Hannah crazy with their little disagreements. However, she knew the statements about these children being beautiful and well behaved out in public to be very true. It was especially wonderful to hear it from others.

Hannah's little girl had the eyes of her father. It was difficult to correct her when looking into those mesmerizing eyes. Hannah was always amazed at people, even those who had daughters of their own when they would tell her that her daughter was the prettiest little girl that they had ever seen. Her son had the dark, but bright blue eyes of his mother and he too was so very handsome. Hannah was so proud of her children. She hated the fact that she could not provide for them in the way she wished. This was a constant worry upon her mind. One thing that about bugged her to death was the fact that she could not afford the white canopy bedroom outfit she wanted for her daughter, and could not afford the pine wooden bookcase outfit that she wanted for her son. She would spend the rest of her days feeling quilt over not being able to provide for her children in the way that they so deserved.

During Hannah's days, divorced mothers with children were the minority. There were not many of her children's classmates that did not have a father and a mother both at home. Hannah's father was of the belief that sometimes a woman may even be smarter than a man. He had gotten these beliefs because his older sisters had all graduated college and were successful. Plus he had been raised since the age of ten by only his mother. But in these days and times, he also felt a woman needed a man around. He was forever telling Hannah she should have married differently and of how he hoped she would find someone who could be a good father to her children. Most of the time, Hannah was just happy being the children's mother and father both. Her biggest concern was always the finances. She would often think of how nice it would be to have another income coming into her home, but she honestly believed she would never fall in love again. For whatever sick reason, she believed she was still in love with her first husband and she felt that she would surely die with a broken heart. These feelings had now turned into a total love and hate relationship.

Now that the children were getting older and were often outside playing with the neighbor's children, Hannah had some spare time on her hands. She started writing down things she could remember from her childhood. She wanted to leave something for her children to know about her when she was but a child. She would remember and write down things about how awful she felt when she had a weak stomach. Being a farm girl, she could remember her grandmother chopping the heads off of the chickens. The very chicken the family was going to have for Sunday dinner. She would tell of how she would watch that chicken flop all over the driveway and of how she became anemic as a child over the fact that she could hardly bear to eat any kind of meat. This was because she watched how it was all prepared.

She stayed very skinny. She believed this, along with her blonde hair and her dark eye brows are the reason that her father had given her the name of 'Legs and Eyebrows'. Years of skinny little knees and not much need for food had caused her to need iron before the day she had her tonsils removed during her fifth year of school.

Her parents had taken her to a small hospital in a neighboring state. The hospital did not have modern items even for that day, it seems. After weeks of Hannah being given a glass of milk with something in it like iodine, she was ready for the surgery. The little girl hated milk anyway, so her mother would have to hold her nose to force this horrible tasting medicine down. On the day of the surgery, Hannah was taken into the operating room where a can of ether was opened and then cheesecloth was placed over that opening. This was then held over the little girl's mouth and nose and she was asked to count backwards from one-hundred. She remembers the nurse and doctor talking about Santa Claus. Then she was out. All went well with Hannah and she got to stop at the Dairy Queen for a rare treat of an ice cream cone on the day of her release. Sadly the following year a little girl of about the same age as Hannah died in that same hospital while doing the very same procedure. This was due to the fact of giving the child too much ether.

Hannah loved writing down her memories and felt her children may enjoy them someday. She wrote about how her father sold gas ranges. He would give the children the crates in which the stoves were delivered. Hannah remembered one day when she and her cousin Carolyn could have not gotten into more trouble. Split level homes seemed to be the style of the day. The little girls went out into a plowed garden, took their crates and anything else household they could find and proceeded to build their split level home. They were not worried about doing this because they knew when they were done playing they would have to clean up everything. At that time they would rake out the dirt again and all would be well. Hannah's dad came screaming and the girls got into really bad trouble. They found out much too quickly that the father had already planted this garden. The children had just dug up his seeds while they were building their nice new and modern split level home.

Hannah knew this must have been similar to whatever each of the girl's little brothers had done just a few weeks before. At least, it must have been just as serious from the actions of the father/uncle. During these years, it was *VERY* common for people to punish their children by spanking. Often a child would be asked to go and get a switch from a bush. In the Dahl's case it was a Lilac bush. They were to get the stick, only to be spanked with it once they had given it to a parent, grandparent, aunt or uncles.

A few weeks before the little brothers, who were almost the same age as each other, had done something wrong in the house. They ran when they knew punishment was coming. Both ran and crawled straight through the bottom of a screen door, tearing and breaking out the screen. Needless to say, when caught their punishment was severe; even though it was remembered that the boys were laughed at for their trip through the closed door.

Some of Hannah's fondest memories were of that old farm house where she spent her younger years. She loved the two doors that were opposite of each other in the kitchen. She could remember how the wind would blow through these doors while cooling the room where her grandmother had cooked over the old antique wood burning cook stove. Hannah remembered the smell of fresh cooked bread and the memories of the thin curtains blowing in the sunlight. Hannah wanted her children to feel some of those wonderful memories. She would often cry because she felt she was not giving those kinds of memories to her children. They had to grow up way too soon. They often carried the burdens about life right along with their mother. All she could give them was an apartment life and limited funds.

Everything at work seemed to be going along just fine. Hannah put her children in church, but she would not attend very often herself. She often felt God had forsaken her. Even though she knew this to be an unforgivable sin; she often stayed about half mad at God. Then on certain evenings after the children were in bed she would get out her large black notebook and write down another memory. She thought of how God was a constant of her life. She worried she may be destroying any relationship her children would have with God due to her rebellion. She knew her religious family could never understand her dismay. In their way of thinking, if you sin, you pay for it. Obviously Hannah had sinned when she married Ambros. He was of a different faith and had been married before. She could not fault her family for this. That was their belief system, and she did feel pretty darn stupid after everything she touched did not work. She often questioned her own judgment.

Try as everyone did to make Hannah feel guilty, the only things she felt guilty about were the facts that she could not give her children the wholesome wonderful young childhood she once had. Guilt would set in more strongly when Hannah would think of something she enjoyed as a child. She did not want to deprive her children of any of those blessings. She wrote in her journal one night of how nice it felt to squeeze the sand and mud up between her toes when her church would have a baptismal. She remembered how everyone wore white and everyone went barefooted. It seemed so wonderful when the group would slowly walk down the Raccoon Creek bank while singing, 'Shall We Gather At the River'. Or the times of tent meeting revivals when the grass had just been cut and evening was ushering in. The smells were wonderful.

Some memories were those of the excitement of going to the Circleville Bible Camp Meetings. She knew she wanted to share these things with her children. She did not want to raise her children without God. These thoughts always gave her pain. She had a minister father and a minister grandfather. Her whole large family, on every side, was great and wonderful Christians. All of her cousins had now attended Bible College. Many were teachers and many were ministers. All were leaders of their church. When it came to heathens, Hannah guessed she would be considered to be the only one. Oh a couple of the men had divorced, but no one really looked on that the same because they were men.

Since Hannah worked heavily. She would let her children go to Ohio the minute school was out in the spring. She hoped this would give her children the wholesome upbringing they needed to survive in the cruel world. However deep inside, she wanted them to be street wise as well. She never wanted them to grow up with the naïve outlook on life that she had endured. She refused to keep them in that bubble. She hoped they would see the world from all angles and make wise decisions as adults. She did not want them so vulnerable to where someone could rip their heart completely out of them. She wanted to protect her children, but in the summers she knew they were being raised the very same as she had been.

Hannah missed her children terribly during the summer months. She would either deliver her children to her parents or someone would come and get them. Amazingly, no one could or would ever bring them back at summers end. One year this mother panicked when an airplane that her children were on had been reported to having returned to Columbus, Ohio due to mechanical failures. Hannah was scared. She sat in the terminal and cried when she was told the same plane had taken off again. When the children finally arrived at the Atlanta Airport; Hannah hugged them way too tightly and kept kissing each of them. They stared at their mother in disbelief. They did not understand her over reactions. The attendants had given them ice cream, toy airplanes and little wing pins while they were waiting for the unloading of too much weight. It turned out not to be a mechanical failure at all. The stewardess had explained to the children that they had weight comparable to the weight of one elephant too much. Even with that fear, Hannah still knew these trips to Ohio were more beneficial than letting her children play without supervision in an apartment complex all through the summer. Hannah would often hire a baby sitter, of sorts; by paying a neighbor lady to watch her children, only to find the kids spent most of their time playing outside at the pool or inside of their own apartment. As they got older Hannah knew she could depend on her smart children more than trusting others. Strict rules were to be followed and thankfully everything turned out okay.

During the summer months after Hannah's boss had divorced. She spent a lot of time at his house. She found that he and his son were cooking scrambled eggs in the microwave every night. She felt the need to cook for them on different occasions. They loved her cooking and this kept her from being so very lonely without her children. She would eat dinner with her boss and his son. Then she would do the dishes and go home. She would average about one night a week of giving the father and the son a good meal.

Samuel would buy whatever she had put upon a piece of paper before she left work that evening. Then after she had gone home and changed clothing, she would arrive at the Wright home where all of the right ingredients for the weekly meal were laid out before her. She loved his kitchen with all of the most modern conveniences. She knew that Samuel looked forward to these meals with great anticipation.

One such evening, Samuel told Hannah that they must have dinner a little earlier because his son was going to stay with his mother for the weekend. Hannah got the house key from Samuel and left work a little earlier so she could prepare a meal before the son had to leave. This time she did the grocery shopping. Samuel had thrown her a credit card to complete this task. Hannah had pangs of jealously when she thought of how some of the world lives with such privileges, while others have to struggle so badly. Then she felt guilty for such thoughts as she thought of how Samuel was suffering. He had lost a family life and his wife. He was now alone. Money did not seem to matter too much when it came to that kind of problems. Hannah only knew that this man did not ever have to worry about where he would get the money for his next meal. He would never have to worry as to whether the money saved would be enough to pay the rent, the electric bill or buy something needed for school. Hannah knew this was a problem of hers that he, more than likely, could never understand. She often felt so badly for her children when Samuel's son would show them the newest or latest toy on the market. Her children could never be afforded such items.

On the evening of the son going to his mothers, Hannah was doing dishes when the ex-wife arrived. She did not act too pleased to find Hannah working in what was once her kitchen. She must have gotten control over her feelings, because she sit down at the table and was trying some of the leftovers. She gave Hannah a compliment when she said,

"Hmmm, this is good!"
Hannah told her that she sometimes felt sorry for the two when they were eating so many eggs. Then she added,

"You know that is not good for them!"

The ex-wife laughed and said that is about all that they liked to eat. Then she spoke of how she never was much of a cook. She stated that she did not like to cook. She made a joke about Hannah being a little miss homemaker. Then she grabbed her son and left. Everything seemed to be on a happy note upon her departure.

Hannah finished the dishes and proceeded to go home. Samuel showed signs that he did not want her to leave. He made a remark as to what was she going home to and reminded her that the children were not there. She laughed, but still excused herself and headed home. Tonight, she was not even going to turn the TV on. She thought she would call her children, then relax and reflect on the week's happenings. She took out her journal and wondered why she had such a memory. It seemed she never forgot anything. She could remember the exact words, word for word, of something that was said to her twenty years ago. Some would say that she had the memory like a horse. She hoped this would always be true, yet she sometimes wished she could forget certain things. Maybe she would not be so critical of herself and others could she just forget.

Hannah picked up the large black notebook that she now considered her journal or manuscript of the past. Tonight the thoughts of a large bird went through her mind. She had watched monster quest on TV the night before. The show was about a large bird in Point Pleasant, W.VA. They were talking about the bird that everyone called the 'Moth Man'. Later there would even be a famous movie about this monster sighting with Richard Gere as the lead actor. As she watched this show about monsters, she saw people from home. Some that she knew! She listened to a young man whom was once very close to her. He was telling of all of the sightings so many had seen before his time. She had never believed any of this, but it was fun to watch and to see the people from home describing this creature. It was wonderful to see the local area on TV and see how different people had aged since the last time she had seen them. Thoughts crossed her mind about the young man who was talking and his baby daughter. Then she realized quickly the daughter would no longer be a baby. She had not seen this family in years. Hannah pondered on how life is so short.

Hannah took pen in hand and started to write. Often the pen seemed to have a mind of its own. She knew she was blessed with a touch of ESP. She wondered what else she may be blessed with at times. Often stories would pop into her head that she knew absolutely nothing about. Where was all of this coming from? She would ignore stories unfamiliar to her and write only of her past. Tonight a flash hit her brain about that big bird everyone was talking about. Gee Whiz, she believes she knows what they are talking about. Just as all logical people would say, most everything has a solid explanation.

This story had gotten really wild over the years. The strange thing about this story was that Hannah was from that same time period. She could not help but wonder why she did not hear these stories when she was a teen. Maybe she was held so strictly to where she was not out in the world to hear such nonsense. Maybe the twenty miles that she had lived from these sites was enough with the poor communications of the time period for someone not to hear of those going ons.

There were other possibilities in Hannah's mind. She remembered when she was a child of how her father would run into the house once every year and scream,

"He is back! He is back! Everyone come and see him! He looks like he has grown since last year!"

Everyone would run out to view down over the pasture hill, while looking up into the large sycamore tree by the pond. The family would always stay a field away so as not to scare this huge bird away. They would always see this bird in the day time. The legend about the Moth Man was always at night. Hannah laughed at her thoughts while thinking maybe the creature lightened up her farm during the day only to terrorize the good people of Point Pleasant, W.Va. at night. What Hannah and her family were seeing was a very large bird called a Crane. These were very common in the south but very uncommon to Southern Ohio. Hannah's father would estimate that this bird had about a nine foot wing span. However, Hannah's father did realize what it really was. The family was always happy to see this large bird's yearly trip. It seemed to always take the same route and it always seemed to find that old sycamore tree by the pond.

Hannah wondered this night if that was maybe the same bird that the community of Point Pleasant had seen so many years ago. She knew the bird that had landed at her family's farm for so many years had stopped coming after a while. Not knowing the life length of these birds, Hannah just assumed he must have died. Surely this beautiful bird could not have been the bird the legend was based upon. The legend of the Moth Man even gave the monster credit for causing the Silver Bridge to fall into the Ohio River. This was a terrible accident that claimed many lives of friends and loved ones during the 1960's.

Chapter 12

The weekend passed and Hannah let herself stay in her pajamas for the whole day of Saturday. Sunday she went down and sat around the apartment pool. She took a book to read. She often read romance novels only to feel more cheated with her life. She would cry and feel sorry for herself. By now this well trained lady was getting good at picking herself up, dusting herself off and starting all over again. She was also a master of disguise. By Monday morning Miss Hannah was bright eyed, bushy tailed and ready for a week's work.

The dinners, house cleaning, reading books and crying seemed to be the duties of Hannah Jane Dahl Hughes. Summers seemed so long. This year had seemed longer than most. Thankfully the children had finally arrived safely home and all was well with the world once more.

Arriving at the office early Monday morning, Hannah found one of the owners leaning up against the large heater that someone had placed in the outer office for the winter. No one troubled to remove this stove during the summer months and now it would not be long before it would be needed again. Samuel's company partner was obviously hung over from a weekend of pleasure. This morning he pushed Hannah up against the stove with his body. She knew she was in a strange place. His bodily functions were all working quite well and Hannah became scared. She had reasons to believe that they were the only two in this building at this time. If she got nasty with this guy, her job could be in jeopardy. He was one of her bosses. If she did not put him in his place, he would feel he could do anything to her at any time. She shoved him away with a frown, then said something like,

"Gee, did you have that good of a time this weekend to where you cannot stand up on your own? Do you have to lean on someone?"
Quickly adding,

"If so; I can get one of the fellows to help you into your office."
All of the while knowing there may not be anyone arriving for work for another ten minutes or so. Then she said,

"I am not strong enough to carry you!"
All of this was said with a nervous laugh which thankfully somehow made him snap out of some of his still drunkenness. Then he said, while pinching her on the cheek,

"Don't frown pretty lady, you will cause wrinkles in that beautiful face."
Hannah smiled at him and put her arm in his arm as she led him into his office. She was about to close the door behind her while leaving, when he said,

"Hey Hannah, you do know you could be driving that big Corvette out there if you play your cards just right!"
Hannah was embarrassed now with his comment and the referral to the other boss's car. All she wanted to do was to just leave. She realized the whole sickened mess this morning was more than likely caused by jealousy over Samuel and her friendship.

As the day wore on, the one boss sobered up. He was not such a happy camper now and he wanted to pick a fight with just about everyone.

156

Hannah had gotten busy and talked only business with this man for the rest of the day. Once in the afternoon, he looked out of his door when Hannah passed by and said,

"Hey, I'm sorry!"

She leaned into the door by placing both hands upon the casings and said,

"That's okay, you know I ignore you!"

Both laughed and the day went on.

3:30pm rolled around and it was time to get the children from school. The boys had been working in the shop some after school and Hannah's daughter was extremely detailed, so she often helped her mother with timecards, putting checks in numerical order or filing. Today when Hannah picked up the children, Samuel's son blurted out something his father had said to him. He said,

"My Dad said that you are the most beautiful woman he believes he has ever seen!"

Hannah said nothing to the nine year old child. Okay, how does one react to that? Great, she was never going to be able to face her boss again. She knew that she found him very attractive. She found him to be everything that any woman could ever want and felt his ex-wife had to have rocks for brains to have ever left such a man. She also knew this was her boss. She had no hopes of ever being anything to this man but a friend and an employee. Any other thoughts were quickly erased from her mind.

Then one evening a few weeks later, the shop was very busy. No one was going home on time tonight. Everyone had to work possibly into the weekend. A large job was on the floor and each employee had to stay until it was complete.

Hannah could have gone home earlier, as the actual factory workload constituted no urgency on her workload. Her children were there and seemingly having fun, so what was the rush. She could catch up on some of her duties and she was going to try to leave around seven.

Then around six thirty, Samuel's parents showed up at the shop. They were going out to eat and wanted to know if they could take all of the children along. Hannah agreed to the dinner idea, but then was ask about the night. The children were begging to go to their friend's grandparents for the night. They had visited there before and it must have been like Disney Land because they always wanted to go back. Usually it was just Hannah's son who would go, but tonight her daughter was begging to go as well. Samuel's mother had asked for the daughter too, while saying it would be fun for her while the boys were all together. She stated that she and Hannah's daughter could just be the girls and do something special together. She said she was often alone when the guys all got together. She told Hannah that she would love to have the little girl's company. So, Hannah agreed to let both children go. They had keys to their house and the grandparents had promised to take them by there to get fresh clothing.

Hannah had turned off the ceiling light in her office. She was using only the green glass covered desk lamp for her needs. Samuel came in looking very tired. He and his partner were not above working for a living. They would stay in their offices very briefly each day. It was nothing to see one of them out in the shop with their dress sleeves rolled up while they welded, sawed or whatever needed done.   Tonight Samuel was obviously in a joking mood. He had lain down upon a leather couch in the outer office a few minutes earlier. The front desk girl was still there completing an assignment. Hannah heard Samuel say something and then she heard the young girl say,

"**Ah-h-h-h-h**! Did you just say what I think you just said?"

Hannah had just picked up some papers from the young lady and was walking back into her office when she heard Samuel say,

"No, probably not, I am just talking to myself. You better watch what you think you heard and what I think I said, and maybe you thought you heard."

Hannah walked back into that outer office as her high heels clicked upon the tiles. She laughed and said to the other girl,

"Did he just say what *I think* he said?"

The office mate said,

"Yes, and I heard what he said the first time too. We're off duty now so you cannot fire me for this Mr. Wright."

Then she looked at Hannah and said,

"When you walked by him a while ago, he said, she sure has pretty legs."

Now Hannah wished she had just gone back into her office and kept her big mouth shut. Her face was red and she could think of nothing else to say but,

"Thank you, I think!"

Hannah put up her work and was reaching for her purse when Samuel came into her office. He was tired and very funny tonight. He scooted into her office chair with her while they both hung over the sides. His face was so very close to hers as he looked her in the eyes. He said,

"Well, well, Miss Hannah are you thinking about leaving me here all alone tonight?"

She laughed and said,

"I think so Mr. Samuel!"

Just about that time, Hannah could feel his breathing upon her face. He was so close she could hear his heartbeat. Suddenly their lips met. Samuel placed the longest, most wonderful, smooth kiss upon Hannah's lips. When he withdrew, Hannah said something she thought she should have never said,

"Lord, I have been waiting so long for that!"

Without taking his arms from around Hannah, Samuel said,

"Me too! You know why I couldn't, don't you, me being your boss and everything. I had no idea what you might think. I was afraid I would lose you forever. I could only hope that if I got the nerve to make a move that you would hopefully feel the same way."

Hannah knew his eyes almost never left hers when they were in a room together. He had a way of changing the colors of his eyes when he was feeling affection. Hannah melted every time he looked at her. She had shamed herself over the feelings that she had gotten on the day that her old company was moving in with the new. This was way back five years ago when Samuel had purchased her company. Everyone was involved with the move and Samuel was dressed in jeans that were threaded on the bottom of the large bells. He had on a stripped tank top due to the heat. Nothing was left to the imagination as his golden

160

muscles were shining. Not only was this man extremely handsome, he also had the body of a Greek God. Hannah could only think of the statue David when she looked at his body.

For lunch the new boss had taken all of the employees, who were helping move, to a pizza place. As fate would have it, Hannah ended up on one end of the long table and Samuel ended up on the other. He had stared at her all through lunch. This was only the second time she had seen him. She worried that maybe this was a disapproving stare. He never smiled. He just stared a hole through her. Then she thought maybe he was staring at her because she could not keep her eyes off of him. She learned quickly after that, that he was married. He had introduced Hannah to his lovely wife shortly after her placement at her new job. So, all thoughts were erased. She had a talk with herself and blamed it all on a fact of hers She said,

"Hannah, you have just been without a man way too long."
Then one time shortly after Samuel's divorce, they were in a room full of people and Hannah wanted to go into another room. Her boss had stood in the door opening, while blocking the way. He did not let her through the doorway on her first try. She noticed his eyes on that day and she thought at that time that he may be having deep feelings about her. That was, of course, depending upon whether she was reading him correctly or not. How could she be sure? She was in love with him now and she had known that for a really long time. She only knew she could never act upon it. Now, it was there. Everything was out on the table. He had kissed her. She floated on air this night.

With trembling hands, Hannah picked her purse up from the floor and started for the door. Samuel leaned over and said,

"If we get done here, can I come over later?"

Suddenly she realized that Mr. Samuel Wright was most likely behind the parents coming after the children. Hannah's hands were shaking when she whimpered out a shallow,

"Yes!"

She was afraid to believe, but had she found happiness? All she really knew was that she had fallen completely in love again. This love, this time was in a more adult kind of way. She was so very happy this night.

When Samuel finished working, it was about one o'clock in the morning. He had called Hannah at about nine o'clock and had asked if she would leave her door unlocked. What was she doing? Why were her actions as they were? She never hesitated one bit. Actually she had put on the nicest of lounging clothing that she could find. She had lit candles and made sure every drop of her make-up was on correctly. She had gotten sleepy and made very sure to lay her head upon the living room couch pillows so as to not mess up one hair. She was not going to go to bed. That would have been way too much of an invite. She laughed at herself when she thought that at least she had that much decency left about her.

Hannah had finally dozed off, only to awaken by being lifted from her slumber. Samuel had picked up the top part of her body and was holding her ever so closely. He had lifted her so gently from her slumber. He had placed her head upon his strong shoulder and was holding her tightly. He realized she had awakened when he whispered,

"I am in love with you Hannah!"

Hannah's dreams had come true. Never could she feel more love than she was feeling this night. As Samuel placed a soft wonderful kiss upon her lips, she knew she had never been kissed this way before. She could feel the gentleness and the love from this wonderful man. Another gentle, long kiss and Hannah was lifted from the couch into the strong arms of her lover. He carried her to the bedroom and laid her softly upon the bed. This night all of Hannah's dreams did come true. Samuel and Hannah were deeply in love. Samuel did not go home until the wee hours of the morning. The couple did not sleep. They only bask in the enjoyment of being together.

The next morning was Saturday, but Hannah had to go to work. It was month end and she had slacked with some of her duties this week. She arrived at her regular work time. She walked out into the shop at just the time when Samuel arrived. He walked through the large roll up doors. He was dressed as she had never seen him before. He had on a Poncho over his tight fitting jeans and upon his head was a large Sombrero Hat. Everyone laughed as they saw his get up. The dark complexioned man could have passed for a foreigner this day. Hannah tried to be most discreet when she said,

"Good morning Sam! Like your outfit!"

She then walked back into her office and went to work, only to have her other boss come directly to her door and ask,

"What did you two do last night?'

He must have picked up on the looks that were exchanged by Samuel and Hannah. She felt her face turn red, she could feel the heat. She was finally able to answer with a guarded sentence,

"Nothing! Why do you ask?"

He then said,

"Because, I have never seen him act like this. He is floating on air! As you very well know, he is not a drinker like me! He seems like he is just too darn happy today. Maybe he just won a lottery or something!"

Hannah was just happy to have the boss walk away. She had to gather her composer enough to be professional. She too was floating on air. She wondered if it really was that obvious to everyone that they were each sitting on a high cloud this morning. If so, they had best keep everyone from knowing it was the very same cloud.

Samuel did not come into the offices at all this morning. He had taken off his attire and was now busy at work. Everyone was hoping to be finished by noon. Hannah knew that was the time she had planned on finishing her duties.

Noon came close with nothing but work in this manufacturing company. Hannah had the whole office to herself. As a matter of fact she had not even unlocked the front door. She had come in through the large opened roll up doors when she arrived this morning, just as she often did. This entrance gave her a chance to speak to all of the workers and start each day off with a friendly note.

Shortly before noon someone was knocking on the front door. Hannah had been so busy trying to complete her work to where she had not looked out of the large storefront type window. She had adding machine tape all over the office floor and

164

she had to step over it. She looked around to see who was at the door. She did not recognize the gentleman. As she opened the door, the man just stuck his head in and handed her a large beige envelope, while saying,

"Please give this to Mr. Samuel Wright Tell him that his delivery has been delivered to the address of 356 Belmont, per his request."
Then he added,

"The keys are in there too."
Whatever that meant, while he pointed at the package.

Hannah knew this was Sam's home address, but did not question what he may have had delivered. She had planned on sneaking out of the office so as not to disturb Samuel. She was very, very happy, but was a little uncomfortable with the next communication she would have with her handsome boss. He must be uncomfortable too, since he had not shown his face even once in the front offices today. Maybe he was just too busy! Or worse, maybe he was sorry and felt that he had made a big mistake! Hannah was shattered over that possibility.

Now the dutiful office employee must take this package to her boss before leaving for the day. Hannah was dressed in a cute outfit that was not that unlike her boss's attire of the morning. She had on a light green colored slack outfit. The top was made in just two pieces and rounded at the bottom. This caused wing type sleeves that had a rope tied in front that kept the pieces together under each arm. Printed in the front and the back of this top was Indian sculptures with things one may find on a totem pole. The top came only an inch or so below the waist. The slacks were of this same thing like material and they had a full bell bottom. The softness of this material showed every curve of Hannah's perfectly shaped body as it flowed over her skin. Upon her feet, she had on laced Indian Moccasins. She believed these to be the most comfortable shoes she had ever owned. They did not have much of a sole upon them, so they were almost like wearing nothing. This also put her down much shorter. She liked this, considering she believed herself to be way too tall at 5' 7' and 3/4th's. She also knew that Samuel liked this outfit, because long before this day when she had worn it, he had come into the office on a more casual day and smiled when he said,

"I don't think I have ever seen a blonde Indian before!"

Now Hannah must go face her fears. Why did she question everything? She had just been given the most precious of gifts. Why was she so scared? She knew the answer to that question. She felt she had been used and abused by her first husband, now she could only hope Samuel Wright was not just toying with her affections. If this would turn out to be true, she would feel like a cheap woman. She would be a destroyed woman with no cheer left.

Hannah gathered up all of her belongings with the intentions that if things did not go well, she would have her purse and her brief case in hand. She could be ready for a quick dart through those big rolled up doors. She walked quietly up to her boss while he was working on a large machine. He had on safety glasses and was drilling a large hole into a big piece of metal. It was as if he had eyes in the side of his head because when she walked up too close, he put his arm out to stop her until the machine slowed down. Once he had taken his foot off of the pedal, he seemed to snap at her when he said,

"I wish you would not do that! You are going to get hurt walking up on these machines like that."

She wanted to say she only did that sort of thing because she was always afraid someone may not hear her. He was right, she knew that, because just the other day she had little burned holes all over her favorite gold colored satin blouse. This was caused from walking up too close to a welding machine. She had been warned about looking into the flames as well. She was told that there were reasons why the men had to wear such heavy shields, safety glasses and other things to protect themselves.

Knowing she was wrong, but still hurt over the tone of voice, Hannah said,

"This just came for you."

Then she handed him his package. She then said,

"I'll see you later."

That sentence came out in a hurt kind of voice.

Samuel put down his safety glasses and started walking out to her car with her. Just as she got into her seat and shut her door, she rolled the window down. Samuel looked around to see if anyone was watching, then he stuck his head down into the car and placed a kiss upon Hannah's lips. He said,

"Do what you have to do, then meet me at my house in a little bit. I will be done here soon. I have a big surprise in my front yard."

Hannah went home and freshened up. She was so relieved with Samuel's actions. She now knew she was going to have a wonderful rest of the weekend without her nerves being shattered. She believed that Sam's son was going with his mother this weekend and knew she would have to pick up her own children shortly. Therefore, she assumed she and Samuel would not be spending a lot of the time together this weekend. But, she also realized that this man did not like to be alone.

Before Hannah got to her front door, the phone was ringing. It was her children and they were begging to go to the cabin with the older couple for the rest of the weekend. Samuel's son had obviously talked his mother into this. Hannah knew that her daughter had never been to the cabin and figured she did not want to go, but she chimed in by saying that she was having fun and ask could she please go too. Hannah agreed reluctantly. Weekends were the only true time she had with her children. When school was out, they would be going to Ohio for the whole summer. She wanted to spend as much time with them as she could during the school year.

Within a couple of hours, Hannah pulled into Samuel's long drive way. There were so many tall pine trees in this large front yard. Lining the driveway were beautiful flowers and shrubs. The house was of a red brick and it was very large. It was all on one floor and had big Florida windows in the front. A big L shape went around the back and it had a large three car garage. Habit was to pull into the driveway and go to the back door which was in the garage. This practice caused everyone to end up in the dining room first. This garage had the proud honor of a medieval looking chandelier hanging from the ceiling right in the middle of it. It was just like the one in

Samuel's office.   Strange place for a chandelier, but Hannah thought it was pretty.

Today, Hannah could see a brand new Corvette sitting out in the grass.   The shadows through the large trees made the car shine like glass.   She did not see Samuel, but she now knew this is what had been delivered to this address today.   The color was that of a dark pearl beige that faded into a lighter toast color on the top.   A smoked glass T-top finished this beautiful car off.

Hannah stopped in the driveway.   She got out and walked over to look at this beautiful new car.   Just as she got close, Samuel spoke from the hammock that he was snuggled down in,

"*Well*! What do you think?"
Hannah was taken aback because she had no idea that Samuel was out in the yard.   He must have been home for a while, because he had changed and was now adorning a pair of blue jean shorts and wearing nothing else but flip flop shoes.

Hannah said,

"I love it! It is so beautiful!"
Samuel stayed in his laying position as he said,

"Get in!"
She nervously opened the door while trying not to damage it in any way.   She had never been in a car such as this.   She even worried about her long fingernails.   She knew that her boss bought a new Corvette at least every two years.   He had done this ever since the day she had met him and she was very sure he had been doing the same thing for a really long time.   He had owned at least three new ones during the time that she had known him.   She had joked about how he never ran out of a color to choose from.   She also knew that the last Corvette purchased had gone to his ex-wife,

leaving Samuel with the older one for himself for some time now.

Samuel noticed her hesitation when he said,

"Hey! It is just a car!"

The tall thin lady let her body drop down into the plush leather seat. She put her hands upon the steering wheel and said,

"Wow! This is beautiful!'

She looked over to see Samuel's eyes dancing. He was smiling and he said a silent, yet sincere,

"*Y-E-S, Y-E-S, Y-E-S!*"

She looked at him again and said,

"What?"

He said,

"I knew you would look beautiful in that car. I bought it that color so it would match your hair."

Hannah felt her flesh get hot and it felt like forever before the color came back into her face. As she snapped around to look at Samuel again, he had not moved. As she looked at him, he said,

"Take it for a spin!"

Hannah said,

"I'm scared. I have never driven a Corvette before and you have always said so many people do not remember that there is another three feet out in front that they cannot see! What if I wreck your pretty new car? Please come and go with me on this so called spin!"

Samuel rolled out of the hammock and started walking towards the car. He did not go for the driver's side as she had hoped. He instead got into the passenger's side. He was determined to have Hannah drive. Now she wished she had not insisted that he go along. If she made any

170

mistakes he would surely notice and she would be so much more nervous.

As she pushed in the clutch, she wondered how he knew that she could even drive a straight stick. Maybe she had told him over the years. All she knew was that most women did not know how to drive one. Hannah shifted into first gear and turned around in the yard. She was headed out of the driveway, but she was determined not to drive very far. She thought she would just drive around in the subdivision for a block or two, then hand the controls over to Samuel. He had not planned the same as she. He told her to turn towards the interstate. She did as he asked and climbed ever so slowly onto the interstate ramp. Then he told her to let it out. He said,

"See what she does!"

Hannah was not unlike Samuel when it came to speed. She loved it when she had control of the vehicle. She shifted, then she shifted again and off she was going. This was a six speed and with each shift the car seemed to fly. Before she knew it, she was up to ninety miles an hour. *Gee this was fun!* Hannah's nerves seemed to settle down after a few miles. Driving this beautiful car was a real pleasure.

The couple kept riding because Samuel just never said to get off any ramp, nor did he say to turn around. Once Hannah got comfortable, she looked over at Samuel and noticed that he looked completely relaxed. They rode straight into Atlanta. She was more comfortable with the handling of the car after driving the sixty miles she had just driven, but she was nervous about the Atlanta traffic. This time she did not ask, she just drove off at one of the first exit ramps she came upon. It was as if these two people did not have to even speak. They communicated in some other way. Each got out of the car. Both went to the restroom and both got a drink. When they came back, Samuel reached down and took the T-tops off of the car. He then slide into the driver's seat and flipped through the CD player while hunting for a song. Hannah relaxed into the passenger's side as her handsome driver adjusted his mirrors. When he put his hand down upon the gear shift, Hannah reached over and placed her hand upon his. She thanked him for a wonderful day. They settled comfortably into the luxury seats and both basked in the warmth of each other's company.

Samuel drove slower on the way home while the wind blew his and Hannah's hair. Little was said, but both were smiling and looking at each other. Hannah had finally found happiness. She whispered a 'Thank You' to the Good Lord above and thought in her mind's voice,

"I have finally found Heaven."

She somehow knew deep inside that she had found her soul mate. She had found Samuel.

Chapter 13

Summer came and Hannah had to make a trip to Ohio. Once she arrived, everyone seemed so happy to see her. Many said that she looked radiant and so very happy. They ask if there was something new in her life. She lied and said,

"No!'

Her relationship with Samuel was way too new and she did not want to jinx it in anyway. Besides this relationship could either made or break Hannah and her life. If it should end, she would probably not have a job. Then another way of looking at it was if it continued, she could probably not have a job. Both ways, she had no idea as to what could happen and she was scared. She was treading in high seas. All she knew was that she was in love and right now she was very happy and she would cross the other bridges when she got there.

By the fall, when the children were to return, Samuel and Hannah was a fixed item. They were together all of the time. People at work were now aware of their romance. This seemed to be okay for awhile, but then Samuel's partner became upset. He explained to Hannah his dismay. He and Samuel could not come to an agreement over Hannah. The partner told her that when they had incorporated the company with the three original owners, they had placed a clause into the records that said none of their wives could take any control of the company. If one should die, the company was to be sold to the other partners and that partner's share of money would be given to the widow. But, the wife or wives were not to have any say in any happenings of said company. One partner had wished to move out west and had now sold his share to the other two.

Hannah was starting to feel unwanted. The other partner informed her that even though she was not a wife at this time, she was still too close to one of the partners. Since she was also the actual Secretary to the Corporation in the Corporation books, this made everything that was going on between her and Samuel a conflict of interest. Hannah loved her job, but knew rather than causing conflict between the partners, she should resign as Secretary to the Corporation and leave the company altogether. Samuel would have none of that. Hannah told Samuel that she could understand his partner's dismay. Samuel could not understand. He stated that his partner had always trusted Hannah during all of these years and there was no reason for any mistrust now.

Well, the problems did not get resolved and before Hannah realized it, there were a group of gentlemen in her office asking all sorts of questions. She realized the other partner was leading these men through all of the offices as if they were on a tour. Samuel stayed in his office the whole day and did not even come out to talk to Hannah. She could tell he was very upset. He had left his usual notes upon her calendar pad this morning, but had not said two words to anyone all day.

Samuel was of a habit of drawing an eight figure upon Hannah's calendar pad each morning before she arrived. Below this sideways eight were the words,

"Always and Forever!"

These words always warmed Hannah's heart and let her know she was much loved. He also had the habit of just writing down a group of letters and letting Hannah figure out what they were. This morning the letters were,

"T.M.B.L. - Y.M.S.V.M.T.M."

It took Hannah a while to figure out what Samuel meant by this note. But when she finally did figure it out it made her very happy. He had meant,

"To my beautiful lady, you mean so very much to me!"

This was always a fun work game that started each day off on a warm and happy note. Hannah was always anxious to get to work to read her calendar. The calendar had been written on so much by the end of a month to where one could hardly see that the year was 1978, much less what day it was. The recent note was the reason that Hannah knew Samuel's quietness this day could have nothing to do with their relationship. At the end of this day, Samuel came into Hannah's office and said,

"Clean out your office!"

With a big shocked look, Hannah said,

"What?"

Then and only then did Samuel inform her that he had just sold his share of the company, the company that he had started so many years ago, the company that meant so very much to him. Now, Hannah was feeling it was all her fault. She said,

"Oh, Samuel, why did you not just let me leave? I could have gotten another job. This company means too much to you! Don't let me cost you your company!"

The partners had fallen out completely and no matter what Samuel was saying; Hannah still felt it was because of her. The other partner _did_ come into her office after she had gone to the back of the shop where she could get some boxes. He looked at her sharply as he said,

"I'm asking you to resign. I would like to keep you, but the new owners have a CPA in their employee, so your services will no longer be needed!"

Hannah knew he was being a smart butt about this. Otherwise, he would have never said anything like that when he could see that she was leaving anyway.

Samuel and Hannah had ridden to work together this morning. Samuel went out with a mad look upon his face and jumped into one of the company trucks. She was to learn later that this company truck was part of his pay for his share of the company. Now the self-made company was going to be run by complete strangers. The other partner was a hard worker. He was also a hard partier. He also did not have the skills or the (want to) to know how to run the finer points of a company. As Hannah picked up her belongings and ran to jump into her car, she could not help but think of how this much loved company was headed for disaster.

Hannah became very depressed. What was she to do? Samuel was more than likely financially stable. She was not. She lived from pay check to pay check and she had two children to rear. Now she had no job. Jobs were not plentiful in the small town where the company was located. Hannah knew in her heart that she would have to move to Atlanta. Samuel knew it too, because within days he suggested that they take a drive to Atlanta. He was a man of few words, but he always had a plan. When the couple arrived in the outskirts of Atlanta, Samuel drove directly to an apartment complex. This apartment complex was next door to a school. He had done his homework thoroughly and he was taking care of Hannah.

Samuel jumped out of the car and went into the office of this apartment complex while still not saying one word to Hannah. He returned within a half hour. In his hands was the contract and the paper work needed for the lease of an apartment. Still saying nothing, he pulled around a couple of buildings and got out of the car. He came around to let Hannah out of her seat. She stepped out and Samuel started up some stairs. At the top of these stairs, he placed a key inside of the key hole. They were suddenly inside of a nice apartment. Hannah was very satisfied. The carpet was a pretty beige color. Custom drapes were upon the windows. The living room was big and the windows were large. The kitchen was nice and the three bedrooms were cute. Hannah knew that she and her children could live quite nicely here.

Since no questions were asked and no statements were made, Hannah knew this was Samuel's way of protecting her and her children. This was his way of saying that he cared. He knew the sale of his company could not be a good thing for Hannah and her children. Hannah looked her new home over. She reached over and placed a big kiss upon Samuel's face. She whispered,

"This is nice. Thank you! Everything is going to be okay!"

Change was hard on Hannah, as it was going to be for her children. They were never fond of moving from one school to another. Could she blame them? She had never changed schools more than one time when she was a child. Her parents had moved to Florida once for a short time, then right back home again. That was devastating to her, so she could imagine how awful her children must feel about this, still another move.

Within the week, Samuel had moved all of Hannah's furniture and belongings into her new apartment. The children were soon enrolled in the school that was now next door. This was very nice for the small family, because the children could walk to the nearby school. Now Hannah must find a job. She looked in the paper, and she went downtown to different employment agencies. Luckily she found a position within days. Samuel, having a good education and being an engineer also had no problem acquiring a good position in Atlanta. He would not be moving to Atlanta because he still kept his son most of the time. He would be driving the distance from his home each day. This saddened Hannah, but she knew she would see him most every day, either before or after work. There had been no reasons to stress out because before long Samuel was spending a lot of time at the apartment. He was there every time his son visited his mother. Life was adjusting well.

Hannah settled into her new position and she liked it very well. She was enjoying the working in the downtown area. It was exciting! She had one big worry, and that was about her children. This was because they were not quite old enough to supposedly take care of themselves. Hannah always worried. There was a term for her children. That term was called 'The Key Children'. A parent would place a key around their child's neck and pray for the best. Grandparents could never understand this standard of living because in the 1950's and early 1960's most mothers did not work. Now in these years a lot mothers worked, even those who had not been divorced.

To add to Hannah's grief, concern and guilt, shortly after she had acquired her new position while riding a bus to downtown Atlanta each day, something horrible happened. During this time her son became very sick one evening. She thought it was only because he had been at a pool party all day and maybe he ate too many hotdogs or other goodies. With the limited funds that Hannah and her family always endured, she watched diligently over her son, but she did put him to bed. She stayed up and watched TV for a short time and then she went into the child's room to kiss him goodnight. She had left the nightstand light on during her trip to tuck him under his covers earlier. She asked her son if he liked his cowboy room that she had painstaking decorated upon their move. She was talking about these things to try to get her child's mind off of his tummy ache.

As Hannah walked back into the child's room to kiss him goodnight, she noticed he was still awake. This time she saw big dark circles around his pretty eyes. She panicked! What was she to do? She felt she had been on her job less than one month, but she wasn't sure. Insurance would not take effect until after one month of service on her job. Yet, the young mother knew that she could not ignore the horrible signs her son was having. She thought of her options for a second. Then she ran into the other bedroom where she awakened her daughter. The small family loaded into their car and headed for the nearest hospital.

It was now around 12:30am and the emergency room was almost empty. The little boy was rushed right in. Immediately the doctors surveyed the problem and reported to the worried mother. They stated that the child was on the verge of a ruptured appendix and he would need to be operated on immediately. Now Hannah felt deep, deep pangs of guilt. 'What if's' started running rampantly through her mind. What if she had tried to doctor him herself at home? What if the worry over their money situations had kept her from going to the hospital? What if she had made the wrong decision? Was she that irresponsible? Why had she moved her children away from her parents? Why was she trying to make it on her own? She was scared and feeling really stupid for everything she had ever done. Why did she have to work so hard for her pursuit of happiness? Others did not seem to have to do that. Her looks were far above average according to everyone who made remarks. She was always told of how pretty she was by everyone. She did not believe that because if these things were true, why did she have to work so hard at just being what she thought was normal?

The night was spent at the hospital with complete worry. The operation went well, however the doctor told Hannah that should she have waited until morning it may have been too late for her child. This was because her son's appendix was hot. There would have been a much more serious situation by morning. Hannah knew now that her fear over not having enough money to do anything could be very dangerous for her little family. Times were not as they became in later years. There were no free services for people who worked and made any kind of a living. Though often completely at the poverty level, working mothers could easily be evicted from their apartments. They never received help with medical bills or education. They always made just enough money to be either right at or right above the line of help.

The following morning, Hannah had to make a very big decision. Her son was going to have to stay at the hospital for two to three days. She was brand new on her job. She felt she would surely lose that job if she did not go to work. She talked of this with the hospital officials the whole night through. Finally, when she knew she could not wait any longer, a nurse came in and said,

"The extra bed in this room is not going to be used. You go on to work and you can call all day long if you wish. You daughter can stay in this extra bed until your son is released. Your children seem very well behaved. They can watch TV together and I will look after them until you get off work."

Hannah could not thank her enough. Yet, she felt so devastated that she had to leave. She beat herself up all the way to work and the whole day long. Thankfully Samuel got off work much earlier than she and he had gone straight to the hospital.

Fate was helping behind the scenes, even though Hannah could not tell it. Her boss or someone had hurriedly put her on the insurance package at the company. Someone brought her forms to sign and she was now on the company insurance. At the end of the work day Hannah hurried to the hospital with the needed forms to take care of her son's hospital bill. When she walked into that hospital room she felt so terrible. She said to herself,

"What kind of mother am I? How could I have left my children all day in this hospital without me?"

The children were okay. Hannah was not. She was getting really good at bashing herself. She had lost all of her self-respect. She had learned from her first husband how to find all kinds of fault within herself. She really did not like herself very much.

The children were very smart and very resilient. The lad and his sister were home within a few days. Once again there was the big worry of going to work and leaving them home all alone. Hannah had very strict rules for her children. She told them that they must call her the minute they arrived home from school each day. They were also to stay in the apartment with the door locked until she arrived home. They were not to open that door to anyone, no matter what may be said on the other side. Hannah would always regret the way her children had to live. She knew this was because she was a divorced mother, but what could she do about that?

So many children of this era had both a mother and a father. One of those parents would most usually meet their children at the school or at their home. Life was so much easier in the smaller town while working for Samuel. There, life was almost normal where the children could be with her at work and so on. Hannah could now only teach her children and believe in them to have common sense. They were such intelligent children to where this plan did work, no matter how inadequate Hannah felt as a mother. She spent the biggest part of her life beating herself up and hoping for her life to change. She always hoped for tomorrow. She always hoped things would get better. They never did.

Hannah's life would not change before her children grew up and left home. She worked all of the time. She often held two or maybe even three jobs at a time just so she could make ends meet. <u>The ends never met</u>! Hannah struggled, the children struggled, but they all got by somehow.

Samuel and Hannah had become somewhat distant a couple of years after the company had sold. Samuel's visits became less often and any financial help he might have given did not come along. The only time Samuel had helped much at all was that first day when he rented the apartment. He had paid the deposit and the first month's rent. Hannah was much in love, but wondered if she had maybe caused the distance between the two showing her hopes of getting married. Samuel never mentioned marriage anymore. She realized this man had a bad taste in his mouth about marriage after the loss of one.

One night as the couple laid upon the large couch together, the song, 'I Will Always Love You' came on the radio. Samuel looked at Hannah with the softness he often got in his eyes and said,

"I will always love you darling!"

She did not know how to deal with this. She knew she was loved. She knew Samuel wanted and needed her, the same as she wanted and needed him, but he would not commit to her. Hints seemed to be that he was afraid of losing what he seemed to have with his son. Hannah could not understand this either, because the group had become a family. Everyone loved one another and everyone felt they were connected. Maybe this man did not want the responsibility of raising two other children. Yet, she knew he loved her children. She just could not put her finger upon it.

Hannah really never understood why Samuel never married her. She was rather gun shy too and asked herself why she wanted to fix something that was not broken. She and Samuel had a Heavenly relationship. Financially she and her children would have been so much better off if Samuel had married her. Oh, Samuel helped her if she became completely devastated about a money problem or when she would tell him she was in trouble, but she would never know the bliss of having the money she needed to survive. Her children would never know what it was like to receive the items or the care the extra money had bought Samuel's son.

Chapter 14

Samuel and Hannah had become so distant by the year of 1980 to where visits had stopped completely. Hannah was devastated. She did not know what had happened to what she believed to be her 'Forever'! The children had left right after school and were once more spending their summer in Ohio with Hannah's parents. Thankfully the children would not see their mother cry. Crying seemed to be Hannah's biggest pass time of late. Work at her office position was always a wonderful outlet and she enjoyed that very much. She always filled her evenings with a second job as a waitress or other part time job during the summers to help with the money needed once the children returned. One would have thought this would keep Miss Hannah very busy and exhausted. It did most of the time, but there were other times that she could not sleep. Times she would cry for hours until she would have to get up and change her pillowcase. It was during these times that she tried to draw her mind away from her loneliness. She would wipe her mind of the current activities and she would recall days of her childhood!

Summers were hot in Georgia. How could anyone recall winter snow days? Hannah let her mind wonder back to the days of shopping with her family in the small town of Gallipolis, Ohio. She could almost smell the roasting peanuts under the large glass cases that lined the large Murphy's Five and Dime. Saturdays were spent shopping in this beautiful 1700's town. Hannah's parents would park in the Kroger parking lot and walk through the lower five and dime. This small town shopping stripe had two Murphy's Five and Dimes. Why? Hannah never understood. But, this town boasted of two. The family never stopped to shop at the lower one upon their arrival. They just walked through the store to the sidewalk. They would proceed to the North, larger five and dime store where the old wooden floors would sink down below the front door stops. Large fans would hang overhead and rows of merchandise filled the store.

Hannah's father knew everyone in the whole county it seemed, and he would stop and talk constantly with everyone along the way upon these shopping trips. The mother's cousin was the president of one of the banks, so a conversation was always inevitable when the banking was done. Dr. Shane was on a side street beside of the North side of the park. Visits were often there, or on up the street to Dr. Wareham's. Many times they would go to the children's doctor, Dr. Brown. Dr. Brown's office was in his house a block behind the shopping area. A large Chevy garage was between the doctor's offices, so the family would often stop to see the latest cars, even though this family was Ford people. These Saturday's were set aside for just this thing. The whole day was spent shopping and visiting in the downtown area of Gallipolis, Ohio.

As the family would work their way down the street, they would stop at many stores. There was a small diner where they rarely stopped. But there was a nice restaurant to where the family would most usually eat their lunch. However, the children preferred to eat in the drugstore further down the street because it had a soda fountain, red stools and black and white floor tiles. It seemed more of a fun place for the children. The best of all treat was that it had juke boxes on every table. The children could always get cherry cokes or shakes from the fountain. This would have always been the children's favorite place to eat. After lunch, the family would shop their way down to the lower dime store where they would search for bargains. This large store had sky lights high above. Big fans blew strongly throughout the store. The manager was also a cousin of the mother's so the family would always visit with her a spell. Christmas's were always exciting because each downtown store gave away tickets for a new car that they would have sitting in the middle of the city park. Someone was going to be the lucky winner of this car.

Finally an exhausted, but happy family would take their hot peanuts and candy and walk down the wide sidewalk to any store that they could walk through so as to end up in the Kroger parking lot. They would take their time in this venture while finishing their goodies. Once every bag was placed into the car and it was locked up tight, the family would go inside of Kroger and do their grocery shopping. This was a ritual that was done each and every Saturday in each and every week and each and every year of Hannah's youth.

Hannah thought about that for a minute then she realized that her family probably did not lock their car. They did not seem to lock anything during those times. Everyone must have been totally honest or something.

Hannah could close her eyes and see the large wooden sleigh and the eight reindeers made of wood that decorated the beautiful city park.

The city park sat right in the middle of downtown. All of the stores were on one side of the street because the park was on the other. This park met First Street that was along the Ohio River. In the heart of this park stood an old two story gazebo. This gazebo dated from the 1800's. It was covered in carvings and lattice work that the townsfolk keep painted a sparkling white. Hannah missed Santa Claus and his sleigh the most. The past few years the city had replaced these with more modern plastic or metal type decorations. In Hannah's book, nothing could take the place of that large old wooden Santa and Sleigh

Hannah could close her eyes and place herself in that park. Or she could feel the warmth of her loving childhood home. She could almost hear her father cheerfully saying his little night time poem while he was helping her mother put the children into their beds. His poem went like this,

Let's go to bed said sleepy head
No let's wait awhile said slow
Put out the pot said greedy gut
We'll eat before we go.

Or she could hear her mother singing,

Playmate come out and play with me
And bring your dollies three
Climb up my apple tree
Look down my rain barrel
Slide down my cellar door
And we'll be jolly friends forever more!

Hannah missed her family so terribly bad. She missed her home town so much and often wondered what she was doing in such a far away state. Yet, she knew she now seemed to have two homes. When she would visit Ohio for any

188

extended visit, she would be happy when she arrived back home to Georgia. When she was in Georgia, she would get homesick for Ohio. Hannah's life had turned into, what she believed to be, a mixed up world. One guesses she could be qualified as a misplaced individual. She felt so pulled between the two homes.

Many lonely nights Hannah would let her mind wonder to the days gone by. As she was folding clothes one evening she noticed the rose print on the white sheet she was folding. This brought back the memory of her eighth grade graduation dress. Hannah's school held a ceremony for the eighth grade students the very same as the ceremony for the high school graduates. The only difference was that these children did not get to wear a cap and a gown.

For this eighth grade graduation, Hannah's mother was going to make her a beautiful dress. She did not buy her material at her usual place in the basement of a store in Gallipolis. She had ordered the material from a catalog. Hannah chuckled to herself as she wondered what her mother's back up plan had been; because on the day of the graduation the material had not arrived. The minute that Hannah jumped off of her school bus, her mother sent her to the post office where her aunt was the postmaster. She prayed that the material would be there. Upon the arrival at the post office, Hannah was greeted outside of the door by her aunt who was holding out a package. She screamed,

"Grab this quick and run home fast Hannah! I don't know how your mother is going to do it, but you run as fast as you can!"

Upon arriving back at her home, the mother franticly opened the package. She cut the fabric and started to sew as fast as the old manual sewing machine would let her sew. Her feet were pumping and pumping as if she were running.

Suddenly there was a beautiful white taffeta and nylon dress completed. The plan was to tuck up clumps of the white nylon material and sew a small white cloth rose at the base of each clump. This would have taken a large amount of time because it would have to be done by hand, so Hannah was sent to the small town's general store where she was to purchase small gold safety pins.

Hannah's thoughts ran rampant when she thought of how that general store must have carried everything. She was always able to come home with whatever her mother sent her to that store to get.

Time was running out. The graduation would be in a few short hours. Mrs. Dahl preformed miracles that day. She pinned each and every tiny white rose upon that beautiful dress. She placed ribbons around the neck and the sleeves. A tailor made dress was finished and upon the little girls back in time for her cherished event. Her mother was tired, but very proud. Hannah would always remember that day and the blessings of having her mother. Now she was sad again because she missed her mother.

It seemed everything Hannah would think about would bring tears to her eyes. She missed her children terribly while they were away each summer. No matter what she was telling herself, she was missing Samuel terribly as well. She had believed that she had met her true love, her soul mate, and her passion. Now she had not seen him since early April and she did not understand why.

The shocking truth was about to unfold. One bright morning while sitting behind her well lit desk, a phone call came in unexpectedly for Hannah. The receptionist had said a Mr. Wright was calling. Hannah replied by asking,

"Samuel?"

The young lady had said,

"No, it sounds like a much older gentleman.

As Hannah picked up the receiver, her hands were trembling. Why would Samuel's father be calling her? What was wrong? Why would this elder gentleman, whom she did not know very well, be calling her at all now that she lived in the city and now that she and Samuel had become so distant? She nervously answered the phone. A cheerful, nice voice came over the line when Samuel's father said,

"Hello Hannah. How is the beautiful lady on this beautiful morning?"

Hannah said,

"Fine Sir, how are you?

He then said very little more except that he would love to take her to lunch this day. Hannah did not know what to think, but she knew that she had caused a much too long silence over the telephone line. She finally accepted and the father told her what restaurant to meet him at. This caused much anticipation for the rest of the morning. The elder gentleman had stated that he wanted to talk with her. She was at loss as to why this man would wish to speak with her.

Hannah finished her morning work rapidly and hurried to the restaurant to meet with Samuel's father. Upon arrival he greeted her with a big hug. The couple sat down around the table. The elder gentleman began to talk. He said he knew she was questioning as to why he would have the need to talk with her. He started off by saying,

"Hannah, I have always liked you. I was happy my son had found a nice girl like you and I had hoped it would work."

Now Hannah was concerned. She knew she had not seen Samuel for a couple of months but had hoped there would be a good explanation. Of course there could be no explanation for the not calling her to explain what was going on.

Finally the elder gentleman took the pretty girls hands into his and a sad look came over his face. He said,

"Honey, have you heard from Samuel?"

Of course the answer was no. He continued with,

"He has been going up to the cabin about every weekend. We can see that he has been there. I like you and do not want to see you hurt. I can tell you love my son and I believe that he loves you too. He has told me as much. Lately, I do not know what to think. I am finding women's attire up there. I heard that you worked weekends while your children were away, so I knew most these items could not be yours."

Hannah did not know what to think. Samuel was always offering that cabin to anyone who wanted to go. He knew his parents liked to go often as well, but he usually scheduled trips so as not to interfere with their visits. Her first reaction was to believe that the father was over reacting. Just as suddenly as that thought crossed her mind, she realized this man was serious. She realized he must know something he was yet to tell her.

Hannah played down the fact that she was miserable and missing Samuel terribly. She put on her professional face and asked,

"What do you think is going on? You know Samuel loans out that cabin often!"
The older gentleman just hung his head as he gripped tighter upon the hold he had of Hannah's hands. He continued,

"I don't know how to tell you this honey, but I know what is going on and I don't like it. Your boyfriend is spending weekends with his ex-wife."

Hannah's mouth flew open. She was shocked. The old man looked her in the eyes and she could see great sympathy in his eyes. Why was he telling her these things? Did he come to Atlanta just to hurt her? He stated,

"Those two have about driven me crazy over the years! They fight over everything. They probably have their child so confused to where he does not know what to do. I do not want them together. It would head for disaster once more! There is nothing wrong with either one of them, they just were not meant to be together. All they do when they are together is destroy their son."

What could Hannah do about this? If this is what Samuel wanted, then this is what Samuel should do! Hannah was terribly hurt and shocked, but she must not let it show to Samuel's father. She was falling apart inside. There is no worse feeling than the feeling of possibly being a toy to a man who has just returned to someone from his past. One feels as if they were nothing to that person.

Samuel and his ex-wife had married as teens, so naturally there would be a deep connection between them. They fought like cats and dogs, but there was some kind of connection that obviously could not be broken. Hannah knew they were still fighting over property. She knew they went back to court over and over again about custody rights for their child. She knew all of this had been rough on Samuel. Now he must have found a solution.

The lunch went well and Hannah realized that the older man wanted her to somehow put a stop to the mistakes he felt his son was making. She knew that she could not interfere. She had known something was wrong when Samuel totally disappeared. This is the reason she had not tried to contact him in anyway. Her pride and ego would get into the way. She would never beg.

The following week Hannah thought much about that lunch meeting. She finally decided that she would call Samuel. So, on another lunch break she went to the bank and got some rolled change. She then went to a pay phone and called Samuel. He answered cordially enough. He asked how she was doing. He asked how the children were. He never explained or volunteered one bit of information, however he did tell her that he would come to talk with her on the following Saturday. Hannah left it at that and waited for the rest of the long week to end.

Saturday came and around 11:00am Samuel knocked upon the door. He walked in with his son in tow. Hannah was hurt and somewhat mad at the site of the man who had left her to wonder what he was doing with his life.

Samuel had tried to quit smoking and for a release had taken up chewing on the small straw type stirrer one gets in a to-go cup of coffee. This morning he was chewing upon one such stick. He had plastered on his professional face and was acting very nonchalant. This unnerved Hannah even more and actually made her mad. She started to question just where the H---- he had been! She was getting louder with each sentence. She was not planning any of this. Where was her professional face? Why could she not control her anger? She could not shake the feeling of being used! No matter how hard she tried; she could not keep her mouth shut. Samuel reached down and got the remote control to the TV. He turned it to a station he knew that his son liked and turned the volume up very loud. He got Hannah by the arm and led her to the bedroom.

Once inside, Hannah started badgering Samuel with all of her questions. This was not intended, but Hannah was realizing now that she was really mad inside from this man leaving without a word and then not coming back for all of these months. She was hurt and she was mad! Finally during this heated one sided conversation Samuel sit down upon the dressing table stool. He looked Hannah square in the eyes and said,

"I love you!"

Okay, what was Hannah to do with that information? She started to calm down and then she started to cry. Samuel did not move from his stool. The man who would have comforted her in days gone by was sitting there stiffly while Hannah's world was falling apart.

Samuel stared for a few minutes from his distance and just let Hannah cry. One could not say that Samuel was torn. He showed that he was solid in his decision. He refused to let the passion of the minute interrupt what he was about to say. Hannah was now crying to where it was more of a whimpering. She hated to be in this position. This made her come off as the weaker sex. She wanted to scream more at Samuel. She wanted to tell him she was boiling mad at him. She wanted to slap him or hurt him for hurting her so badly. Nothing could come out of her mouth now but a shallow,

"Why-y-y-y?"

Samuel hung his head as he said,

"There is no answer to that question except that little boy in the other room, Hannah! It's just that little boy in that room!"

With that, he got up from his seat and left the room. Hannah followed as Samuel collected his son and walked out of her door forever. She stood at the door with her face pressed tightly against it while she cried uncontrollably for what seemed like an eternity. Her heart was broken. Her very soul was destroyed. Why had God forsaken her once more? Why could she not hold onto happiness? Why was *Happiness* always just one reach away?

Chapter 15

Summer was over and the time came for Hannah's children to come back to Georgia. This mother had been given two months to do nothing but think. She had a very dark two months. She was states away from her family and she was hurting. She had never socialized much with anyone because of her burdens with money. Her responsibilities were so great. She found no time to make friends. She was devastated! Her dreams were destroyed, her life was saddened and she was all alone.

Hannah did not know whether she was making a proper decision, but all she knew was that she needed someone around her who cared about her at this time. She thought everything over and decided that any chances she may have had with Samuel were gone now! It was over! Like that old song, 'It's all over but the crying'! She realized that her whole world had been wrapped around Samuel and her children. She would never be happy without him, but she could make her children happy by giving them a stable home and putting them back in the guidance and protection of her family. So, she decided instead of her children coming home this fall, she would just move back to Ohio.

August the first of 1980, Hannah calmly moved her furniture and belongings back to Ohio. She left the world where she had found true love for what she believed to be forever. When she was not feeling sorry for herself, she realized that she was luckier than many. She had fallen very deeply in love twice in her life. How often does that happen? She had heard so many people say there is only one soul mate. There is only one true love in anyone's life. Hannah felt she had two.

Hannah knew she could only be at her parent's house temporarily. There were no positions in that small community for her. She had tried after her divorce from Ambros to acquire a position in her family's county, only to result with her living with her parents for close to two years without any income. She knew she must move immediately to the city.

Hannah could afford no more time than a few days to visit and adjust. School would be starting soon and she must get her children enrolled in school. She knew she had to go straight to Columbus, Ohio. Strange, but the weather was already getting cold this year. After Georgia's weather, Hannah knew she must adjust in that department as well.

Immediately after arriving in the big city that Hannah remembered so well, she headed straight downtown. She parked her car and started walking the wide sidewalks in her high heels. She was of a habit to always half run and half walk. The stylish candy type heels had no back on them. The very first red light where she had to cross, she tripped upon a medal lid to the underground of the city and fell down. She noticed no one tried to help her. She knew people were pretty much the same all over, but today she was feeling sorry for herself and thought of how if she had been in Georgia, a dozen people would have come to her rescue. She assessed her damage and saw that she had not disturbed any of her clothing nor shoes. Her elbow may be black and blue tomorrow, but today she could still look for a job. Twice this day she caught a city bus that ran up and down High Street. She was remembering where some of the employment agencies were and was hopping into each one and leaving a resume. She also wanted to go to a temporary service. She had been placed quickly many times by doing just that.

Midday, Hannah purchased a newspaper and sat down in a corner restaurant. As she sat there in her Southern Attire, she realized it looked and felt very cold outside. It looked like it may even snow. She could see every angle of the street out of the restaurant windows as she viewed the heart of this capital city. When she had ordered a coke and settled down for a working break; she gazed out of the corner window. Depression was setting in. Everyone on the streets at this time of the day looked as if they were homeless or disturbed. She was not being fair. She knew all downtown areas had bad parts and she also knew this was a beautiful city. In her younger days she had once loved this city. To top off all of her depression, she thought of how the weather even looked ugly. The buildings surrounding her looked so grey and so sad. THERE WAS NO SUNSHINE in this world. *THERE WAS NO SAMUEL.* Hannah knew what her problem was. She knew her heart was completely broken. She could feel the tears forming under her eyelids. She knew she had better snap out of it. There was no way that she could mess up her make-up. She had to go to work, and soon!

Hannah knew that she had to be strong, but she was feeling the magnitude of the move. She just had not realized how badly the change would hurt. Besides, her last years in this city had been very painful. She had nothing but bad memories of this city now. Her first husband still lived in this town as far as she knew. He did call her parents often. Strange, but he often called her father for advice. He had made many mistakes in his life and often called the Reverend to discuss his problems and to request prayer for himself. This was a good gesture and it showed that maybe he did really have a heart. However, at this time in her life, she hated this man and felt she would most probably go straight to Hell for hating him so terribly much.

Hannah often wondered at her coldness towards her ex-husband. He had done her so very wrong on one hand, but on the other hand she could not understand how she could be so cold and so uncaring. She guessed that maybe that old saying that love turns into hate must be true. Ambros had been shot six times by someone in a bar and he was in the hospital for over six months. He almost lost his life. She heard that he had made the remark that the one person he believed who would have been there was Hannah. This statement only made her mad. She questioned how she could hate as strongly as she had loved. By this time, the ex-husband had been married a couple more times. His life style could not contend with marriage.

Hannah had a determination that living in this town would not cause her to ever have to cross his path. This city had to be big enough for the both of them. She had not laid eyes upon this man for eleven years now. Besides she was only in his city because she had to be. She was there because she knew she had no future. She was there to work and raise her children while close to her family. She was there to forget.

Hannah had heard once that her first husband had always known where she and the children were. He had the money and the connections to have private investigators inform him of her whereabouts. She heard that he had said that he had kept a detective busy trying to locate Hannah with her many moves. He would make his brags that he always knew exactly where she was and that she could never hide from him.

For years, Hannah had received dark wine colored roses that she loved so very much on her birthday. She never knew who sent them. Now she felt she knew who may have left these roses' years ago. After her move to Georgia she had still received the same roses for each and every birthday. The difference being that a delivery person would bring them now. The roses would always have an unsigned card. The card would read,

"Your Secret Admirer."
This was unlike those that had been pressed into her car door handle so many years ago without any sign of a card. However, there still were twelve wine colored long stemmed roses arriving from whom, she did not know. She started making jokes to her fellow employees when one year she got only six. She said,

"See my secret admirer is caring for me less, or the economy has gotten to him. See, I only got six this year."
She thought a minute, but then realized if it were Hugh, he would have never had a money problem. So, there still was a question as to who sent the roses.

Hannah would never ask and she would never know who had sent these roses. Finally after several years of living in Georgia, the roses stopped. She could never get over the fact that she had left Columbus, Ohio without telling anyone but her family of where she was going. She did not want her ex-husband to know. Yet someone from there she had to assume, had been sending her roses for many years on each birthday. The first year the roses had scared her, being placed inside of a car door handle as they were, especially when she was all alone. She was very shaken and this had unnerved the young lady. Someone had to know her quite well, because the roses were the very color she had always loved so much. Hugh and her were separated at that time and as far as she knew, he had moved back to Cincinnati. He had made no claims, at that time, that he still wanted his marriage to work or that he ever wanted anything else to do with Hannah.

While Hannah tried to put all of her thoughts collectively into one spot; she could not help but blame herself for all of her problems. Why was she not a smarter person? How could she make so many stupid mistakes? Why had she not gone to that Bible College? Why had she rebelled? Why had she not become a missionary? All of these thoughts would cross her mind. She knew in her heart this was exactly the way her parents felt. Oh, they felt sorry for her and they helped her all that they could. But, they also had such firm beliefs. They believed with their hearts, had Hannah chosen the path that they had laid out before her, she would have not been going though all of this pain. None the less, she would not have her beautiful children had she not taken the path she had taken. So, even though she was hurting, she would stand up, wipe herself off and start all over again. She knew she had to be a survivor!

After letting her thoughts run rampant while staring out of those large restaurant windows, Hannah realized it was now time for her next appointment. She was somewhat relieved because her mind was going in circles about her past mistakes and the mistakes of others. She jumped up from her seat and went to the cash register to pay for her drink. Today was going to continue to be a most stressful day.

Hannah jumped on a bus and rode down close to the Lazarus Department Store. She arrived at a most beautiful office which caused all of her negativity of the street views to go away. Hannah believed that her interview with the employment agency went well. She was now scheduled to go to a CPA firm for an interview. She jumped back on a city bus and went to this scheduled appointment. She tried to think only of happy thoughts. She could remember being turned down for a position one time in this very city due to the fact that the potential employer felt he could read much unhappiness on her face. She knew that attitude played a large part in securing a good position. So, she thought of her children. This was always her happy thoughts. She thought of how when her little girl was small, she could not say city bus. She would say.

"Nitty Bus!"

This put a smile upon Hannah's face. How precious was that? What would Hannah's world be like without her beautiful children? She always knew it was just she and the kids. She always knew her children were her world. She was selfish in her belief that she loved her children more than other people loved their children. She knew she was loved as a child, but she also knew her parents had so many other involvements. They had the large extended family and they had the church and the church children. They had each other and sometimes Hannah believed that would have been more than enough for this much in love couple.

Hannah knew when all was said and done, she had her children. She was thankful for her two wonderful blessings. She believed that she and her children would be closer for the rest of their lives than any other family. She thanked God every day for giving her such wonderful gifts. When all was said and done, the other problems in life were a small price to pay. Maybe God had given her a choice to have these beautiful children or a calm life. She did not know if God operated in those ways, but she knew she would go through it all again if it meant the difference of having or not having her precious children.

Thinking of her children put Hannah in a happy mood by the time she got off of the elevator to go into the CPA's office. Luckily for her, the interviewers liked her resume and they liked her. So, they hired her on the spot. Work was to start the following week. She had to get moving to prepare for her children's move and the readiness for school. Now, she must find a place for the family to live immediately. She jumped back onto the city bus with a lightened heart. As she got off at the stop where she had parked her car, she could feel the weight of the world lifting from her shoulders.

Chapter 16

For four years Hannah worked and made a life in Ohio. She loved being close to her family for the first time in many years. She could attend reunions, holiday visits and be there for all events. She enjoyed every visit with her loved ones.

The children were teenagers now. Ambros had once more come into their lives. Hannah had hated him for so many years, but became soft hearted on the day he walked into her home and looked at his beautiful teenage daughter and his six foot three inch son and said while tears were running down his face,

"Children, I would like to introduce myself, I am your father!"

Eleven years had passed and this man had not laid his eyes upon these children. This day marked a very notable date for this family.

By this date, Hannah had taken a better paying position as a Controller of a Country Club. This position was about thirty-five miles outside of Columbus. She had put off the request of the school to bring papers to prove that she had legal custody of her children for far too long. She had tried to explain to the school that all of their records were right there in their city and that the father had never left. He lived right there! But seemingly, nothing like this was going to please the school. So, one day the children brought home a paper that said the officials were going to remove the children from school should their mother not prove that she had the right to have these children? Hannah was disgusted. These children were *NO ONE'S* but hers. But rules are rules and she guessed many people who did not have custody of their children must be moving from state to state to remove their children from the rightful custody holder.

Moving as much as Hannah had moved, plus with her mother being a clean freak, she now had no idea where her custody papers may be. So, on the evening of getting the letter, she got the bright idea of how she could solve her problem. She knew there would be no problem finding Ambros. In a hateful way of thinking, she told herself all she had to do was go down to a certain street in Columbus, Ohio and she would find him in one of the bars. So, she got into her car and began her search.

Hannah was in luck. Everyone in town seemed to know Ambros. The very first place she stopped she was directed to another. Upon arrival at this club, Hannah was pleasantly surprised. This was a nice neighborhood family bar. It served food and the atmosphere was pleasant. She walked in during these early evening hours to find only three or four people watching TV and eating their dinner. A pretty lady jumped up from one of the tables and walked behind the bar as she said,

"Hello, may I help you?"
Hannah said,

"Yes! I am told Ambros Hughes comes in here a lot."
The lady got very quiet but finally said,

"And you are? Why are you looking for Ambros?"

Thinking this line of questioning to be strange, Hannah was reluctant to continue with her conversation. The lady noticed her demise and forced a smile upon her face, then said,

"Yes, this is his place. He should be here shortly!"

Now Hannah started to get really nervous. She had not laid eyes on her first husband in years. What was going to happen in the next few hours?

During the wait, the nice lady stayed on the other side of the bar. She even pulled up a stool and started to talk with Hannah. She was really asking a lot of questions. Had it not been for the kind way in which she was asking these questions, Hannah would have been even more uncomfortable. Finally she thought, what's the difference? It may make Ambros blow sky high should she tell his business to anyone else, but who cared? She had seen his temper before, and after all of these years, who cared? She decided to confine in this lady. She said,

"My name is Hannah."

With just that statement the lady walked off and said,

"Wait a minute. I thought that was who you were!"

She went over to the cash register and picked up something besides of it. When she returned, she had a picture of Hannah's children from way back when they were three and four years old. Of course these kinds of pictures were the only pictures Ambros would have of her children. He had not seen them since that time. The picture was tattered and looked as though it had been shown and handled many times over the years.

The lady said,

"Hi, my name is Sharon! Are these your children?"

Hannah said,

"Yes!"

Then the lady started telling her of how Ambros was so proud of the picture. She told of how he showed everyone his children's picture. Hannah was taken aback. This did not sound like the self-centered Ambros that she knew from so many years ago.

Hannah was realizing she was stepping into a territory that she should probably remove herself from. She suddenly realized this lady was connected to Ambros in some romantic way. So she started to explain. She explained why she was looking for him. She said,

"I have a fairly new job and the school is driving me crazy. I have explained to them that I have always had custody of my children, but they are not settling for just my words. I called downtown and ask for copies of my divorce papers and the custody papers only to be told that the papers had long since been moved to the annex and I would have to come down to retrieve them. I explained that I could not take off work to do that, but they had no sympathy."

Hannah could see that this nice lady did feel sympathy, but could also feel a strong jealousy lurking underneath. She knew she had to put this lady at ease, so she said,

"Ambros and my relationship was over years and years ago. I was so young and so naïve. He was so worldly and so removed from my world. We could have never had anything in common. I have not seen him in eleven years. I want nothing from him and I am sure he wants nothing from me. I just thought he could handle this with maybe just a phone call. All he has to do is to tell the school that he is the father and that his ex-wife has custody of his children."

This blunt statement seemed to put the lady at ease. Luckily the timing was correct, because just as those statements got out of Hannah's mouth Ambros walked in. Hannah could not help but be taken back by this man's ever handsome self. Jeans were now the style and Ambros was wearing his in the most fitting way. He walked through the big doors while the sun shined behind him. His broad shoulders were covered with a long sleeved shirt that was opened in the front while showing a dark knit tee underneath. Other than graying, years had not changed this handsome man. Every hair was still in place. He was still very much a drop dead gorgeous kind of man.

As Ambros walked up to the bar, a strong worried look came over his face. What was he to expect. He had not seen this woman in over eleven years. What was wrong? What was she here to do? What did she want? Hannah read his concerns and blurted out her needs immediately. Ambros jumped up from his half sitting, half standing position that he had taken upon the stool next to Hannah and walked to a lighted area between the bathrooms. She watched as he picked up the telephone and proceeded to have a long conversation with someone. When he returned he said,

"I have an attorney that I keep on a retainer. He will get the paper work needed and everything will be taken care of! Don't worry!"

With that distant level type conversation, Hannah excused herself with a 'Thank You' and walked out of the door.

Days later the children brought home a paper stating that their status at the school had been reinstated. Hannah was once in her life thankful to Ambros for taking care of this problem. This favor became two fold before long. The following weekend a knock came upon her door. Hannah should have known the power that could be behind her ex-husband. He knew how to get what he wanted. He had somehow gotten her address. She was shocked and a little mad when she opened her door this Saturday morning to see none other than Ambros Hughes standing there.

Hannah's son had always said he would like to knock his father's lights out should he ever meet him. Her daughter just never said anything and Hannah knew there were many times that this young lady would have liked to have had a father. On this day of the meeting, nothing was said or done in a negative way. Ambros cried and hugged his children. Hannah watched with a mixture of love and hate flowing through her. She knew this was bigger than she. She knew there was no fighting this. Blood runs deep within one's soul.

Hannah's daughter had shown many signs of strong ESP through the years. Possibly in this case she had a very strong memory that took her back to when she was three years old. She had told her mother that she had seen this same man at her school. She said she was watching out of her classroom window when this man got out of a Lincoln Continental and walked into the school office. She told her mother that she could feel that she knew him. She had the strangest of feelings as she watched him get out of his car and walk into that building. Then that Saturday she found that he was her father.

Being close to Christmas, Ambros and his wife Sharon had come to visit. Now Hannah understood the questioning she had received from this lovely lady. The couple asked Hannah for permission to take the children shopping. Hannah was nervous in doing so, but realized she felt comfortable with this nice lady named Sharon. She agreed to this outing.

After the long day was over, the children came home right on time, just as Ambros had promised. They were toting many gifts. This Christmas was going to be the most expensive Christmas Hannah's children had ever received. She was soon to find out that the club she had gone into to find her ex-husband was owned by Ambros and his wife. She was also soon to find out that the couple was fully determined to play Santa Claus to her youngsters. They were going to do everything in their power to win the children's love and to make up for all of those lost years. Christmas was very nice for everyone.

Before long, Ambros had asked permission for his children to come to visit him and Sharon. The children seemed to enjoy these visits. Things were getting better for Hannah's children. She was thankful for all of this. Within the following years there were gifts like a diamond ring, a Camaro car, trips to California and a poodle. Life seemed to be good for Hannah's children.

Then one day Sharon just suddenly died at a young age of forty-two years old. She died of a brain aneurysm and everything seemed to slow. Ambros went into a long mourning period and the children and he became very distant once more. Hannah knew that Sharon had been the one woman in Ambros's life whom he loved more than himself. She knew he had finally realized true love and that he was hurting beyond belief. She also knew that Sharon had been the factor in getting him back with his children. Within a few months, Ambros had gotten rid of their luxury townhouse and had moved into an apartment above his bar. Later months he had talked with Hannah's Reverend father about how he was fighting suicide. His world was shattered and he crawled into a bottle where he stayed for a very long time. This caused much strong distance once more between his children and him.

Chapter 17

Hannah was taking stock of her life. Her children would soon be graduating High School. Having only fourteen months between their ages, this was going to happen very fast. Hannah enjoyed their teenage years. She was always happy to have all of their friends visit her home. The children's friends thought her to be cool. A big group of teenagers were always at Hannah's house. This was good because Hannah knew where her children were at all times. She did not have to worry much in this department anyway because her children were extremely smart and both had their heads on rather straight. They might get into silly little troubles now and again, but as a whole, Hannah's children were very well behaved and respectful to their mother.

Hannah watched many of her lifetime friends and family. Her thoughts would wonder as to how different her life could have been had she married a local boy or one of those from that Bible College as her father had so desired. She felt that she would more than likely still be very naïve without the hard knocks of reality. Possibly she could have been happy.

As Hannah was approaching the age of forty, she started to feel sorry for herself and feeling as if her life was over. Her children were grown now and soon would be gone. They both planned on going to college. This was something that Hannah had never let them un-think. She had embedded this need very deeply into their heads. She wanted so much for them. She also knew that had she not received the small amount of extra education that she had received, she would have never been able to have raised her children. It was extremely tough as it was. An education was extremely important and at the top of her desires for her children.

Hannah had not been on a date in years. Her brother had a friend from down in the woods who seemed to be attracted to her. She went out with him a few times. Her way of thinking now was that maybe if she had married one such guy she would have been happy. If she had been allowed to date a local boy when she was in High School, she may have had the kind of happy life all of her high school friends now seemed to have. So with Hannah feeling her chances in life were now going away, she started dating this farm man.

A short time into the relationship, Samuel and his son came to visit. Samuel had called Hannah sometimes everyday while she was on her job. If she refused to talk with him he would call her children. They adored him and he would often try to talk them into coming to live with him. He too, would always have ways of finding out where Hannah was. Hannah knew she was still very deeply in love with Samuel and seeing him only made things worse. The children were so very happy to see Samuel and his son. Although he never told Hannah as much, she had heard he had remarried his son's mother. She felt he was more than likely visiting her without his wife's knowledge. The two had come to Kentucky for a Corvette show and had politely traveled on to Ohio to visit Hannah and her children.

Hannah watched as the pretty new Corvette pulled out of her driveway. Tears fell down her cheeks while those old feelings and all of the old pains shot through her body. She told herself she would never see these loved ones again. Once more, her heart was breaking. Oh, the pain of loving someone when you know you can never be with them again.

This visit caused Hannah to once more make a mistake. She phoned the farm boy and told him she was ready now to be only his. She was putting her past behind her and she was determined to make a life for herself. This idea was very short lived. As she was trying to comment herself to a life with the farm boy, she realized she had lived way too much. She had been everywhere. She had knowledge of a broader world. She and her farm boy went together like oil and water. She could never go back to that innocent world of so long ago. This sweet man had never left. This sweet man was unspoiled. He lived just the same as he had in his teenage years upon his father's thousand acre farm. He went fishing every day. He stared at the stars. He took long walks through the woods. He loved his gentle life as he had always known it. Hannah had too much baggage. She had been through too much to ever conform to this man's way of life.

Hannah was determined to try the country life. But, even while going into it she knew it would never work. Suddenly, reality hit. She said to herself,

"What am I doing?"

She went to the store and bought a record. That day, all day long, she listened to that Dolly Parton song called 'I Will Always Love You'! She cried while she missed Samuel. She was having a day of totally feeling sorry for herself. She could hear and see Samuel as he said in his loving voice on that night of so many years ago,

"I will always love you Darling!"
She was so hurt. Would her heart ever quit breaking?

Hannah had tried to start a new life. She was going to forget the past and start a life that she had missed out on in her youth. She changed jobs and moved to her parents where she proceeded to have that new life. She had tried to lose contact with Samuel, but he had called her old work and got her new work number. Then one day he called. Hannah could tell by his voice that all was not right in his world. He said immediately and in a panicked voice,

"Anna has been killed in a car accident!"
Anna was his wife. Dear God, how sad. She was but thirty nine years old. Hannah's heart bled. She had at one time had good times with this woman. Loving the same man had caused large distances between them by now, but losing her to this horrible accident was so sad. Hannah cried.

Hannah always knew Samuel could not live alone. Within weeks he was begging her to come back to Georgia. She knew she must be the stronger of the two. She kept telling him that she could not do such a thing. She informed him that the proper thing to do in any wife's death was to wait one year before approaching any kind of a relationship.

Many months and then a year passed. Hannah found that Samuel had met someone else. She knew now that her life had to remain the same and she would stay connected to her farm boy, even though she knew all along that this was not fair to him. However, he was her strength. He is what was keeping her from running straight into Samuel's arms with all forgiven and all pain running away. She did not want to do that. She now had a deadly fear of getting hurt even more. Possibly in the deep parts of her soul she wanted Samuel to suffer. Why? He had suffered enough. No matter what she and Samuel had together, he had to have loved his wife very much because they had been together for so many years. Hannah was starting to understand the fact that people can be in love with two people at the same time. Even though the loss of Samuel had about killed her, she now felt happy that Anna was able to have spent her last years with the man that she loved. Some wise old woman had told Hannah after her breakup with Ambros that people do not fall out of love. They only fall in love with someone else. She had said you will always love someone you once loved whether you realize that or not.

After a year and one-half, Hannah started realizing that Samuel's adventures with the other woman were purely his desire to be with someone. Anyone! She knew he wanted her back and would take her back at any cost. Finally after two or three phone calls per day, Hannah caved in. Her son had been attending Ohio State University while taking Electrical Engineering. He had always loved Georgia and had voiced the fact that he would love to go back to Georgia and attend Georgia Tech. This helped Hannah in her decision to return to Georgia. Her daughter had now graduated high school and had not decided which college she wished to attend. She had friends and a boyfriend of whom she did not wish to leave. Therefore, she would be staying in Ohio with her grandparents. This saddened Hannah.

In October of that year, Hannah and her son took off for Georgia. Her teenage son was driving a Rider moving truck and she tailed behind. She was not going to live with Samuel at this point even though he had wished her to do just that. She intended to be self-sufficient as she had always been and was moving to the Atlanta area once more to live in an apartment. She had been to visit now a few times and she and Samuel were once more getting close. She had rented a very nice apartment. The apartment was so unlike those she had to have while her children were growing up. This was new and more on the luxury side. There was a lighted pool, a hot tub and many nice things about this gated community. Life was going to be different. Hannah had acquired a marvelous position as a manager with a large employment agency. She would hire seven to nine people and have a complete satellite office, while her boss and others would be in their Menlo Park, California office. Hannah just knew she was going to love this position.

On a cold October night they arrived at Samuel's house, Hannah would never forget the greeting she was to receive. Samuel had told her that he would leave the door open since it would be in the middle of the night when she arrived. As she and her son pulled into the long driveway, they were very tired and ready for some much needed rest. The many hours of driving had taken its pain upon their aching muscles. The October night had a large chill. Hannah had just left a much colder area and was dressed in a short white fur coat. Her son took to the front bedroom almost immediately. They had not awakened a soul in this house. Hannah walked down the long soft carpeted hall to

Samuel's bedroom. She leaned over his sleeping body and placed a kiss upon his forehead. Months had passed since the two had seen each other. Just as Hannah's lips met Samuel's forehead, he wrapped his arms around her while placing a passionate kiss upon her lips. He said,

"Oh Baby, You're Here! I love you so much! I've missed you so-o-o-o much! Please don't ever make me live without you again!"

Hannah melted into her lover's arms hoping to never leave them again. She always knew that Samuel loved her completely. She had just felt they had met too late in life. They had not been meant to be together. It saddened her to know that Anna most surely knew that Samuel loved her as well. She also knew in her heart that Samuel had loved Anna through it all. Both women had to wonder which one he loved the most. Hannah would always have a thought run through her mind that obviously Samuel loved Anna the most. He had gone back to her after a few years with Hannah. She also knew that this wonderful man was always torn between what was right and what was wrong. Being raised Catholic; she knew that he felt his being with Hannah had been a sin.

Chapter 18

About two years after Hannah's return to Georgia she and Samuel had finally moved in together. This had been a slow process for many reasons. The children were in and out sometimes leaving home, sometimes moving back in. Hannah's daughter had now moved to Georgia. This made Hannah very happy. She was attending Georgia State and all was well in the world. Hannah was being little Miss Independent and for once in her life she could say she was very happy. She loved her job. She had other jobs in the past that she liked very well. She had always thought the position at the country club would be a hard position to beat, but she found out quickly that her new position was like no other. She really loved her job.

With her position Hannah got to travel constantly. She was responsible for the accounting for eighteen offices in Georgia and many more in other Southern States. She had offices in Alabama, the North and South Carolina's and Florida. She had the total of forty seven offices. She was forever traveling to each of these offices to hold seminars and train new employees. Once per month she would report in to her Menlo Park, California office where she would be trained in the latest techniques and meet with her boss. Then, once a year her boss would fly in and take her to lunch while giving her that yearly review. At first she was afraid of flying, but soon began loving every minute of it. Each year the company would take each of their managers on a vacation/training trip. One year they went to Hawaii, another to Switzerland. They entertained their employees in the best of fashion while traveling to these exotic places. Hannah loved this high prestige position. She loved the office that she had picked out and rented. She loved her employees and she loved the security she now was feeling.

Samuel always held very high positions as well. With his three degrees and his seasoned knowledge as an engineer, he was in much demand. He owned three condos upon the beaches of Panama City, Florida. Each weekend that they were both available they either by themselves, or with the children, would go to Florida for the weekend. Life was grand for this self-made family.

Several months into living together, Samuel ask Hannah to please not go into work the following morning. She had no idea why, but reluctantly agreed to not go to work that day. A few days before the couple had gone shopping. This was not that unusual, Samuel always loved buying pretty things for the more conservative Hannah. She would often tell him that she needed nothing until she would upset him to the point that he would just start pulling things off the racks and loading them into a cart. On the most recent shopping spree, Samuel had purchased a navy blue suit for Hannah. One that she was sure she would not like. It was navy and of a shining broadcloth. She felt the skirt was way too short. On the rack it looked one way, but once it was placed upon her back it looked like a million dollars. It was amazing as to how Samuel could always do that.

On this morning of neither going to work, Hannah could not help but wonder where they were going. Samuel had told her it was a surprise. He had dressed in a beautiful expense suit and asked her to please wear her new navy suit. They got into his Corvette and then headed north. This seemed strange to Hannah. All of their work life and life in general was always south.

With Hannah's trust and belief in Samuel, she settled down into her comfortable seat and planned on what she believed to be a long ride. She said,

"Samuel, you know I cannot take off from work for long. This is not a long vacation or something you are planning, is it?"

Samuel kept driving without saying a word. As they arrived at a store in a small town called Ringgold, Georgia somewhere between Atlanta, Georgia and Chattanooga, Tennessee, Samuel pulled into a convenient store. He handed Hannah a nice little wrapped box with a ribbon around it. Hannah thanked him and watched his eyes dance while he was planning something wonderful.

When Hannah opened the beautiful little card on the top of the box, in Samuel's handwriting she saw the words,

"Will you marry me?"

She replied with an immediate,

"Yes!"

Inside the box were beautiful wedding rings. Samuel pulled out his and handed it to her while taking the one out of the box for her. Samuel had asked this very same question many, many years ago and nothing ever came of that. She had said yes then too, only to have her heart ripped right out of her. He told her that this time he was taking no chances of anything messing up his plan. Hannah laughed and said,

"Alright Mr. Wright, what would have happened if I had said no?"

Samuel hung his head and said,

"Well then I guess I would have had to drive this car off a cliff and put both of us out of our misery!"

Hannah reached over and slapped him. He then said,

"We would have turned around and gone home and I would have cried all of the way! I love you Hannah and want you to be with me for the rest of our days!"

Ringgold, Georgia was the same as that little town in Kentucky where Hannah had said her 'I Do's' light years ago. What on earth was with her life? Could she never be married in a church? Recently she had been asked to go to Ohio with her daughter and her fiancé for a weekend. She had explained to her daughter that she could not go because of her short notice. Her daughter's beautiful Irish eyes were dancing. She had her father's powder blue eyes and Hannah had learned long ago not to look into those eyes if you wanted to correct or disagree with them. Those beautiful Irish eyes could make you melt away completely. Hannah had never in her life seen prettier eyes anywhere than those her ex-husband and her daughter owned.

Finally after much persuasion, Hannah had packed a bag and gone along with her daughter on the long weekend trip. There would have been no way she could have missed going on this trip, because unbeknownst to her, the daughter had already reserved the church and ask her grandfather to marry her in a Saturday evening wedding. Hannah had exactly one day to put together an open church wedding. Being a small town and everyone knowing everyone; the church was full and the wedding ended up being beautiful. Hannah was able to persuade a friend of hers who had a photo service to come as a quest and to take the professional pictures. He did not do that sort of thing anymore. He hired that done. But after much begging, Hannah had him at the wedding and on time. She knew that she would have to go with artificial flowers at this late date, so she and her eleven year old niece ran to town and shopped as fast as they could.

Hannah started with the arrangements while her pretty little niece, who was also to be the flower girl, helped her curl the ribbons and worked as her third hand. Her daughter's friends had been in so many of each other's weddings and so many proms to where they had beautiful dresses to wear. Hannah's niece and nephew were owners of some very nice clothing that had been worn on Easter or some other special occasions. The flowers were beautiful, the wedding was grand and everything went on as if it had taken months to prepare. Hannah had even decorated the church. She had placed a white rolled paper down the center floor and placed large, pretty ribbons upon the seats. Candelabra's had been rented and candles were lit everywhere. Two large flower arrangements upon the altar were only one sided, but Hannah was sure no one would notice that except her father.

The bride wore a beautiful white wedding gown that she had purchased for this very special day. Her grandfather was marrying her and as luck would have it, or maybe the daughter had planned it that way, Hannah's son had gone to Columbus, Ohio that very weekend for an alumni banquet. Her daughter had called the son and asked him to please go find their father. She wished him to walk her down the aisle.

Ambros arrived in a cashmere suit and all went well and wonderful. After the wedding the father took everyone out to eat. The only catch was that a pianist was not available. Hannah had to do these honors herself. Earlier Ambros had asked her if she wished to have a drink. While she was married to him she had screwdrivers on occasion. He had remembered this. Being a bar owner and knowing his ex-father-in-law would never have any alcoholic beverages to celebrate the wedding, Ambros had come well stocked for the after, after party of his daughter's wedding. He too had to plan in just a few hours. When Hannah missed a note on the piano while Ambros and their daughter were walking down the aisle, both chuckled. Lord, it had been twenty years since Hannah had touched a piano. Even though Hannah had refused Ambros's offer of a drink earlier, he still ribbed her when she sat down beside of him. He said,

"You should have had that orange juice!"
Both laughed when they, the parents, complained about such short notice of the wedding! They were told of how nice it was of their daughter to relieve them of so much stress while planning a wedding for a long period of time. This way, it was quick. This way no one got stressed out for more than a day.

Now, Samuel was doing Hannah the very same way. By now two of their children were married. Just a few weeks before this date, Hannah and Samuel were arguing about something when all of the children walked in for a visit. The daughter and her husband had been four wheeling in a dried up lake and were solid mud just a while before. Their expensive leather boots and the daughter's cashmere sweater were caked with mud. Samuel had hosed them down before allowing them to come into the house. As the two sons, one wife, daughter and her husband took seats, they were listening to this silly argument. The daughter said,

"I do wish you two would grow up before we do completely! Wouldn't that be nice?"
She said this as she looked at the young men. They all laughed. Maybe Samuel had taken heed of this advice and decided to marry her.

Regardless, and for what quick reason, Samuel and Hannah were married at 2:12pm on July the twelfth. No honeymoon, no nothing; just home again and then off to work the very next day. Nothing was said to anyone. Not even the kids. But, neither could have been happier. They were about to explode with happiness. It was a long time coming. It had been close to twenty years. Many mistakes and much unhappiness had come along through these years, but as of this date Hannah could now hold her head up high and say she was finally Mrs. Wright.

Chapter 19

On the very Christmas after Samuel and Hannah had gotten back together, Papa died. Samuel's father had a stroke on that Christmas morning and was dead within a couple of days. The family had taken turns staying with the sick man in the hospital the few days he was alive. On the night he died, it was Hannah's turn to stay. She was pulling out a chest type bed for herself to lie upon when the man went into convulsions. Hannah had never been with anyone when they died before and this was a horrible, stressful situation. This was a day before cell phones and it seemed like forever before Samuel and his mother arrived home only to be asked to return to the hospital.

The funeral was sad and very hard on everyone. Samuel would seem to be in deep thought much of the time. Sadness was showing upon his face. His mother did not know what to do with herself, except cry. Shortly thereafter, Samuel the same as forced his mother to stay with him. Right after the death of her husband she had a head on collision due to the fact that she would not stay with Samuel as he had requested. He and Hannah both worked in Atlanta and were not there during the day to monitor what she was doing. She claimed that she did not know how to use the showers. So, she was going home to take a bath each day. After this tragedy, Samuel decided his mother was not to drive at all and he insisted that she move in with him and Hannah permanently. Hannah had not realized the magnitude of Samuel's decision.

Mrs. Wright had become contrary in her older age. She had lost her oldest son in recent years to 'Agent Orange' caused from when he was in Viet Nam years and years ago. He never married because of his worry about his health. He had died at thirty-nine years of age. Then, Samuel's wife, her daughter-in-law, had the horrible auto accident at the age of thirty-nine as well. Now her husband! She did have reasons to be sideways with the world. Now Samuel had taken away her freedom and placed her in his home with his new bride. She seemed to not have much use for Hannah anymore. This was strange to the young woman since once upon a time Samuel's mother had really cared for her. But now the tides were turning. She showed signs of not having much use for anyone who was not of her blood. Dealing with this old lady was the only problem Hannah felt she had with her wonderful marriage. She knew in her heart most of the problems had been brought on by the deep grief that this poor old woman had suffered. Hannah would and could deal with this because she loved her husband so very much.

December 24th, 1988 brought about a much appreciated gift. A beautiful little boy was born to Samuel's son and his wife. Samuel and Hannah were now grandparents for the very first time. A more handsome little man no one had ever seen. Then in little over a year on Feb 07, 1990, Hannah's daughter had a beautiful little girl. Oh, she was so extremely pretty. She had her mother and grandfather's powder blue eyes and adorned a little China Doll face. Samuel and Hannah could not be more proud. But just as Samuel had done his son over the years before; he was Hell bent on spoiling these youngsters. He bought the two anything and everything any child could ever want or need. The young parents tried to slow the shower of gifts, but appreciated them just the same.

These children were left with Samuel and Hannah often while the parents worked or played. These grandparents would have it no other way. They would demand time with their grandchildren and get in discussion fights with their children when they wished to take the grandchildren home. The proud grandparents enjoyed every minute of this time together.

Samuel had recently been offered a position in Panama City, Florida. He, along with six other engineers was going to be given the task of designing robots for the auto industry. Samuel loved this idea. He loved no other place like he loved Florida. He had often said he would love to spend the rest of his days counting each and every sand pebble upon the beach of Panama City, Florida. Hannah was devastated. She loved her job. She loved being close to her children and the grandchildren. She was going to have none of this. She was mad at Samuel for even thinking of such a thing. They lived in a beautiful home. They had everything they needed and life was wonderful. Samuel had given two of his four acres to his son who now had built a log cabin facing the other road behind them. The closeness of this family and the city of Atlanta where the other two children resided was perfect for Hannah. She would never want to move.

Regardless, by the beginning of that summer Samuel had accepted the position and was on his way to Florida. Hannah stubbornly stayed in Georgia as long as she could. One thing was that she had signed a contract with her company that she would give a month's notice should she ever leave. This gave her the much needed excuse to hold back her move. Her boss obviously noticed she had no desire to go anywhere and he strung out her notice until it was the end of September. Samuel and his mother had moved into a rented a home during July and he had started his new position. Even with all of the love, marriage problems were lurking. Weekend visits almost always ended in some sort of a disagreement. Hannah almost refused to move.

Hannah had no desire to leave her grandchildren and children. They were too special and dear to her. The little ones were too little and too much a piece of her heart. None the less, she had to move to Florida or get a divorce. She had to make the move just as the biggest part of her life was feeling pulled between those she loved so much. She was Samuel's wife and she loved him. She had to go! But on the other hand she loved her job, her kids, her grandkids and her world. She loved her life just as it was. She also knew she could not live without Samuel, so after much reluctance and dragging her feet, Hannah moved to Florida.

At first, the couple and the mother lived in a nice rented house upon the beach of Panama City. There was a large deck overlooking the ocean. Hannah would run up and down the beach for exercise each morning after her husband left for work at an early hour. She knew she would need to find work soon, but as of right now she was truly enjoying the vacation like atmosphere. Her only problem seemed to be the missing of her family.

After living in Florida for a few months Hannah started her own wholesale business at the request of Samuel. She was now to be self-employed and she thought she may like that. This freed her up to travel with Samuel and kept her free to travel to visit her children. Travel, they did constantly. Samuel would often go somewhere on a plane twice a week. Hannah enjoyed the trips on which she could tag along.

Within six months of renting, Hannah and Samuel decided renting was not what they wanted. They purchased the most beautiful of homes upon the bay. Their home was in the old city and faced the bay. On a good day, one could see the famed Shell Island off in the distance. The home was over six thousand square feet and had everything anyone could ever dream of having in a home. There was a sauna, a large deep Jacuzzi tub, a steam shower, five bedrooms, five baths, a sunken living room, a large den, a dining room and many large sun rooms that reflected the ocean water all through the house. The yard was manicured beautifully to where it looked like it had just been moved off of a magazine cover. A beautiful ocean drive ran in front of the house at the bottom of the pretty brick steps.

The next door neighbor was a widowed bank president's wife whom set off her alarm system on a regular basis. There was a circle alley type road running behind the house and Samuel and Hannah's yard had brick walls of about three-feet tall that sheltered there picnic play area. Hannah would get the biggest charge out of her grown son when he would say,

"Here comes Driving Miss Daisy! Mother you are about to lose more bricks."
This had become a large joke because the neighbor lady was very elderly. She had a butler/chauffeur who was just as elderly as she. She also owned a black Rolls Royce that she would be seated in the back seat as the couple would try to turn the circle around the Wright's backyard. This was so much fun to watch to where the family would never complain about a couple of the loose bricks falling. Someone would politely go out to the back of the yard, pick up the bricks and place them back into place. Samuel said he did not wish to cause damage to that beautiful old car so he refused to have the bricks placed back in place permanently.

The family settled in nicely. Hannah had to admit this was most surely her dream home. She did love her house. It was very comfortable from every stand point. Her mother-in-law seemed to be very happy as well. Being unhealthy and using a walker, it was wonderful that she could walk the long six-thousand foot, one floor home. This gave her the exercise she much needed without the need of going outside in the heat of the Florida sun. She had a large bedroom and a private bath with a dressing room in between that became her own private suite. All seemed to be well with this family. Samuel traveled so very much to where he received many travel miles; thus giving the children opportunities to come and visit often. Hannah's daughter had since gotten a divorce and had moved to Ohio to be with her friends and her grandparents. Hannah was always so thrilled when her daughter and granddaughter came to visit.

On one of these visits bad news came their way. Hannah's son and daughter were both at her house when a call came from Hannah's sister bearing bad news. The voice came softly over the phone,

"Something terrible has happened Hannah! It is all over the news! *Ambros has just been killed!*"

It was now late and everyone was in bed. Hannah did not know how to respond. She talked with her sister longer and got all of the details. Someone had robbed Ambros's club, at which time they set fire to the building, obviously to hide their crime. Since the death of his wife, Ambros had lived upstairs in one of his apartments. Two other gentleman rented apartments there as well. One man had escaped, but Ambros and another man were trapped and killed. Hannah was shocked and devastated! She took this so badly to where she wondered if Samuel would question her sorrow in the wrong way. Why was she taking this so badly? She honestly believed that she had no feelings for this man. All she knew was that Ambros had broken her heart so very badly years ago. Then she remembered what that wise old lady had told her when she had said,

"You do not stop loving someone. You only start loving someone new!"

Hannah realized this night that a big part of her heart would always mourn the death of Ambros. Now she must straighten herself up enough to go and tell her children!

Hannah talked some with Samuel. He stated of how that would have been such a horrible way to die while bringing up the fact that there would surely be no way of getting out of something like that with all of the alcohol stored within that large building. She had not thought of that and she was not going to relay that bit of information to her children.

Hannah slowly put on a robe and started down the long hallway to her children's rooms. The shocked look upon their faces broke Hannah's heart. Although these children had grown up most of their years without their father, they would never have a chance to know him now. All of their hurt and all of their resentments from the past could never be washed away now.

Hannah's daughter started to tell of how just yesterday, she was going to take her baby to see her father. She had arrived in Columbus, Ohio that very day and thoughts crossed her mind of changing her flight and going to see her father. He had never seen his granddaughter. Hannah's heart sunk. Had her daughter done this very thing, Hannah knew her father would have talked her into leaving the next day and she and the baby would have been in that horrible fire this night. Hannah thanked the good Lord above for protecting her daughter and her granddaughter, while knowing had her daughter not been traveling on Samuel's frequent flyer miles she would have definitely changed that flight. Thankfully Hannah's children had dodged this tragedy.

Time passed and Ambros's death was still under investigation. Hannah wondered if the crime would ever be solved. Life went on for the others. If anything good could have come out of Ambros's death, it was the fact that his children came together. Although they had all known each other in the early days of Ambros and Hannah's marriage, most could not remember. They finally

234

met each other and found that they cared very much. Seeing all of the children grown up, Hannah once more realized the extreme reach of Ambros's good looks. He had the most beautiful children. Every one of them was so very pretty. Many had Ambros's beautiful mesmerizing eyes. Many had his unforgettable hair.

Life got back to pretty much normal and everyone seemed to be fairly happy with their lives. Hannah was now aware that there probably is no world, like she used to think there was, called normal. Later that same year more tragedy struck the Wright family. Living on the waters as Samuel and Hannah did, brought much vacationing from the extended family members of both sides. Hannah was blessed with her children and nephews coming to visit often. The very year before the entire family had gone to Shell Island on a boat with a fellow employee of Samuel's. This was such a wonderful day. Hannah knew her children swam very well and she had not worried about her tall handsome son sitting upon the rails of the boat as it raced across the waters that day.

The following year Hannah felt so blessed that this time her son and daughter were not visiting on Memorial Day weekend. Both children had made other plans. Samuel's son and his family were visiting. Samuel and Hannah had accomplished something many families cannot accomplish. Possibly this was because the other mother/grandmother had passed on. Then the other father/grandfather, who had never been a very big part of Hannah's children's lives, was now also gone. Samuel and Hannah had developed a solid wonderful family. Their children were theirs. Their grandchildren were only *THEIRS!* They belonged to no one else. They felt that they were just strictly theirs the same as if Samuel and Hannah had been married to each other forever. Oh Hannah did not want to take the place of Anna. She knew she never could. Anna had always been there and was a good mother to her son, but Samuel and Hannah had been in their children's lives since they were small. When it came to the grandchildren, they would never know any grandparents but Samuel and Hannah. The couple was very happy. They showered their love upon these beautiful children.

Memorial Day weekend had promised to be a Heavenly day for this family. They had purchased a nice boat for the day of fun. The boat they had purchased was used, but it looked like it was in an excellent condition. It had been stored in dry dock and only had the problem of a destroyed motor. Samuel had taken the boat to a reputational boat repair shop. Here he purchased a new motor and paid over two thousand dollars to get the boat in tip top shape for its maiden voyage. The family was going to go to Shell Island for the full day. They packed a picnic lunch and took plenty of drinks. The grandson was but two years old and Hannah had gotten him a sand bucket with shovels and rakes to make his day a fun one.

Originally, Samuel's eighty-four year old mother, who was not feeling well this day, had no intentions of going along on this outing. The only people who were going were Samuel, Hannah, the married son, his wife and their son. The daughter-in-law was six months pregnant. At the last minute Mamma decided she wanted to go too. Her daughter-in-law and granddaughter-in-law stood in the window as they watched her being helped into the car. They both realized this would slow their day on any long walks or such things they may wish to do. So they seemed to be a little disappointed that the elderly woman wished to come along.

The boat had been cleaned and readied the night before. On this morning all that needed done was the loading of the food. Hannah had covered a large couch cushion to go over the large storage box on the back of the boat. Samuel had waxed and cleaned the boat. Everything looked great.

As the family backed the boat into the water, everyone was with large smiles upon their faces. Stepping down off the dock into the boat was a little more nerve racking to Hannah because she really did have a deadly fear of water. She could not swim. The good swimmers and the strong did not put on their life jackets immediately. Hannah, the elderly lady and the grandson were the only people to have on life jackets upon their departure out into the ocean waters.

Being somewhat new to this adventure, no one had checked the weather reports. Samuel suggested that they should have checked, because he felt the waves were exceptionally high this day. That passing thought was relieved when they could see boats all about them. This was a holiday weekend and much fun was to be had by all.

As the boat flew over the waters it was quite choppy. They seemed to be in a path that all of the boats were using to get to the island. After awhile the island was in site. Samuel noticed there was a large shrimp boat in the path he wished to take. He realized they would have large nets all around them. Therefore, he took a very broad path out away from the shrimp boat. Hannah looked back at the happy family and she saw a large smile plastered over her eight-four year old mother-in-law's face. She was being splashed with water, but everyone could tell that she was loving it.

Suddenly the son started screaming at his dad. He screamed,

"There's water coming into the boat!"
Samuel and Hannah looked around to see the back of the boat was full of water and filling fast. They were sinking. Samuel had long enough to get off a flare. The boat swayed left and then it swayed right and it was over. All Hannah could see was the top sided boat and the light of the sun coming through the water. She had been thrown deep into the ocean. As her life jacket brought her body up to the top of the water, she knew they were in terrible trouble. She tried laying on her back as she had been told to do, but the waves were slapping her so hard in the face to where she turned over again to look for her family.

The boat was still partially afloat and you could still see the pointed part of the nose. The son, with all of his young strength and muscles had somehow put on his life jacket at this time. Like Hannah, he could not swim either. Somehow the young man had locked his feet into the back of that boat and rolled with it until it brought him back up. This left him standing over the upside down boat.

The expecting mother had grabbed her son and swam away from the danger with him. Realizing she did not have on a life jacket she swam back to her now apparently safe looking husband and handed him their son. She then grabbed the cushion that Hannah had created and held herself above water until it became soggy and sank. At one point she said she would swim to the shrimp boat for help. She actually tried to swim a ways, only to realize that the shrimp boat was much further away than it looked from their view.

Samuel was busy working very hard while holding onto the front of the boat. He kept diving under the water. Hannah was too far away by now to understand what he was doing. She kept screaming at him to please put on a life jacket. She knew he may not have a clue where one may be at this point. All of their food and belongings were floating all over the wreck scene by now. It seems the current had moved Hannah and her daughter-in-law far from the boat. After the pillow had sunk, the daughter-in-law swam to a gas can. She held onto it to stay afloat.

Hannah was finally able to dog paddle herself closer to the boat. She knew now why Samuel was working so furriest the whole time. Oh dear God, she could see her mother-in-law just below the water. Was her life jacket not working? She was face down about two feet under water. Samuel looked like he may drown any minute, but he would not stop diving to help his mother. He kept diving under the water and pulled and tugged on something that was holding his mother down. After what seemed to be forever Hannah knew in her heart that the woman was dead. She screamed and begged Samuel to stop. She told him she was sorry but he had to realize for his own safety that his mother was dead. Samuel acted as though he did not hear one word she was saying. So, white faced and breathless as he was, he went under the water again and again.

Suddenly there was a rope floating out from the boat. Hannah grabbed it so she could stay close by. Samuel was screaming for everyone to try to stay close to the boat so if someone came to rescue them it would be easier to find them all. The waves were just too strong and too large. Hannah could not hold onto that rope for very long. Suddenly she was drifting away from the boat again. Thankfully she was close to her daughter-in-law once more. She was now believing no one was ever going to come to help. There were no boats that could be seen upon these waters. Finally the family also realized that the crew of the shrimp boat was most surely asleep, because they would have been fishing all night. Besides, they were more than likely too far away to see the family in their distress. They started to believe and to know that they were all going to die out in the ocean this day. Hannah knew she must be strong.

Hannah heard her daughter-in-law crying. Sometimes it was more of a whimper. She fought the waves to get close enough to hear her. She begged her daughter-in-law to hang on just a little longer. The beautiful young lady cried and said the gasoline was burning her arms and she did not think she could hold on much longer. She said,

"I'm not going to make it! I just can't hold on any longer!"

Hannah realized that she had somehow lost most of her fear by now and she became so worried about her loved ones. She wanted everyone to be safe. She started begging her precious daughter-in-law to please hold on. She said,

"You've got to hang on baby, you know you do. Hang on for your beautiful family and that precious little life inside of you. You have got to hang on. Talk to me! Talk to me honey! Come closer if you can and please hang on and talk to me!"

Hannah could barely see the boat by now. She could see that it was sinking ever more. The son was now up past his waist in water. He was holding the beautiful little grandson high above him upon his shoulders to keep him from the nasty tasting water. Dear God, thought Hannah! She had seen this before. Hannah had a touch, as does everyone, of ESP. She would rarely have a dream that she somehow knew was not really a dream, but instead a picture of something to come. There was never anyway she could quite understand these dreams and they did not do her any good to have them. She could not stop a tragedy. But she sometimes felt that she could see a little into the future by having these crazy dreams.

Years ago when the young man standing so strongly upon the back of that boat this day was about nine years of age, Hannah had a dream about him and his father. She had always had a fear while driving home late at night along the Ohio River. She would often leave Georgia after a Friday night work week and head to Ohio. By the time she got onto the tiny state route of about sixty miles that she had to travel along the river she would be so tired and sleepy to where it would make her very nervous to drive. She hated the places where there were no guard rails. So, she had always contributed this one dream to those fears.

Samuel's father owned a two toned pick-up truck at that time. It was dark beige and white. Samuel would often borrow this truck and he, his ex-wife and his son would ride around in it. In Hannah's dream she had dreamed that Samuel had ran this truck off of the road and into the Ohio River. She panicked as she saw Samuel holding onto a tree while holding his son high in the air above his shoulders. She remembered screaming,

"Where's Anna!"

Of course after Anna was killed in a car accident, Hannah believed this may have been a warning of that accident to come. She believed this dream was trying to tell her that there would be no Anna in the future.

This day, Hannah saw the truth. As the young man stood there holding his son high to the sky, Hannah realized this was the scene she had seen so many years ago, but it was the son and the grandson, not Samuel and his son.

Hannah looked back to see her husband laying his head and shoulders upon the tip of that sinking boat. He was holding his mother with one hand. He was exhausted and he looked pale as he wrapped his arms around what was left of the boat still above the water.

After much time, Hannah realized she was passing out. She had turned over on her back again because she knew that was what she was supposed to do. Fighting the flow of water coming into her mouth was not really working in whatever position she was in. The waves were too high and they were slapping her with great force. She would black out for a while and then snap back. She would tell herself that she had to stay alert.

After what seemed to be days, Hannah could hear a boat motor. Someone had come to their rescue. She was so far away from the accident by now to where she could not see over the waves to see who had come to their rescue. She heard a man scream,

"Does anyone know CPR?"

This told Hannah that they had gotten her mother-in-law on board. Then she heard the son and grandson speak as they were helped onto the boat. She was so thankful to hear the half crying, half talking voice of her very special daughter-in-law. Hannah loved this child so much. She had become the very same as any daughter and she knew she could not love her more had she given birth to this young lady. Then she heard her husband as he climbed aboard this boat. A wave of complete relief swept over Hannah. She knew that she had floated so far away from the rest of her family to where they may not be able to see her. The waves were causing her to come in and out of consciences. Once again she passed out. When she came awake again, she could hear the faint sound of the boat leaving in the distance. She listened until she could hear it no more.

Hannah was so pleased that her family was all safe. She felt a wave of relief cover over her. That seemed to be her blessing. She was okay with the fact that she was likely to be no more. Being a minister's daughter, she was shocked that she had not prayed. She did not pray like one would think she would have. Instead she was feeling blessed that her family was on that boat and away from danger. A feeling of tranquility flooded over her. However, someone up there was looking out for her, because after passing out and coming back around, she could hear her husband's voice coming from afar. He was giving the people on the boat complete *HELL*!

Hannah realized now that the rescue boat was a private boat. It was not the coast guards. She could hear what sounded as though there were two couples upon this boat. One of the wives or a girlfriend was screaming from fear. She was fighting her loved one about trying the rescue. She was screaming,

"You have to let her go! You will drown yourself! We will sink our boat!"
Hannah could hear the seer panic in this woman's voice. She heard her say,

"You've saved most of them! You've done all you can do and you are still alive! I'm Sorry! I am so very sorry, but you have to give it up. You just have to let her go!"
Then in a calmer but still loud voice Hannah heard the lady say,

"We can go back to the shore and tell the coast guards. They will come and hunt for her!"
It was as if neither Samuel nor this lady heard each other over their own voices because Hannah could hear Samuel screaming. He was screaming,

"I see her! I see her! Get closer! Get Closer!"
Hannah could now see and hear the boat fairly close by. She tried to scream, but she had no voice. She could not get a word out of her mouth. Samuel realized the waves were too strong and that Hannah had floated out into the strong channel which carried all of the bay water out into the deepest parts of the sea. He knew the owner of the boat was afraid to try this dangerous route with their small boat to rescue his wife. He also believed if he let these people leave he would never see his loving wife again. She was his whole world and he was not ready to lose her. He

could not let that happen. He could not let it be. He cussed, he begged, he offered every cent of money he had or ever would have if these people would only attempt to save his wife.

All of a sudden, Hannah heard complete panic and screams! She heard someone scream,

"Oh My God! Stop him! Somebody Stop Him! He is going to jump!"
Hannah watched as her wonderful husband jumped from the back of that boat into the sea. She realized that he still did not have a life jacket upon his body. She watched in panic as he swam as fast and as hard as he could towards her lifeless body. Judgment of distances upon the high seas can be very confusing. Samuel had misjudged the distance to his wife. More possible was the fact that he was blinded by determination.

Samuel using all of the strength that he could muster was able to get about half way out to Hannah. This alone was a miracle while he swam through the eight to ten feet high waves. Hannah could feel the complete love and devotion that her husband had for her. She knew he would gladly give up his life to save hers. She did not want him to do that. She wanted him to live. She tried to scream,

"Go Back Darling! I'm Alright! Oh God, please go back!"
She could not even hear her own voice. She was now very scared. She was now scared for the both of them.

Samuel finally realized that he was not going to be able to reach his beloved wife. Hannah had never heard that tone of hopelessness in her husband's voice before as she heard him scream,

"I can't make it baby! I just can't make it! I love you Darling!"

Hannah could hear the pain and despair in this wonderful man's voice. Hannah hurt. She hurt for herself and for her husband as she watched Samuel swim back, whipped and beaten while using all of his strength just to get back to that waiting boat. She finally heard someone say,

"Thank God! You should have never tried that. We could have lost you too!"

Then she heard the boat take off in the opposite direction. She now knew that she was going to die. People who have never experienced this near death experience could not know the feeling that came over her. She accepted her fate and she even felt calm.

Hannah passed out once more only to be awakened by the sound of a boat. This time it was within feet of her. A large man adoring a life jacket was in the water now. He was coming towards her. She felt his arm wrap around hers and felt herself being dragged through the waves. She was weak, so very weak by now, but when the man asked her to please get a hold of the ladder to pull her body up; she was able to grip her hands around the rails. Strange, after all that she had been through this day, now she panicked. By now she was kicking and pushing her rescuer under the water by putting her feet upon his shoulders and fighting to get into the boat. The screaming woman was losing it. She was screaming with great panic for the fear of losing her loved one.

Finally, they both were on board. The other gentleman loosened his grip that he had upon Samuel. He was a larger man and he had wrapped his arms around Samuel who was completely exhausted at this point. He held the weakened Samuel tightly until his wife was on the boat.

Hannah looked down to see her mother-in-law laying on the floor of the boat. She realized that she was dead. She looked into the faces of her loved ones and saw complete sorrow and pain. They seated her upon a bench beside of her daughter-in-law. Due to the entire trauma, Hannah began to vomit. No one seemed to care or to move. It was as if everyone was stiff and robot like on this long ride back to the shores.

Suddenly Hannah looked around to see boats everywhere. Now there were boats on each side of their rescuers. They were in front and behind them. The boats were that of the coast guard. They were covered with red flashing lights and sirens were blasting as they escorted the boat carrying this tragedy stricken family to safety. Someone on the boat said that the coast guards had seen the flares but could not find the boat because Samuel had taken a different route out close to the channel. Lucky for this family the other boat had done the very same thing because of the shrimp boat. They then had seen the loaves of bread, picnic baskets and debris floating across the waters. Little did they know that they would become someone's heroes this day?

As the boat pulled up to a large covered dock Hannah could see ambulances, TV units, reporters and cameras everywhere. A large crowd of people was being asked to please step back by the Panama City Police Department. When the Wright family left for a wonderfully planned holiday pleasure trip, little did they know that they would become front page news on this day!

Samuel refused to go to the hospital with the others. Following his lead, the son refused to get into an ambulance as well. Samuel stood stubbornly by while the County Coroner pronounced his mother dead. Samuel, as any son would do, did not want to believe what he was hearing. So he argued with the kind old gentleman and ignored the urging to please go to the hospital with the others to have his health checked.

As the ambulance rushed through the city, Hannah finally thanked God for saving the ones He had saved this day. She also said a silent 'Thank You' for the fact that the other children were not on board. She was so very thankful that her son, daughter, nephews and granddaughter were unable to come to visit this weekend. She sat on an arm of a chair while she rubbed the hands of her expecting daughter-in-law. What could this do to her and the baby?

Upon arrival at the hospital the daughter-in-law was rushed right in upon the cot the workers had placed her upon during their arrival at the docks. Hannah did not want to leave her and her grandson, but the doctors insisted that they check her out as well. She was feeling fine now. She was so worried about the others. When all was said and done Samuel and the son arrived at the hospital to collect their loved ones. The doctors decided to keep the daughter-in-law and the two year old overnight for observation. They stated that both had much water on their lungs.

Hannah stubbornly let them x-ray her lungs, but would not stay for the results. She did not want Samuel to be alone. She melted into his arms in the hallway of the hospital and walked hand in hand out the door and straight home.

Upon their arrival home, officers were there to take statements. Samuel had called his sisters and other family members to tell them of his mother's death. For a woman who had stayed so calm during the disaster, Hannah could not stop crying now. So Samuel had put her to work to occupy her mind. He asked her to call all of the credit card companies and tell them that their cards had been lost at sea. If she had been of a rational mind she would have known he could not be worried about the credit cards at this minute. No one was going to steal them from the bottom of the ocean. While she was operating the phone, a call came in. It was the hospital asking her to please come back to the hospital. She asked why and pretty much refused to leave her husband at this time. The lady on the other end of the line was getting impatient with Hannah, so she said,

"You need to come in because you could die! Your x-rays show you have very much water on your lungs!"
Hannah thought, well yes, I would have water on my lungs! Then she asked more questions. She was finally told that she could stay at home with her grieving husband on one condition. That was if she would not lay down at all. She was not to sit more than a few seconds and she needed to walk. She was told if she went to sleep that she could still drown in her sleep. Hannah did not find this to be a problem because she knew she could not sleep this night. She was wound up tighter than a drum. All she *COULD* do was walk the floors.

While an officer was at the house, the report came in. Divers had been in the water and found that the entire back of the boat was missing. The large motor had torn off the whole back of the boat. Unbeknownst to the repair shop, rotten boards had been above the boards where they had attached the motor to this fiberglass covered boat. The motor was bigger than the old one and the power pressure had been too much on rotten boards. The officers reported that the waves were, yes in fact, eight to ten feet high this day. Thus putting more stress upon the damaged boat. The coroner's office had also report to the officers that there were marks upon the mother's ankle that showed them that the rope meant to hold the boat secure on a dock had wrapped around the aged woman's ankle. This had held her just below the waters. Hannah shuttered when she realized that Samuel had, too late, been able to loosen that rope. She realized now that was the rope that she had most probably grabbed onto herself while trying to stay close to the boat.

Chapter 20

The family traveled home to Georgia for the funeral of Samuel's mother. The long trip back to Florida meant they would walk into a house that she loved so much, only to not find her there. The following days Samuel spent long hours in his mother's room. He claimed this was to look over her belongings, but Hannah could often see him sitting on the bed, while mourning. He was the baby son of his family and he was going to miss his mother very much.

The children had often joked about this large old house being haunted. One son had a friend that loved to come to Florida. He would sleep in his car because he was afraid of the large house. He claimed he got lost in it on one occasion. After purchase, Samuel and Hannah did find that the builders and previous owners had been dead for nine years. The house had sat empty for all of those years. When they moved in, there were still pictures of these people upon their walls. It could be spooky because of its size. Both the daughter and the daughter-in-law had joked about how they had seen an old woman walk into their bedrooms on occasion. Then in Samuel and Hannah's fifteen hundred square foot master bedroom suite there was one night Hannah felt someone had knocked her out of her bed. In each corner of this large room were planters deep into the floor filled with dirt. There were large greenhouse lamps upon poles to help with the growth of the large live plants. This night Hannah had fallen down into one of the planters, while hitting one of those lights. This left a horribly large black and blue mark upon her side. One other time Samuel woke up with large scratches all over his back. The couple joked about these things and let them pass. They said the kids were nuts for thinking of such things and always remembered how much they loved their beautiful home.

Now Hannah was starting to rethink the after death experiences. For about a month after the passing of her mother-in-law, she would be shocked at the yellow haze that seemed to linger in her mother-in-law's bedroom. True, the walls were of a golden wood that glowed with the sunlight coming through the large windows, but this looked mostly like a yellow fog. Then one day after Hannah had completely redecorated her mother-in-law's room, it just went away.

Samuel and Hannah were deeply saddened by the loss of Samuel's mother. But shortly thereafter they were blessed by the birth of still another beautiful granddaughter who would never know how close she came to being lost in the ocean waters. During those times Hannah was always getting a phone call that she had lost still another wonderful aunt or uncle of her family. She attended the funerals that she could and grieved in silence for those she couldn't. Hannah's parents came to visit. Then Hannah and Samuel went to her parent's fiftieth wedding anniversary celebration in Ohio. Shortly thereafter Hannah's son married. The beautiful wedding reminded one of a 'Gone With the Wind' type wedding ceremony. The wedding was held in Georgia where the entire family attended.

Samuel and Hannah traveled. Lord, did they travel! They went to England; they went to Bermuda, Los Vegas, San Diego and anywhere else they wished to go. They had been to every state in the United States at least once. They loved and lived the life that so many people could only dream of. This couple was so much in love and so very, very happy with their self-made life.

After several years Samuel's job was complete in Florida. Knowing there would be no other positions of this magnitude in the area, the decision was made to sell their home and return to Georgia. Their home in Georgia had long since been rented. They were not going to move their renters out of their home at this time. Hannah had loved this home, but she also knew it was built for Anna. This had always been Anna's home. By now Samuel had inherited many old homes from his family in the town of his ancestors. The decision was made to take the smallest home and make an office out of it for Hannah's wholesale business and her new accounting firm. They would then fix up the old homes that had not been lived in since the deaths of Samuel's grandparents and his great-grandparents. Some would be rented. One very Victorian home would be renovated for Samuel and Hannah's usage. They went about purchasing claw foot antique tubs, stained glass windows, antique wood, and door knobs. In the meantime the couple could stay on a futon in the office in front of the gas fireplace or stay in their Winnebago.

Although their home in Georgia was beautiful and the one in Florida was gorgeous, this couple was so much in love to where they would have been perfectly happy living in a tent. As usual Samuel was very employable. He had a position with an engineering firm in Atlanta even before the move. Hannah boosted her business and started even more. She started a newspaper, of sorts, to advertise her wholesale business and accounting firm only to cause the joking, advertising paper to grow faster than the accounting firm. Before she knew it, she was printing a paper called 'Hanging Around' for five different small cities. Life could not have been better for this loving couple.

In 1996, Hannah got a call she never wanted to receive. In February of that year her father was hospitalized for still another heart attack. By May he was dead. Late in the night her beloved daughter had called her from the hospital. On the first call she had said,

"Mother, they have brought Grandpa into the hospital."
Then she hesitated and said,
"It is bad mother! It is really bad!"
Hannah could hear someone talking to her daughter and her mother. Then the phone went dead as her daughter's voice just trailed away. She had dropped the receiver! Hannah called franticly to the hospital of her home town. She knew this number by heart. Finally she was directed by someone she knew had to be a family friend, but she did not know who sent her to the family room where her mother answered. She said immediately,
"He's gone! Honey, he's gone!
Hannah's heart broke. She ran to tell her loving husband, who hurriedly helped her get her clothes together. He begged her to let him take her to the airport. He said that he would go to work the next day and tell them he would be out of town. He said he would come to Ohio as soon as he could. Hannah only knew, in her current frame of mind, that going to the airport meant heading south to

Atlanta and she wanted to go north. What she thought she could do for her father at this point was beyond understanding. So, at about 3:00am in the morning, Hannah took off for Ohio in her Corvette.

While making this trip, Hannah remembered often that the road seemed to not be there. She knew that when she went through some of the mountains of Kentucky an officer had been in the left lane when she passed him as if he was standing still. The inside light was on in the officer's car and she remembers him looking over at her very strangely. Stranger still, he did not follow her. She wondered if he was able to channel in on her many cell phone calls to her loved ones. Having no idea how fast she had driven, on the way home from the funeral Samuel ask a question. The son and his family had traveled along with Samuel to the funeral and were now driving their other vehicle home. Samuel and Hannah were all alone when Samuel asked,

"How fast will this Corvette run Hannah?"
She answered by saying,

"How should I know?"
He said,

"You do know because you left home at three in the morning and you called me as you were crossing the Chesapeake, Ohio Bridge at eight o'clock in the morning."
Hannah panicked. How could she have driven that fast? Samuel told her not to worry now, but he worried himself and wondered why he had allowed her to do such a thing in her state of mind.

The whole family was saddened by this great loss. Hannah's daddy was a bigger than life person. He had been a much loved minster and a businessman. He was a pillar of his community and a dear loving individual. No one worried about where this man had gone. If there was in fact a God, He had welcomed this beautiful man into his open arms to keep him forever. A more perfect man no one had ever known.

Life went on for Samuel and Hannah. Within days after Hannah's father's death, another beautiful granddaughter was born. This time the beautiful baby was born to Hannah's son and her daughter-in-law. Hannah and Samuel were so very blessed. Considering death being a part of living, this couple coped and went on with their lives. As a whole they were very happy people who traveled around the world and traveled often to see their grandchildren and loved ones.

The next couple of years passed by quickly! By now the grown children were getting older and acquiring very good positions of their own. They were highly professional with good educations now and they were coming into their own. The parents could not be more proud of them. In 1998, the oldest grandchildren were already in school. All were doing well. The oldest granddaughter had never missed a day of school and each year she would receive a trophy stating that fact. Hannah's daughter held a very high position in her city and was to go to Alabama for a seminar during the first week of October. Hannah saw an opportunity to see her daughter and her granddaughter. The granddaughter did not want to miss any school, therefore she wanted to stay with her great-grandmother and ride to work with her mother's cousin who lived next door. The cousin would then be able to deliver the child to school in that same town.

Hannah will never know why she was so adamant about this visit. She begged and she begged for her daughter to please bring the granddaughter along. She told her daughter that she would go to the City of Birmingham with her and play with the granddaughter each day long. Finally after much pressure the daughter caved in by saying,

"Okay mother, you will have to talk her into it!"

Hannah talked to the youngster and saw that she was getting no where with her. So, she suddenly spoke up and said,

"I promise to buy you one-hundred dollars' worth of toys at Toys R Us. I will even buy you a trophy if you will come to see grandma. We will have so much fun. We can ride the trolley car and I will take you to the museum!"

This finally worked on the eight year old child and she agreed to come south with her mother.

The visit and the trip were wonderful. They stayed in the most wonderful hotel. Hannah had one scare while they were there that she could not understand. She left the room to go down many floors to get a snack one evening, only to find her door of the elevator opening to a concrete wall. Then the night before they left Alabama she had a horrible dream. Once again this did not feel so much like a dream. Hannah was in a rail car sitting high up in some sort of a cage. She had on a heavy coat and she felt trapped. The dream scared her and she awakened fast.

The next day the family was to return home. The plan was for the daughter to deliver her mother home and stay all night. She then would get up early the next morning and head back to Ohio. Once the family arrived at Hannah's and Samuel's home, Hannah and her granddaughter sat down at her desk beside of her computer. The little girl wanted to play a game that her grandmother had purchased her. They began playing scrabble. Hannah told the little girl that she did not want to play anymore after a while, because they kept coming up with words like, "dead, dying or death'! Hannah laughingly told her granddaughter that this was morbid and she wished to stop playing. It was time to put the little girl to bed anyway and the daughter and Samuel were having a very good visit with each other in front of the fireplace.

The little girl ran off to be with her mother and grandfather. Hannah realized she needed to check her computer for messages. It was set up to receive all phone messages as well as e-mails. Once she turned up her volume and started to listen to the messages she realized from the view that she had many messages from her mother. The first one she listened to was the last one her mother had recorded. Her mother had given up with the idea of not giving the shock statement that she had to give over the phone. She said,

"Annie was killed tonight!"

Instead of listening to any of the other messages, Hannah picked up the phone and called her mother immediately. Her mother was devastated. She said,

"Annie was killed in a car accident tonight!"

One realizes how the mind does not grasp things that it does not want to grasp. So, Hannah said,

"Is she going to be alright?"

With that her mother burst into tears. The reality was setting in. Hannah's daughter was close enough to have heard the conversation. Her eyes were getting large and a shocked look came upon her face. Hannah handed her daughter the phone while the grandmother told her the details about her cousin's wreck. Hannah's niece had been killed by hitting a semi gas tank truck this very evening.

The women hurriedly got out of their night clothes and packed to head in a rush to Ohio. Hannah's daughter and this young lady had been so very close. This was Hannah's baby brother's only daughter and she was only ten years older than Hannah's granddaughter. She had just graduated High School. She was in college and she was getting married. She had taken a job with Hannah's daughter for the summer. Hannah had just spoken with her a few hours ago while the family was still in Alabama. She was with child and extremely happy about that. Young people of this day did things differently than those of old. She and her fiancé were buying a home, finishing school and waiting until after the baby was born so that they could have a church wedding. This way Annie could wear that beautiful white wedding dress without the baby bump showing.

Just this afternoon while still in Birmingham, Hannah's daughter had stepped out of her car for one reason or another. She had left her cell phone in the car. It rang and Hannah answered. On the other end of the line were her daughter's boss and Annie. They were on a speaker phone and with Annie realizing she was speaking with her aunt; she hollered in and said,

"Are you going to buy me something?"

Hannah spoke up and said,

"From Alabama?"

She was meaning, in a joking way, that she would not want anything like Alabama sports items and so on. Annie had then said,

"I'm decorating my son's room in 'Winnie the Pooh'! Get me something like that!"

Hannah had agreed and told her only niece that she loved her. That was just a few hours ago and now she was gone. Now once again, Hannah and her daughter were making an all-night trip to Ohio.

When the family arrived the following morning, they found that the news stations were all carrying this tragedy news flash. The beautiful niece had been traveling home on a fairly untraveled highway that the family had used all of their lives to get to Gallipolis, Ohio. Her other grandparents lived in Bidwell, Ohio and Hannah's mother and brothers lived in Vinton, Ohio. This accident happened just above her maternal grandparent's home on Route 160, just above Porter, Ohio.

No one will ever know what caused this accident. There was not enough left to be investigated. The driver of the truck somehow got out, but he was traumatized so badly to where he would never be able to drive again. Annie had somehow crossed paths with this close to empty semi gas tanker truck. The driver was not able to stop and ran over her vehicle. Both vehicles exploded. Windows in cars behind and in front of them were blown out. Windows in homes were blown out. It took more than forty-five minutes before fire fighters could begin to put out the fires. A more tragic accident this county had never seen.

By the time Hannah and her daughter got to

Ohio, the TV was flashing the beautiful senior graduation picture of the darling girl. She was beautiful with long flowing blond hair. Then they were flashing a picture of the vehicle. The family should have never seen this picture because there was nothing left of this vehicle but the chassis.

Hannah's heart broke even more when she heard about how her brother and her sister-in-law had heard of the horrible accident. The community in which Hannah was born was a close family community. Everyone knew and loved each other. When Annie did not arrive at home on time, the parents became worried. Her father always kept a police scanner playing in his home. He always knew what was going on in his county. This evening he heard of a terrible accident upon the highway. Time passed and he started to feel this could be his daughter. It was either that, or the horrible accident was keeping her from getting around it to get home. He decided to go and investigate. Call it ESP or whatever one wants to call it. The closer he got to the accident, the more he began to believe it could be his daughter.

Knowing everyone in the county and being a member of the Dahl family. This Mr. Dahl was very well known in his community. Unlike his sisters he had never left home. He and his family were actually living in the old grandmother's family home. He had now purchased that old magical farm from his family. The closer he got to the accident, the more worried he became.

Arriving at the accident scene, he insisted on going closer. Knowing him as the officers and fire fighters did, they would have ordinarily let him get fairly close to any accident. Tonight an officer stopped him while calling his commander who was up front at the accident. He tried to be discrete and quiet, but Mr. Dahl could hear what was being said over the walkie-talkies. The young officer said,

"Mr. Dahl is here and he is insisting he wants to come through!"

There was a deep breath and a hesitation on the other end, when the commander said,

"Let him in, I don't think you could stop him anyway!"

Hannah's brother was of a very large muscled man. He stood six-foot-six and was made of solid rock. They were very correct! They could never have stopped this mountain of a man from coming through if he thought that could be his daughter.

"He told of how all of the firefighters, police officers and the highway patrolmen stepped aside while forming an aisle way for him to walk down. Each one of them took off their hats and bowed their heads. Many of these men were crying. Then at the very end of this long line, there stood the commander who had to face his friend. Mr. Dahl looked him straight in the eyes and said,

"Tell me that's not my baby!"

There was only silence from the commander. It was as if he could not speak! Mr. Dahl got louder and screamed,

*"**Please! Dear God! Tell me that is not my baby!**"*

He already knew the answer to that question. He dropped to his knees in front of all his neighbors and friends, put his head in his hands and nearly died himself.

The mother had just purchased a new truck. By now she was also getting that ESP feeling. She jumped into her truck and decided to go see about the accident that was about ten miles down the road. She had spoken to her parents. They told her that they had heard an explosion from their home several miles away, but had not gone to investigate. All they knew was that this was a most horrible accident.

Just as the mother was going through Vinton, she passed her son-in-law to be. They both backed up in the street to talk with each other. He told the mother he had taken another way home because of a horrible accident. The mother said,

"It may be Annie! She did not come home!"

He jumped into his mother-in-law's to be truck and they flew towards the scene of the accident. Traffic was backed up for miles. By now, the mother knew in her heart that this was her daughter. She took her new truck through ditches and shrubs while tearing it to pieces to get to the scene of the accident. These poor parents found their worst nightmare to be true. They had lost their only daughter this night. They had lost their beautiful baby girl and a grandson whom they had already named, bought sweet things for and were so very excited about his arrival. A worse pain, no one would ever know.

Hannah's husband and the rest of the family came from Georgia the next day. She had believed, as everyone else in this county had believed that her father's funeral was the largest ever held in their county. Annie's funeral was massive. Many reasons contributed to this. This beautiful daughter, granddaughter, cousin, fiancée and niece was a member of the Dahl family who were pioneers to this county. She had just graduated from a very large school where she had many, many friends. She had been a Volley Ball Champion, and had made such high grades to where she had been chosen to be a Junior Legislator for the State of Ohio. She had been attending college as well. Then she was working with all of the officials of Gallia County.

Hannah had thought while she and the family were walking out of that church, of how they could get that many people into the church. The parking lots were covered with what looked like thousands of people. Then it hit her, this was a closed casket funeral. The family had to leave first. That church and all of the rooms were still full. One thing about this family, when they had a loss, they could count on the crowds of people from all walks of life. This caring county showed up for Annie's funeral from the dirt farmer to the bank presidents. Even the county's biggest pride showed his respect and devotion to this sweet, sweet girl.

Now, this next generation of the Dahl family had received more grief and pain than it could endure. Years ago and in this very house, Mr. Dahl's grandmother had lost two of her children and her husband in less than two years. Those children had slept in his daughter's very bedroom. Those children who were his aunt and uncle had died at very young ages. This old house had seen this very same grief before.

For months this family grieved alone and together. Someone found that Hannah's brother had taken a gun with one bullet in it out to his barn every evening and clicked it at his head. When told this, Hannah remembered one night before the funeral of her and her sister finding him in the garden with a gun to his head screaming,

"God, if you are trying to get my attention, you are going about it in the wrong way!"
Now, with all of the pain each member of this family was feeling, they had the added worry that they may lose still another family member. This family fell apart. Each grieved by themselves most of the time. The fiancé and the mother seemed to be tight and they could comfort each other. The son had a girlfriend who was soon to be his wife so he went to her for comfort. The grieving grandmother, who lived next door, had her church. But nothing would ever be the same on that Dahl hill again.

Time passed, the brother married. He and his wife had a beautiful little boy. He was the family's salvation. Hannah could not help but see her baby brother, the little boy's grandpa, melt with the site of this child. The child was beautiful. He had that same pretty blonde curly hair that she remembered her baby brother having so many years ago. This little boy was smart as a tack and he is what saved his grandfather. He brought life back to that magical old farm and gave back the hearts to his loved ones. Many things stayed the same, like Annie's pretty little red car that she had not driven that day just sat in the same spot of the grass where she left it while it slowly rotted down. Her father could never bring himself to move it. Her bedroom was boarded up with everything she owned left just as she had left it on that day. But this little boy was sunshine and he brought much happiness into the Dahl world.

Hannah was having a blessing at this very same time. She had a beautiful little grandson born to her son just six months before the birth of her brother's new grandchild. The Dahl family was being blessed once more. Nineteen ninety-eight had about killed the whole family, but nineteen ninety-nine was bringing new life. The powers above had brought along two beautiful little baby boys for this family to love.

Chapter 21

Hannah's niece had been gone less than two months when she received a phone call telling her that her grandfather, The Reverend Herms had died. This saddened Hannah greatly just as it did the rest of the family but no one was able to grieve. The whole family was still rocketing with grief over their precious eighteen year old Annie. The grandpa had lived a very nice long life and he was dying at the age of ninety-four. Annie's parents could not even bring themselves to go to the front of the church where the family was expected to sit. The Great Grandmother Dahl could not even cry for the loss of her wonderful father that they were putting into the ground.

The elderly gentleman had been in a nursing home of late. He had times he could not remember anything, but on the day of his great granddaughter's funeral he seemed to be very alert! The Herms side of the family had returned to Marion, Ohio and had stopped to visit the aging man. Of course they were all dressed in suits and their finery. The flower shops of Gallia County had stated that they each had over thirty arrangements in their shops that the funeral director had ask them to just keep for the family so that they could collect the flowers or the cards. No one could handle more flowers. Therefore the decision was made to give the flowers to hospitals and nursing homes to beautify their surroundings. So the Herms family had brought along many flower arrangements for this nursing home to enjoy. They were not aware that the father would be so alert on this day. He looked at his family and said,

"I know something is terribly wrong in my family! I also know you think if you tell me it will kill me. So, I don't want to know!"
Within the following month, he was dead.

This time Hannah and her ten year old grandson drove the long distance to Ohio. She would not be staying long. Her business had suffered with all of these losses and the days she could not bring herself to go to work. There were days that all she could do was cry. Then Samuel felt he could not miss any more work asking off for still another funeral. He felt the company would start questioning the truth in his requests. This saddened him badly because he had come to love Hannah's grandfather over the years. Their personalities were very much alike and they loved and respected each other very much. Hannah and her grandson said their goodbyes at the church and were leaving to head back to Georgia. Just as Hannah started to step down into her Corvette she heard the undertaker say something to her. She looked back at the church to this also family friend. He repeated what he had said,

"Hannah, why don't you come up for a picnic or just a visit sometime? I am getting so sick of visiting with you like this!"

Hannah traveled back home to Georgia and tried the next day to reconnect with her daily routines. Then that night she sat abruptly up in her bed. She was having a dream! This was no ordinary dream! It was *SO VERY REAL*! The shocker was that she was still having this dream even after she was upright on the edge of the bed and while believing she was awake. She knew immediately this was not just a dream.

Suddenly, Hannah saw a large beautiful tree and a large pasture of green acreage behind it. A greener green she had never seen. She somehow knew that this tree was along the side of a river even though she did not see down into the river. Several people were what she liked to call moseying behind the person she knew to be her father. He was wearing a dark grey suit and he was way out in front while leading this pack of people to the river bank. Up the riverbank came her grandfather. He was wearing a black three piece suit. She watched him lean forward to climb the steep bank as the wind blew the tails of his coat on his brisk walk to see his much loved son-in-law. The Reverend James Dahl threw open his large arms and took his father-in-law into them as he said,

"Hello Dad, it sure is good to see you!" Smiles were large and you could feel the love. Then one by one each person of the crowd walked up to greet the Reverend Herms. There were many Hannah did not recognize, but she knew that she should know everyone in one large group who walked together to greet her grandpa. This group was all of the siblings of the Dahl family. She saw her Aunt Elizabeth, and then she saw her Aunt Mabel and her uncles who had gone to Heaven before this date. She recognized from old pictures, the uncle and the aunt who had died so young in the nineteen thirties. Then she saw a very pretty middle aged lady whom she did not recognize at all. Being half asleep and half-awake she questioned herself as to who this pretty lady could have been.

Up to this point, Hannah knew this could have been classified as only a dream, but then it happened. Her beautiful niece came from another direction from down the river shores. She walked up alongside of her great grandpa ever so silently. He was greeting and visiting with the others whom he had not seen in years, so he did not notice his great granddaughter. The wind was blowing her beautiful golden long hair. She had on a beautiful dress that was made of an almost organdy type material or a very thin cotton. This dress was a tan or beige in color and it had little colored flowers ever so far on this dress. It was an empire waist style dress and it was long in length. The wind was blowing this dress behind her and she looked absolutely beautiful. Upon her feet was a leather sandal.

The niece walked up to her great grandfather, put her hands on his face and turned it towards her face to show him who she was. While she was standing there with a big beautiful smile, the grandfather turned sharply around and he said,

"WHAT ARE YOU DOING HERE????"
He was shocked and shaken by disbelief. He did not seem pleased that her life had been cut so short. He acted as though this was the very last place he wished to see his beautiful great granddaughter at this day and time. Hannah could tell by his expression that he wished for this lovely granddaughter to have lived a long and nice happy life upon earth

Hannah shook herself and went to the bathroom. Then she lay awake for several hours while thinking of this dream or vision or whatever one may call it. She suddenly realized that even though no one had told her grandfather of the granddaughter's tragedy, he was most surely aware of it now.

The next day Hannah tried to erase this dream or vision away from her mind. If this was a gift, and some believed that it was, she was not so happy to have it right now. All these sorts of dreams or visions were doing to her was confusing her. She finally excused it all and credited it to the fact that she had endured so very much grief in these nineties to where she was possibly losing her mind. No matter how hard she tried to bury herself in her workload and try to forget this dream, she could not shake it.

Then while Hannah was on the phone talking to a client the next day, a thought hit her and she suddenly realized who the woman was that she did not recognize. She lost complete connection with what she was supposed to be talking about with her client. That pretty woman was none other than her loving Aunt Edith. The family had lost her to cancer many years ago. She had been gone so long by now to where Hannah could hardly remember what she looked like, until today. Then she started telling herself of how weird she and some of her family members seemed to be. She had never told anyone that on the night of this aunt's death, she had dreamed at the very hour that her aunt had died that instead it was her father who had died and she awakened crying. She only excused this later as if this was now an acceptance of strange, foreknowable things. She believed that she only thought her father was dead because this aunt and he had been so very close in life. She brushed this dream off as if it were only a normal occurrence to anyone normal. Hannah and her family were anything but normal when it came to this sort of thing. This aunt was one of the baby sisters whom her father tried to protect and had shared his life with. This big man loved his little sisters so very much.

As weeks went by, Hannah tried and did finally forget about the dream. By stating that she had forgotten only meant that she could do other things instead of constantly thinking about it as she had so much in the days shortly after. Then she went to Ohio to visit. Although wounds were still very raw and saying anything about this terrible pain of loss felt like someone was placing salt into deep cuts. Hannah told her mother of the dream. The mother stared in shock and left the room. Hannah felt so badly now for telling her mother. This may have been more than the poor woman could bear. She had been so close to her granddaughter. She lived next door and had cared for the child while her parents worked. The very day of the wreck, the young lady had stuck her head in through her grandmother's front door that morning and asked her to save a piece of cake for her. Hannah was sure she had disturbed her mother very badly. She was wishing so that she could take it all back.

Just as quickly as the mother had left the room, she walked back in while holding a picture in her hands. It was a picture of Annie at the church's mother daughter banquet held that same year. Now it was Hannah's turn to go into complete shock and bewilderment! There on that shinny piece of paper was her beautiful niece looking back at her dressed in that tan colored dress with tiny flowers on it. Hannah almost fainted! She had *never* seen this picture. She had never seen this dress. All of her visits to Ohio were when her niece was casual and playing. She had not seen her niece in anything but shorts, jeans and comfortable shirts since she was a little girl.

Seemed every time Hannah was visiting her family, the young lady was jumping on a trampoline with Hannah's grandchildren or on the back of a four wheeler with her boyfriend and rough housing in every way. Hannah could not remember when she had last seen her niece in a dress. She recollected that her niece had on a dress at her daughter's wedding because she was small and the flower girl. Then she had on a dress at her grandfather's funeral but Hannah believed that it was black with some kind of a white background. No, Hannah had never seen this dress. Yet there it was as plain as day and just the very same as it was in that dream.

Now Hannah felt she must tell her brother. Once she started talking to him she knew she should have not told him at all. But for some odd reason she could not stop telling the dream even though the brother had jumped up from their mother's couch as if he was running away and he was walking very fast towards his own home. It was as if Hannah had to tell him as she walked just as fast alongside of her much loved brother.

Hannah went back inside to her mother with a very heavy heart. Had she made a horrible mistake? Had she hurt her precious brother even more? What kind of an idiot was she anyway? She looked for consolation from her mother but there was just too much grief. She and her mother agreed that Hannah would have absolutely no reason to have ever seen that dress before. She just lived too far away. Visits were far and in between. Hannah explained to her mother that her niece had grown up without her being there, other than visits from afar. They concurred to the fact that Hannah would have never seen that dress.

After some time Hannah was looking out of her mother's front window when she saw her brother heading back towards her mother's house. She was determined to not bring up anything ever again about her dream. This time however, her brother wanted to hear more. Hannah told of how she saw his daughter reach over and turn her grandfather's face towards hers. Now this was getting spooky. Hannah had never seen Annie do that to anyone. Now her brother and her mother started telling her that the young lady did that very thing all of the time to get someone's attention. They said this had become a signature with her and was all in fun. They said it was as if she was saying,

"Hey look at me! I'm talking to you!" Now Hannah was beside herself. She realized that Annie had never done this to her and she realized she had never seen her do this jester.

Now the dream was even more real. Hannah suddenly realized that she had witnessed her grandfather's arrival into Heaven. *But why?* Why would God show this to her. She was not the best of Christians. She was not close to God like so many others in her family. She hardly ever walked inside of a church. She used to say the only time she walked into one was for a wedding or a funeral and even then she would look up to see if the ceiling was going to fall down around her. With shame, she questioned why God would show her such a wonderful thing. For months she pondered that question. Then one day she thought she had it all figured out. She imagined God knew no one would believe this wild dream should it be someone who lived close by and saw Annie on a daily basis. The dream or vision would have been excused as others could have somehow seen that dress and only forgot that they had seen it. Others would have known that Annie had developed a habit of taking someone's face into her hands and turning them to see her. Hannah did not! She realized that God had given her this vision to prove that it was true. With all of the horrible pain this family had to endure, the God is good part of God wanted this loving family to know that their loved ones were safe with each other in His hands.

Chapter 22

Life got back to almost normal for Hannah. It could never be the same anymore. Hannah and her family had lost too much. Hannah now understood the pain that her loving Grandmother had suffered so many years ago when she lost not one, but two of her children. Hannah started wondering why such horrible things could happen to such a God fearing and loving family. The older members of this family had walked the straight and the narrow. Living by faith and prayers all of their lives. Why should so much sadness come their way? Just a few years ago one of Hannah's cousins had lost her daughter to a car accident. She had been a nurse in another state and was driving home late after one of her shifts and had a head on collision. Hannah questioned as to why this would happen to the very same family generation after generation. Why were there so many young ones who would not be able to fulfill a long successful life upon this earth? Hannah, not going to church as she should, started to feel that the God she was taught to love and respect was surely a cruel God. Yet, she knew these feelings were that of complete grief over the loss of her loved ones.

After a while Hannah realized she must go on with her life. She did truly enjoy her children, grandchildren and her husband. She enjoyed her company and the constant travel she and her husband did. She tried to think happy thoughts while honoring those gone away with her wonderful memories of them.

Hannah found that the best way for her to deal with her grief was to remember all of the days gone by. She would let her mind float back to the days as far back as the very wonderful part of her childhood. When she was very young she remembered the all-day meeting home comings at her church and a neighboring church. She remembered the many reunions she would attend as a child with all of her extended family members. One of her very fondest memories was that of the homecoming food on the grounds at the Fairview Church. This tiny country church was way out in the country. Had one not been from this community, one could never find this church? Hannah loved the tables under the very tall pine trees and the feel of the pine straw crunching underneath her feet.

The steep roofed church was straight out of the eighteen hundreds. Nothing had changed about this church. It was tiny. It had some sort of waxed looking designed paper glued to the glass of the windows. Hannah assumed this was to make the windows look like stained glass during the eighteen hundreds. She found this to be most unusual. The old organ, piano and clocks were straight out of a history book. All of this held much interest to Hannah, even as a child. But for some odd reason she loved the tall pine trees and the pine straw beneath her feet. She laughed at herself and thought even that was a preadmission. Something was trying to tell her that the biggest part of her life would be spent in Georgia amongst the tall, tall pines.

Hannah was saddened when she heard that the beautiful old Victorian Fairview Church had burned to the ground in later years. She often felt she must have been born into the complete wrong times, because she loved everything that came out of the eighteen hundreds. She remembered seeing beautiful pictures of her Grandmother Dahl with her long dresses and her high collars. She always felt a special blessing that her grandmother had never changed any of her living styles except for the length of her dresses for the entirety of her life. She had kept her home and her life style just as it had been in her childhood, thus causing Hannah to be raised Victorian for many years. She was surrounded by Victorian things and Victorian ways of thinking. She loved this period and wished life could be that simple once more.

Hannah was extremely creative. Many days she would hunt for vines to make into wreaths. She loved to work on things that she was going to use to decorate the old Victorian home. She loved the small city of her husband's birth. She enjoyed her long jogs that she would take of mornings after her husband left for work. She would half walk or half run all over this historical village called Adairsville, Georgia. She loved looking at the beautiful old southern mansions that were scattered about this town. She loved her husband's history and she loved living in this place she now called home. She had been invited to join an exclusive club that had been for the ladies of this town for generations. She really felt she now belonged. She loved their monthly meetings, dinners, tours of homes and any other project they would have. She and her husband would often take a stroll to the wonderful elegant restaurant that served gourmet meals and was housed inside of an old southern mansion. This restaurant was on the corner across from there soon to be home.

Hannah would lay in her bed beside of her handsome husband on a lazy Sunday morning and listen to the train whistles blowing, the church bells ringing and the birds singing. She would look out of her window to the beautiful valley across the street on her husband's grandparent's property and see the sun shining through the two hundred year old trees. This place made her feel like she was on vacation in another time and another place. Hannah felt at home here and she felt that she belonged. She truly loved her husband. She truly loved his hometown and she truly loved her life.

During nineteen ninety-nine Samuel had expressed his wish to get a position closer home. He had worked most of his life in and around Atlanta, Georgia. He remarked at how heavenly it would be to work closer home. Just as the work market was in Hannah's home town areas, good jobs were hard to find. Someone most usually had to die for another to secure such a position.

Samuel had secured a teaching position at one of the colleges on a part time basis. This was something that he enjoyed because he loved working and teaching everything there was to know about the computer world. So, two or three evenings a week he would teach classes at the local college. Since his day position was so demanding, on the times he would have to travel for his company, he had ask that Hannah be his substitute teacher. This unnerved Hannah because she knew she was not knowledge of the workings and programming of computers. She always prayed that no one would ask her an in depth question. The evenings that she had to teach were few and she lived through them without any problems.

Hannah and Samuel's love of travel would have to slow. They would miss their wonderful trips, but they also knew they would be happy to stay at home and enjoy their family and each other. So, Samuel took a lesser paying position at the end of that year so he could work closer home. There were several problems with this move. One was that Samuel would lose his company car. He had always been given a company car with his positions. Another was that his insurance would not take effect until after three months of employment. Hannah could not understand this since every other position he or she had received had covered each of them shortly after the day they started their new position. In Samuel's case he always had such a large life insurance policy because it was based upon his very high wages.

Life was wonderful for Samuel and Hannah except for the worries over their children. The one son had taken a position first in Boca Raton, Florida which meant he was miles away and visits were rare. Now he was interviewing for an even further away position that would take him and his family to Chicago, Illinois. The daughter had been in Ohio ever since her divorce. She and her family did not get to visit as much as Hannah would have liked. Thankfully Samuel's son still lived close by. Samuel and Hannah had recently gotten the shock of their lives when they heard that this couple who had loved each other and dated each other ever since high school fifteen years ago, were now getting a divorce. This couple had a beautiful home hanging over a mountain and now the son would only be living there. The children were to be joint custody. Therefore, Hannah would go to the son's house on the weeks that he had the children and get them ready for school. She would watch them as they got onto the bus, then she would head to her office for a days work.

In February of the year of two thousand, something had happened to the family van. It was in a garage awaiting repair. Hannah was driving it a lot anymore due to the fact that Samuel no longer had a company car. Samuel was driving Hannah's Corvette to work most days. The son had loaned Hannah a golden colored Camry to use while the van was being fixed.

On the twenty-second day of February, Hannah had the duties of dressing the children this week. Samuel did not have to leave the house so very early anymore. For the first time in a very long time he could stay in bed past five thirty of a morning. He no longer had to take those long trips to some part of Atlanta. He loved this comfort!

Hannah, on the other hand, had to go. She must get the children on the bus in time to go to school. She hurriedly made coffee. She downed a black cup quickly and fixed a cup for her husband. He was now up and looking for his robe. Samuel had a navy blue terry cloth robe and Hannah had a pink terry cloth robe. Samuel had said he would go start the car for Hannah on this very cold morning. This was most appreciated. When Samuel could not find his robe he placed the pretty pink robe of his wife's upon his body and ran out to start her car. When he returned, he stepped up onto the hearth of the fireplace and started fanning the back side of the robe to get his legs and cheeks warm once more, while saying,

"Lord, it is cold out there!"

Hannah liked him standing high above her as he was. She reached up to give him a kiss and he took her into his arms and held her tight. He looked her in the eyes and said,

"I love you Darling!"

She said,

"I love you too!"

Knowing that she had to go, she started to break the hold that gripped her. She looked up at her husband's beautiful eyes when he said,

"No Hannah, I don't think you understand! I really, really, really love you! I love you with all of my heart, my soul and my being! I want you to know how very much I truly love you!"

Hannah being most appreciative of what she knew to be heart felt love, watched as her husband's beautiful eyes changed from one color to the other the same way they had done so many years ago. She knew beyond a shadow of a doubt that her husband loved her. She knew that she loved him. She figured that Samuel maybe just felt that life sometimes got in the way of really letting the other person know how truly one cares.

Hannah started out of the door. As she opened the door, she swung her hair back over her shoulder. Looking back at her handsome husband while he was warming himself by the fire, she said,

"You, Mr. Wright, certainly look sexy in that pink robe."

She ran back and gave him another great big kiss and said,

"I hope you know Mr. Wright how very much that I love you too! Now I have got to go!"

The past two weeks had been spent in Chicago for Samuel. He had to go for some training for his new company. Hannah had joined him on the in between weekend. The couple had seen some sites and ate in wonderful restaurants. They had completely enjoyed each other's company, as usual. Their love life was comparable to no other. The two could sip upon a glass of wine and enjoy only looking into each other's eyes while they danced in the dim lights for hour after hour. They were so very deep in love. Hannah would often question of how she had gotten so lucky to have received everything that she had ever wanted in her life. She had finally found that someone to *watch over her*. She had found her soul mate. She had found complete happiness.

Just before the Chicago trip, Hannah and Samuel went shopping. Samuel, for some odd reason liked to fly out of the Chattanooga, Tennessee Airport. Hannah did not. She much preferred the Atlanta Airport. Odd, but it did not matter which one they used because they lived exactly the same mileage between the two.

A few months back Hannah was going to fly to Ohio to visit her daughter, mother and granddaughter. Samuel booked her flight. She was terribly upset when she found that he had booked her out of Chattanooga instead of Atlanta. Smaller planes were often used out of this nice, new airport. Samuel had decided that Hannah should take the van so she would not be leaving the Corvette in an airport parking lot. So, he had gone on to work and Hannah prepared for her trip. A few hours before she was to leave, she received a call from her husband, who said,

"I'm going to take off and come home from Atlanta to take you to the airport. That way we do not have to leave any vehicle there. Plus, I will be able to see you before you leave."

Not until they were on their way on this sixty mile ride to Chattanooga did Hannah realize that Samuel had full intentions of going all of the way back to Atlanta to continue his work this day.

Hannah had been fearsome about riding the small jet plane that she knew she was scheduled to ride. She did not seem to have much fear of the large commercial jets. Maybe it was false security, but when Hannah could see that the plane was small she would become somewhat fearful.

Today, with the obvious need for her husband to hurry back to work, he did not take his foot off of the gas in that Corvette. Hannah could look over and see his speed. Only one time when traffic looked as if it were slowing way ahead of them, did Samuel drop down to even ninety-five miles per hour. He sat right up there on that one-hundred and more mark the total distance.

Hannah said her goodbyes to her husband and ran into the airport. When she finally sat down in the seat of that small jet plane, she was relieved. As she felt the air leave her seat she said,

"Ah-h-h-h-h!"

The lady next to her ask,

"Tired?"

Hannah said,

"No, it's just after the trip I had to endure to get here. It is such a relief to be on this plane?"

The woman looked at her strangely, but laid her head back down upon her pillow.

Then just the week before Hannah had gone to Chicago to be with Samuel for the weekend.

284

She was coming home from the Atlanta airport when the bottom fell out. A worse storm Hannah had never seen. She was sliding everywhere with the wide tires on her car. Water was very deep in the groves of the highway and she was traveling with much traffic within the City of Atlanta. It is funny how childhood things come back to a person when they are needed. While Hannah was having a horrible time trying to see the road, she started singing,

"Jesus Savior Pilot Me!"

She talked on the phone with Samuel most of the way and she knew she was worrying him to death. He was stuck in Chicago for another week. Finally as she pulled into her driveway she called him immediately to tell him that she was safe and that she was home. She could hear the relief in her husband's voice when he told her goodnight and that he loved her.

Since Samuel had been asked to spend two weeks in Chicago, the week before Hannah had driven him to the airport in Chattanooga. They had left early before his departure so that they could buy him a coat. They found a London Fog black coat to keep him warm in Chicago. A month or so ago they had purchased a nice, Charcoal in color, Christian Dior suit for Samuel. He had many suits and loads of clothes. Hannah did also. This couple did not want for much. All of their clothing was that of a good name brand. Samuel always looked like a million dollars with his neat figure and handsome looks. He had decided to wear this new suit on his plane trip. Not that he had any meeting this evening or that he needed to look his best, but because he had joked about the pants being his 'Feel Good Pants'. This was a family joke now because one of their very small granddaughters had told her grandparents while on a shopping spree that she wanted some feel-good-panties. Most of hers were cotton. She meant she liked those of a silkier feel. Samuel's suit was lined in silk and Samuel said the pants felt so very comfortable while traveling on these long trips. The suit pants were his feel-good-pants!

Wednesday came and Hannah got a call from her husband. He said,

"Meet me at the airport tomorrow at two o'clock. We have finished with our classes and I will get to leave early. I have already changed my flight."

When Hannah arrived at the airport, her husband was already standing outside. She knew that he had told her the wrong time on purpose so as to not make her wait. She jumped out of the car and ran into his waiting arms. She was so happy to see her wonderful husband. He asked her to pop the trunk. She did and she slid back down into the car seat. She watched as this handsome man put his suit case in first, then his suit carrier. She could not help but think of how handsome Samuel looked in his new London Fog coat. She knew that no matter how many years they may have been together, she would forever find that her husband could still make her legs go weak.

As Samuel slid into the car, he reached over and put his hand atop of Hannah's who had placed hers over the gearshift so she could shift. He turned to a beautiful song on the CD player and the couple settled in for the sixty mile drive back to their home. Hannah was blessed! She knew this! She was so very blessed! She was listening to beautiful music. She was holding hands with the man of her dreams and all was well with her world.

Thursday night after dinner, Samuel said his chest was hurting. He said he most have gotten a lung infection in Chicago while enduring that fifteen degree weather. Hannah said something like maybe he should go to the doctor. He had said,

"No it will be alright once I get used to being home and out of that winter wonderland!"

As the weekend passed, Samuel did complain a few more times about his chest hurting, but did not act as though anything was serious. He had said some things to his son and he had said some things to his wife, but neither knew the extent of his pain. Now, on this Tuesday morning of February 22nd, 2000 Samuel had started Hannah's car. He was standing up on the hearth warming himself when Hannah left to go to their son's home to care for the grandchildren.

The beautiful little children had to walk down a long mountain driveway to get on the bus. It was still dark at this time of the morning during this date in the year. Hannah always worried about their journey, because there was a period of time that she could not see the children as they passed through a thicket of trees along the long driveway. So she hollered at them continually from high above upon the long porch. They always said,

"Yes, we're okay Mamma!"
Hannah always found great relief when she heard the bus driver speak to each of the children as they climbed into that bus.

Once she knew they were safe and on their way to school, Hannah would straighten up any messes they may have made. She would lock up the house and then be on her way home.

This morning she had passed her husband on his way to work. There was a small strip where there was a four lane highway between Adairsville and Rome, Georgia. She passed her Corvette going the other direction as she was heading home. She waved, but with the darken windows of the car her husband was driving caused her not to be able to tell if he saw her or not.

Hannah went straight into her office and sat down at her desk to start to work. She had payroll to do this morning for some of her clients. She must hurry so that the employers could pick the checks up around noon. While she was adding up time cards and looking for the amount of the tax deductions, she got a call from her husband. He said,

"Hannah, call and make me an appointment with the dentist for today. I have a terrible tooth ache. What is surprising me is that the tooth that is hurting is one that I have had a root canal in."
In the business of the morning both said they loved each other and hung up the phone. Hannah called their dentist and made an appointment. She had told the doctor's office that this was an emergency and they had scheduled an appointment for her husband at 2:15pm that very afternoon.

Hannah jumped back on the phone and called her husband. She dialed once and then she dialed again and again. Every time she would dial the number, a message would come over the line that said,

"All circuits are busy. Please try your call again!"

Hannah could not understand this, because she had never received a message like that before.

Somewhere between the trying to call Samuel's office, a phone call came into Hannah's office. She picked up the phone hoping it was her husband, but instead it was a lady on the other end. Samuel had been on his job such a short time to where Hannah had never been introduced to any of his fellow employees. The voice on the other end of the line started off by saying,

"Mrs. Wright, I am your husband's secretary. They had to take your husband to Floyd Medical Center by ambulance a few minutes ago." Hannah was not sure whether she even thanked the secretary. She ran to the bathroom to straighten her face and see how she looked. She grabbed her purse and ran to the car. She will never know why she started to cry uncontrollably. She drove just as fast as she could to get to the hospital. She ran over large curbs when she rushed into a parking lot and ask the tenant where the door to the emergency room was, only to be told that she was in the wrong parking lot. She rushed back out into the street and pulled into the neighboring parking lot. She then jumped out of her car and ran into the building. As she stepped inside of the seemly empty emergency room, she ran straight to the small booths with chairs and ladies behind the small desks on the other side awaiting patients.

This day it was as if these ladies were awaiting only her arrival. When she threw open the doors, she watched as the women scattered and all but one disappeared. The last lady stood there to answer any of Hannah's questions. Hannah said in a panic,

"My name is Hannah Wright! I am told my husband, Samuel Wright, was just brought into the emergency room. Where do I go to get to him?"

Before the lady could answer Hannah, she had already headed for the big double doors. She was walking very fast while she was waiting for the woman to answer her. The lady spoke up quickly and said,

"You can't go through those doors, they are locked. Someone will have to come and get you!"

With that, this woman disappeared also.

Hannah could hear someone moving down the hallway with a swift pace. Suddenly the big doors flew open and Hannah later questioned if these doors had been locked at all. A kind lady led Hannah to where she believed that she would see her husband. Instead she was led into a room not bigger than a personal bathroom. In this room were two easy chairs that looked like they had come out of someone's living room. There was one hard back chair and a table in the corner between the deep chairs with a lace tablecloth, a lamp and a large Bible. Hannah wondered why on earth they would bring her into a place like this. She had never seen a waiting room that was this small or that looked like this. She was told that the doctor wanted to talk with her and he would be there shortly.

They were right! Just about as quickly as the lady left Hannah alone, a nice old grey headed gentleman walked into the room. He pulled up the straight back chair and moved it closely to Hannah. He took her hands in his and he said,

"I am so sorry! We did everything that we could do! He is gone! It looks as if it was his heart!"

Hannah started crying and begging for this to not be true. She said to the doctor,

"He is not even sick! He has never been sick! Did you look at him, he is in perfect shape! He is only fifty-six years old. People have heart attacks and they live. He cannot be dead!"

The poor old gentleman looked so sad, but could say no more. He only held Hannah's hands in his while he handed her a box of Kleenex from the table nearby.

The doctor then stood up and started to leave the room. He looked back at Hannah and said,

"We'll get him cleaned up and we will let you go back to be with him."

Hannah walked out into the hallway where she found many of her husband's co-workers there to greet her. Once she called her family, her son had called his father-in-law who was a doctor at that very hospital. He came to be with Hannah until her ex-daughter-in-law could get there. As she stood over her soul mate and her love, she kissed him and cried. Suddenly she screamed,

"He is still warm! He's still alive! Help! Someone Help Him! Do something for him!"

The doctors and those around only hung their heads. Pity could be seen upon their faces. Hannah was destroyed. Hannah had just lost her love. The only man who had ever truly loved her with all of his heart and soul was leaving her. The only man who would ever protect her and care for her, the only man on earth she could ever feel safe with and warm in his loving arms was going away, never to return to her.

Hannah had never doubted her wonderful husband's love from that day when he said,

"I do!"

Now, her beautiful husband was going away. Her beautiful little town was there to comfort her, but there would be no more Samuel.

Samuel's son and children arrived within the hour. Then Hannah's daughter and her daughter arrived from Ohio in the early evening. It would be awhile before the other son could get there. The following morning, Hannah took the son and the daughter with her to the funeral home to make the arrangements. As they walked through the caskets, Hannah insisted upon the very best one they had. She chose a solid mahogany glossy wood casket that had a drawer in the top lid where the family could put memories. Samuel had always loved the best of everything in his life. Hannah was not going to let him go away in anything below his standards.

In this quaint little town of Samuel's birth was an antique shop. Hannah had loved this old town. It was as if one was walking back into history during the eighteen-hundreds when one walked through this beautiful little town. Hannah went to the beautiful old antique home that had been turned into a nice antique and craft shop. In the very back part of this house was a Floral Shop. Hannah picked out a beautiful blanket for her husband's casket. She chose the yellow roses. The big, full of roses blanket was chosen in yellow roses because they were Samuel's favorite of all roses. He would always buy Hannah yellow roses. Decisions had to be made about the clothing. The undertaker was a son of one of Samuel's lifetime friends. This was a small town and the whole funeral director's family of boys had grown up with her wonderful husband. She sent her daughter to the funeral home with Samuel's favorite Christian Dior suit, a blue shirt and a tie. She wanted him to rest in his 'feel good pants'.

Hannah Jane Dahl Hughes Wright was now frail and pale as the color of milk. This lady was but a shell of her former self. She was so transparent to where it looked like the wind just might blow her away. She somehow got through the funeral, although she will never know how. As the Priest spoke, she could not even look up.

The grandchildren had written letters to Papaw and she had placed them in the mahogany drawl designed for that reason. She remembered of how she wished she had read each note but knew that was personal between the grandchildren and their grandfather. She took the three older grandchildren up to the casket with her to say goodbye. As each stood there, the grandmother Hannah got down on her knees upon the stool provided in front of her loving husband so as to bring herself down to the children's level. The oldest granddaughter was crying uncontrollably. She was but ten years old. The eleven year old grandson just stood there while he was in shock. He could not cry. His beautiful eyes were large and looking so shocked and so hurt. The little six year old, who did not completely understand, ask about the lid. She said,

"Mamma, if they close the lid over Papaw, how is he going to get out?"
Hannah felt her heart break right in two. She knew how very much this man meant to his wonderful grandchildren. Their little hearts were breaking right along beside of hers.

Hannah knew that her sad performance had deterred many people from approaching her. The night of the viewing, her women's club had made a wonderful dinner for everyone. They were posted in the kitchen area of the funeral home. The funeral home stood high atop a hill and was an old Victorian Mansion with wrap around porches covered in gingerbread. Samuel was placed in the newer, large chapel along the side of this beautiful home. Hannah was greeting those who were paying their last respects to her husband. Her family arrived from Ohio and when she saw her only sister walk into the room, she could not control her emotions one moment more. She broke into a loud earth shaking cry and let herself fall into her sister's arms.

After the funeral, the family all went home. Many neighbors and friends tried to help. One wonderful neighbor kept trying to feed Hannah. She would bring food, only to show up in an hour to find Hannah had not eaten. Anna's mother, Samuel's first mother-in-law was wonderful. Anna was her only daughter and Samuel always was her son-in-law. The elderly lady came almost every day after the funeral to bring food and to check on Hannah.

After a while people shunned Hannah because they knew not how to deal with her loss. No one seemed to know the right thing to say. She would try not to bore anyone with her stories. She knew that her life would bring them down. One had to beg to get her to talk about such things, but once the conversation started, she would always cry and this would cause the person who brought up the subject wishing they had never spoken of the tragedies. Most people felt diminished in her presence. She was now a woman who had suffered just about everything one poor human could endure.

Chapter 23

Hannah became tempered like steel or annealed like glass. Sometimes she felt ageless. She wore her pain as if it were baked in clay. Her life had burnished and refined her to where she was not sure she even thought like other humans. Her heart had been taken out and it had been stomped upon. It had been placed back into her body time and time again, only to be torn right out once more. She knew she had become a very strong woman through no effort of her own. She also knew she would never be that little country girl who was so wet behind the ears and so very full of adventure of long ago. Life had given her a collective magnitude of experiences that she knew most women had not faced. She knew others most likely had trials and pains of their own, but in a selfish kind of way, she could not help but believe that she had been dealt the hardest of hands.

Hannah knew she must not live on her memories alone. She was considered to be, 'Still Young'. She knew that she must carve some sort of a life out of this stone she had been given. She must try to make something out of it. Her stepson lived close by, but her other children lived so very far away. She had wonderful friends and a wonderful part of her family in Georgia. However, she found she knew not what to do with herself most of the time. Her heart hurt with every beat. Everywhere she looked, she saw Samuel. Her life had never been this destroyed. She had never felt like she did not want to see tomorrow or so completely with no future at all. She was devastated! She would get up mornings and go to the isolated graveyard to spend time with her husband. She would sit upon the ground and just cry for hours. She would talk with Samuel and ask why he would leave her. She begged him to come back and climb castle steps with her once more. Friends and family worried about her spending so much time in the graveyard. It sat high upon a hill behind a church with no houses around. The friends and family felt it was so unsafe on that secluded hill.

Like a puppet on a string and after much persuasion, Hannah moved back to Ohio to live with her daughter. She settled in quickly and she truly enjoyed bonding with the granddaughter who had lived so far away for the biggest part of her life. She was able to meet the other children's mother half way on many occasions and bring her Georgia grandchildren to Ohio to visit. They would stay some in the summers. These were her happiest times. She was still missing her son and his children. He now lived in Chicago and visits were far and in between. When she would complain, her son would sing her the song, 'The Cats in the Cradle' and this would make them both sad. Hannah felt those two grandchildren were growing up with so little knowledge of her. This could never diminish her love for them. Life had to go on.

Hannah loved living on the river and watching the boats as they made their daily runs. She loved the history of the beautiful city. She loved the parts that her ancestors had played to help in the development of this wonderful part of the country. She knew that much of the rich history could be contributed to many of her family members and she was very proud of this. She could sometimes drown herself in her childhood memories with the surroundings of her birth. However, she was not at home anymore. She somehow knew she would never feel at home anywhere anymore.

The pain and loss would come into Hannah's life even when she was doing things that she liked. She could feel so alone even with a room full of people. An old song could bring back memories. She would break down and cry if she heard the song, 'I Fooled Around and Fell in Love' or 'I Will Always Love you' and so many more that she may hear on the radio. She missed her first love as well. She knew there was something weird about her when Ambros's favorite songs would come on the radio back to back. When songs like 'Rising Sun' and 'Hotel California' would come on, she would smile and say,

"Hello Ambros!"

After a couple of years, Hannah was still floating around with no particular aim in life. She decided to move in with her mother after her daughter sold one house and moved into another. She worked and she came home. That was about the extent of her life. While at her mothers, the one golden light of sunshine in her life was her little great nephew. He was born six months after her youngest grandson was born. Her grandson had turned one year old the month before Samuel had passed. The nephew was but six months old. While living with her mother, Hannah would come home and play with her great-nephew. Her mother babysat him regularly. He was such a little doll and Hannah buried herself in his affection.

Hannah finally felt as if she had awakened somewhat again. Two years after the death of her husband, she seemed to wake up and realize that she had not taken care of any business. She had a beautiful home in Georgia with a renter in it and it needed some attention badly. As fate would have it, she was working on a part-time job where a company owner offered her a permanent position several miles below her home in Georgia. She accepted with many mixed emotions. She was of the belief that God must have been behind the things that were happening. He must have provided this unusual offer from a faraway state. Even with regret from leaving her home once more, Hannah believed it would be temporary. Her intentions were to take the job, fix up her home, sell it and then move back to Ohio. As so many of Hannah's life plans, this never happened. She would travel home often to visit with her family, but she never moved back to Ohio. By now her son was in the south and she thought she was going to like that scenario. She would now be closer to the largest amount of her children and grandchildren.

After a few years, the father of the little great nephew was about to remarry. Hannah went home for the wedding. She would never forget how handsome her little man looked on that day. He was in his tux when he ran over to his great grandmothers to get something needed. Then he saw that Hannah was visiting. She said,

"Come here, little man, and give your Aunt Hannah a big hug!"
He said,

"I can't right now. We're getting married tonight!"

Hannah laughed and thought of how very precious this little guy was. He and her beautiful grandchildren had pulled her through the darkest days of her life. They had given her much joy when she felt there was no joy to receive. She loved all of these beautiful little children with all of her heart.

Time passed and suddenly the grandchildren were growing up. Hannah's oldest grandson had married and now he had a child of his own. Her oldest granddaughter was away at college. The other children were growing with every day. One granddaughter was soon to graduate High School and another about to enter High School. Hannah was starting to feel old.

Then on a devastating August day, Hannah's life was shattered to pieces once more. She picked up the phone to hear her sweet daughter's voice on the other end. She had to tell her mother that the beautiful little ten year old nephew had just been killed upon that old farm while playing with his cousins on a golf cart.

Hannah screamed,

"NO! NO! NO! NO! NO! NO!"

until she was losing her voice. She was so very loud to where the neighbors heard her and many came running. Hannah was destroyed. How could this much pain come to any one family. *HOW COULD GOD LET THIS HAPPEN TO THIS FAMILY?* Lord, was Hannah ever mad at God. She screamed at Him. She ask question after question and she lost her faith on that day. She screamed that no God could be this cruel! Suddenly Hannah did not believe in God!

Once again this family had to go through an earth shaking event. Hannah hurt so badly for her brother and his wife. She hurt for her nephew and her mother. She hurt for the whole family. How could this be happening? His grandparents lived in the old house that Rebecca Dahl had moved into over a hundred years ago. When the grandmother had arrived at her new home the house had a tree growing up through the living room floor. Was this old house cursed? Or was it blessed? Was this old farm magical? Or was it a place of disasters? This was the place of Hannah's birth. This was the place of her father's birth. This was the place of the warmth of family and loved ones. This old farm was so much a part of each and every one of the Dahl family. How could things so horrible, so unmentionable happen upon this wonderful old farm?

Chapter 24

Hannah woke up one morning and realized that it had now been one year to the day since her beautiful nephew was killed. She had spent the last year in a shell. She felt her very life breath had been drawn from within her just like a vapor. She felt so beat up. She felt the weight of the world had landed upon her shoulders. Facing a new day was such an effort. All illusions of a better life had vanished. She often cried at least once every day. She would smile when she would think of her loved ones, but the loss of the same would make her cry. She could remember a song that her first love Ambros would sing to her. He would sing,

"We'll sing in the sunshine! We'll laugh every day! We'll sing in the sunshine; then I'll be on my way!"

Hannah felt cheated that her first marriage had not worked and always wondered what it would have been like to have stayed married to her children's father. She thought of how maybe her children would have been closer and life would have been better. Of course she knew with their problems, life could have been a lot worse too. Then there was the fact that she would have never wanted to miss the time she had spent with her second love Samuel.

Hannah had to be thankful for some wonderful moments this past year. She was fortunate enough to have some good times in the last year with one granddaughter graduating from college. She was way to young to have graduated. She always made such wonderful grades. Hannah was so very proud! Then another granddaughter graduated from high school and another wonderful day was enjoyed. Her great grandson was growing up fast. He was a true blessing and such a handsome little man. But as a whole, Hannah felt empty. She missed the children and the grandchildren whom she never seemed to be able to see.

On this morning of remembrance Hannah went to her computer and pulled out the CD with her little nephew's pictures upon it. This was the CD that was used at his funeral. She had not been able until this date to even watch it. She decided that from this day forward she was going to remember her beautiful little nephew in her own private way and start a pattern of watching this CD on the date of his death for the rest of her living days. She was also just as determined not to cry, but she lost that battle on the very first picture. She had to smile as she saw her little nephew lying upon a big tuff, lounging Rottweiler he called Grunt! He often used this dog for a recliner. His radiant smile and his shiny curling hair showed that he was so very special. Then, between smiles of remembrance and tears of loss she saw her nephew so true to his personality while sticking his tongue out as he came down a slide.

Hannah's daughter had put the CD together and at the very end she had placed a picture of the little boy walking through the leaves on Halloween while wearing a black cape. One could only see his back as he was walking away. Then it hit Hannah! *HE WAS AN ANGEL!* Why had she not seen that before? This little boy had been a little angel who had come to help. He came along just in time to keep his grandfather from killing himself over the loss of his daughter. He came along just in time to help his Aunt Hannah through the loss of her husband. He was there to help his great grandmother get through the loss of her husband, granddaughter, her father, her mother, her brother, two brother-in-laws, a niece and a nephew. He had been there to help his daddy through the loss of his sister and a bitter divorce. He had been there to help his grandmother when she could not think of anything but the loss of her daughter and the loss of her mother. His grandmother had walked through Hell before she lost her daughter Annie. She also had lost her only brother to a wreck when she was but a teen. This little angel had come along just in time to save his whole family.

Hannah started realizing the reason for his appearance and her pain seemed to soften. Even as a small child everyone should have realized that he was an *angel*. When someone was upset or hurt over anything, this little lad was there to help. His grandfather had a horrible accident while on vacation in Texas. The little boy stood behind a building until he was sure that his 'Dadal', as he called him, was safe at home. Hannah remembered so many times that the little man would say to her,

"It'll be alright Aunt Hannah! It'll be alright!"

Hannah walked outside of her home to find that her white rose bush was blooming again in August. She could not understand how this lone rose could be upon this almost dead plant. It had been a horribly dry year in Georgia and all of the other roses had long gone away. This was not even a proper time of the year for a rose to bloom.

Each leaf on this plant had dried up and was full of holes. Yet on this August morning there was a beautiful white rose upon the plant. Hannah knew it was from her nephew. Last year when she came back to her home after the funeral she found a beautiful white rose in full bloom. She wondered why it would have bloomed at that time of the year and felt it was a gift from Heaven.

The rose just never went away. It stayed through the month of October. It stayed through the month of November and then when it was still there in December and did not die until up into the middle of January, Hannah was once more convinced of a higher power. Today, she reached for her camera as she walked out to take a picture of what she now knew to be her nephew's rose. Yes, this was her gift from her nephew. This was her little angel who was giving her back her faith. He had given her so much in his short life. Now he was even giving her back her faith.

Hannah remembered the things her minister father so often had said, such as,

"Life is but a vapor! Live it fully! We are nothing but dust in the wind!

With those thoughts Hannah knew she must pull herself out of the dumps she seemed to let herself stay in once more. She had been afraid to care, afraid to love, afraid to give of herself. She felt she could not bear another drop of pain. She felt if she did not contribute to life, she would not have to join in. If she made no friends, then she could not be hurt. She was afraid to pray. She had questioned if there was in fact a God! Yet she knew had it not been for the Grace of God on at least two or three occasions that her oldest granddaughter would have been lost. This precious granddaughter was so close to riding with her cousin on that fatal night. Both she and her mother were so very close to dying with Ambros the night that he died. She also knew of how lucky her family was during the boating accident. She had to be so thankful that more of her children were not along and that more people did not die on that day.

Hannah knew not the reasons for the things that had happened to her family. She wondered about the black cloud and the pain that her paternal grandmother had endured. The black cloud that hung over her seemed not to go away with her death. It seemed that so many of her loved ones had died so very, very young. Although she was not there to see it, the Grandmother Dahl had three grandchildren who had died of cancer before they had much of a chance to live. Now the pattern was following with her great grandchildren. She had now lost two great granddaughters to horrible car accidents. With Hannah's great nephew, she had lost a ten year old great, great grandson. Within that very next following year, she lost still another young great grandson who was an only child to his mother and father. He also left a wife and a nice young family while being lost to cancer.

Chapter 25

Hannah thought of how if God had a plan, what was it? She was so very mad at times! She was sad at all times and very disappointed in the cards that life had dealt her and her family. However, she did know that she must count her many blessings and keep the faith to go on with still another day. Her loved ones who had gone on before her would want it to be that way. As the broken woman stood over the beautiful white rose, tears fell from her eyes and dropped upon her blouse. Just then in her mind's ear she could hear a beautiful, comforting little voice saying,

"It'll be alright Aunt Hannah! It'll be alright!"

"ANGELS COME IN ALL SIZES"

OTHER BOOKS AVAILABLE BY THIS AUTHOR ARE:

Historical Fiction

Could be a trilogy of 'The Tragedies of the Dahl's' yet each book stands as a good read alone. These books chronicle the lives of three generations starting during the 1800's. A family named Dahl, an old farm house, a dirt road and the love of a good book has helped to inspire the rage and desire to write these very inspirable and moving stories.

AVAILABLE where fine books are sold.
Sold at Amazon.com
Sold at Lulu.com
Sold at many other sites on the web
Learn more by visiting the web-sites
www.book-burningsunshine.com or
www.marilynpavlovsky.com